Gran

"D'Arcy Kennedy's search for his brother's killer is a gut-wrenching trip into a world of people left behind by gentrification, forgotten by changing politics and trying to hang onto what little family they have left. It's authentic, it's raw, and it's got heart. It's a trip worth taking."

—John McFetridge,
author of *A Little More Free*

Praise for Ian Truman

"*The Factory Line* captures an entertaining voice in a highly readable manner which relays the exploits of some blue collar factory workers over the course of a day."

—Brian Lindenmuth,
Spinetingler Magazine

"Truman has an incredible ear for dialogue...There aren't two pens like [his] in the writing business."

—Benoit Lelièvre,
Dead End Follies

"Truman's *A Teenage Suicide* follows a group of friends working through late adulthood issues of identity, depression, and lots of tough choices. Set in and around Montreal and in particular its punk, art, activist and student scenes, its down-to-earth raconteur style provides an enduring snapshot of young-adult life in the big city today."

—Expozine Awards

GRAND TRUNK
AND SHEARER

ALSO BY IAN TRUMAN

The Factory Line
Low Down
A Teenage Suicide
Northern Gothic
Crass: Poems of Ordinary Havoc

IAN TRUMAN

GRAND TRUNK AND SHEARER

Down & Out Books
3959 Van Dyke Rd, Ste. 265
Lutz, FL 33558
www.DownAndOutBooks.com

The characters and events in this book are fictitious. Any similarity to real persons, living or dead, is coincidental and not intended by the author.

Cover design by Collective Narcolepsy - Mtl.
Photo by Rocky33

ISBN: 1-943402-90-6
ISBN-13: 978-1-943402-90-8

With exceptional thanks to Benoit Lelièvre.

CHAPTER 1

"Hey, yo," the voice said on the phone. It was Phil calling me at five o'clock in the morning. "Cillian's in the canal."

What the fuck was going on? I didn't know. "You mean he's swimming in the canal?" I replied, wondering if my brother was acting fourteen again. I sat on the edge of my bed, ran a hand through my hair, scratched my beard. I hadn't slept all that much and Phil had better have a good reason for calling me.

"No, I don't mean swimming. I mean, he's dead in the canal."

I didn't believe that my brother was floating in the canal, partly because no one had dumped a body in the canal in the last ten, maybe fifteen years. You just didn't see that anymore. Another part of me didn't believe Phil because he had once called me in the middle of the night saying he had fucked Lady Gaga.

"It's no shit," he had told me. You could almost smell the whiskey over the phone. Agreed, Phil did work a shift here and there for the big touring shows coming through the city, so it was not *entirely* impossible. But, the thing was, Lady Gaga made terrible music but she was way too hot for a guy like Phil. Plus, she was on tour in Scandinavia that day. We actually checked online.

It turned out he *had* fucked a five-three hipster chick,

good for him, but that didn't make it Lady Gaga. You had to check the details with Phil.

"What the hell are you saying? What are you talking about *he's dead*? He's probably at Annie's house, or Isabel or whoever he's been fucking these days."

"I'm telling you, the police are here and everything. They got boats and shit in the water. There's a crowd now, D'Arcy. They pushed us back, but I saw him, man. I saw him before they pushed around the corner. Cillian got stuck in the pillars under the bridge by Des Seigneurs Street."

"The police are there?"

"Trying to fish him out as we speak."

"You home from the graveyard shift?"

"Yeah."

"Drank much?"

"Fuck you! Get over here ASAP."

"This better not be a joke, Phil, because if it is I *will* break your teeth with a hammer."

"Why would I joke on something like this?"

I didn't have anything to reply to that. Phil was a fucking idiot, but he was also a decent fucking idiot. What the hell was this all about, I was still too groggy to know.

"Alright, give me five minutes."

"You gonna tell your ma?" he asked.

"Not until I see it for myself. Where are you now?"

"Saint-Patrick and Shearer," he replied. That was four blocks away from my house.

"I'm on my way," I said as I got up. "You better not be shitting me," I added.

"It ain't."

"Alright."

I didn't know what to think. I would have been surprised if anybody had been found in the canal. You heard your uncles talk about shit like that. It didn't happen anymore. Regardless, the prospect of my brother being dead, however improbable it might be, was something worth getting up for, even at five in the morning.

So I put on my camo shorts, then the same black T-shirt I had taken off a few hours earlier. It still reeked of beer and cigarettes.

"Shit," I said, but I was too lazy to pick up a clean one from my drawer. I put on my poor boy hat and walked out the bedroom.

The kitchen was a mess with dirty dishes, pots and pans filling up the sink well beyond its capacity. The curtains were drawn, I forgot to take out the trash again and the August heat had been working the leftovers.

I pulled out the bag from the can, opened the back door and threw the garbage in the corner of my balcony. Garbage day wasn't for another two days. I opened the kitchen window, put on my shoes and walked out.

The plastic chairs were full of rainwater from last night. The ashtray next to it was full of mud that was made out of ash and rain and beer. My mother had left one of her books on a small table next to her chair and the pages had swollen. I couldn't help but think she'd be sad about that, tried to open it so the pages would dry. And then I stopped myself. *Hey, Cillian's in the canal, let me dry up the pages to this book here.* Why would Ma care about the book if the news turned out to be true?

I felt like I should hurry up but the time of the day warranted a quick stop on Centre Street for coffee and something to eat before I could handle any bad news.

I walked across our small yard, up my dark alley, up front to the wooden gate. It was old and all crooked. You had to push it hard in order to get the lock off of it. I struggled with it, more than usual. An old chip of red paint came off it and tumbled to the ground next to the dozen that were already there.

It's got me thinking, like it did every time, that Dad had said he'd fix this shit before he left over a decade ago. For some reason, I could have mustered the will power to get it done that morning. I saw myself walking into a hardware store, get some thinner and some paint, or a whole new set of planks. *Why not get everything done before Ma would get up?* That would have been fucking nice. But then I sighed and pushed the door open.

I exited on Shearer and walked north to Centre Street. I didn't know if I actually expected anything to be open at this hour. Even Tim Horton's wasn't 24/7 but luckily for me, the local café had just opened minutes before I got there.

"Bonjour. Hi," the waitress said as she was still preparing her day.

"Hi."

"What can I get you?"

"Got anything to go in a minute," I asked.

She looked back at her kitchen. "Not really. Nothing's ready yet."

"Coffee ready?"

She looked at the machine, then said, "Enough for a cup, yeah."

"Just coffee then."

4

"To go?"

"To go."

She turned around, poured my cup of joe in a white Styrofoam cup.

"Milk and sugar?" she asked without turning around.

"Two milk, two sugars."

"So double, double," she said.

"I refuse to use the term double-double," I replied. She smiled.

"I wonder what's the commotion about over at Saint-Patrick."

"I don't know. Some people eager to relive the good old days in the Pointe," I replied.

"You going over there aren't you?" she dared.

"Yeah, I am."

"Funny," she said as she handed me my cup. "Didn't pin you for the nosey type."

"We all have our days," I said. I tipped her a buck. I walked out of there, took a sip on the sidewalk. It was too hot to drink yet.

Centre Street was nearly deserted. Only a few unlucky Saturday drivers were starting their shifts here and there. Most of them were to deliver food or restaurant supplies. The occasional UPS or Purolator truck headed for Wellington, and then downtown, that was it.

The city of Montreal was still asleep, or at least Pointe-Saint-Charles was still asleep. I took another sip and swallowed it even if it burned my throat. The coffee was burning my hand so I switched to my left, held it with my thumb on the bottom and one finger on the very edge of the cup. That's when it hit me, or *finally* hit me I should say.

I got this bad feeling in the back of my head that Cillian Kennedy, my brother, could actually have gotten himself in enough trouble to end up dead in the canal. After all, I hadn't seen him all that much these last few weeks. Who was I to know what he had been up to?

Cillian *had* indeed been a troublemaker. I had met way, way worst troublemakers in my life. Hell, Cillian would be considered a saint in this neighbourhood. I would never believe he'd do something bad enough that someone would kill him off like that, not Cillian. Fucking a guy's girlfriend, that was his style, nothing else. And you might hit a jealous husband every once in a while, but most of the time, you end up in a brawl, nothing more.

My breath got short, I felt deaf all of a sudden. I had this heat flash running through my spine and I started thinking: jealousy, fights, drugs, random gang violence, wrong-place-at-the-wrong-time kind of thing. And here I was, having coffee like I was simply going to work, like it was just another weekday.

Fuck!

I headed north on Shearer and it took no time for me to notice the yellow tape and a few cop cars with their lights turned on. A dozen people or so had walked out in their pyjamas, wondering what was happening.

There were welfare moms in their night robes, barely concealing their fat bellies and ample breasts. One guy was standing shirtless on his balcony, looking over to the canal to see if he could spot anything.

No doubt, the event would fuel the gossip around the neighbourhood for the weeks, months or maybe even years to come.

Among the flock of poor folks that had been born, bred and lived their entire lives in the Pointe were the few odd urban professionals that had bought a condo in one of the factories that used to provide work for the rest of us. They looked out of place. They felt out of place. But they bought the motherfucker, now they had to live with it.

"D'Arcy," someone shouted. I spotted Phil in the crowd, waving his hands from a distance. "D'Arcy. Over here."

I caught up to him next to the police line. I shook his hand and said, "Hey, man."

"I saw him, man. Right over there." He pointed towards the canal. You never saw Phil panic. He just didn't do that. But that morning, he almost did. That much made me worry.

"Where's the body?" I asked a nearby cop.

He was startled at first but then replied coldly, "I'm not at liberty to discuss any details of the operation, sir."

"Hey, look at my face. Look here," I insisted. He was pissed, but fuck him. "Where's the fucking body?"

"C'est son frère," Phil added. "Je l'ai vu en bas, criss. J'te jure je l'ai vu en bas."

The cop wasn't convinced.

"Sir, please," I said.

"Alright." He took his CB. "Sergeant à 1429."

"Oui," the CB screamed.

"J'ai quelqu'un ici qui prétend connaître la victime."

"J'arrive."

The sergeant showed up three minutes later. Looked at me and Phil, but mostly me.

"C'est toi qui a vu la victime dans l'eau?" he asked Phil.

"Exact."

"And you, sir, what's your last name." He was looking at his notes.

"Kennedy," I said. He looked up from his pad. That meant bad news.

He almost replied, but then no words came out of his mouth. He decided it was best not to speak. Not here. He looked at me with as much fake compassion as he could muster and said, "If you would come with me, sir."

I was fucked. No need to see the body. I fucking knew it. He lifted the yellow tape, I slid under. He took me twenty yards inside or so, by the corner of Des Seigneurs and the bridge. It was fucking weird, the yellow tape and the crowd out at five in the morning.

They were just around the corner but the wind blew through the leaves of the trees in the small park and the building sheltered us from the crowd. It was like the entire city was there around the corner but you could only head them as an echo. Even the cops were quiet, felt quiet. Hell, you could hear the water splash against the cement walls of the canal.

There was an ambulance near the entrance on the other side, forty cops or so and a bunch of camera crews on the north end. Half a dozen reporters lined up in front of them.

The cop next to me waved at someone down by the pillars. A young officer in a suit and tie was coming out of a small harbour unit in the canal while swimmers were packing up their gear behind him. He climbed a ladder up to the bridge. He traded a few words with another inspector. There was a second boat on the other side of the drawback. They started the engine, headed out for the old port.

"Who is this now?" the inspector asked as he was walking over. No one replied. "Oh," he added when he was close enough.

Shit!

He took a good look at me. Five-eleven, strong build, freckles, heavily tattooed. "Can I please see some ID, sir." I took out my driver's licence.

"My brother's back there, isn't he?" I asked.

He took a quick glance at my licence, one glance at my face and said, "Mr. Kennedy. I think we better find some place quiet."

CHAPTER 2

I spent a couple hours at Headquarters downtown. They had taken me there, offered me coffee, said they'd be back as soon as possible. I waited there a long time if you ask me. Long enough for two people on two different shifts to offer me coffee. I found that funny even though it wasn't. There I was, sitting in an office with two fucking coffees and no brother. There must have been some irony to that.

I didn't cry when I saw my brother dead on a stretcher. Something inside me turned cold, I can't explain it. They had pronounced him dead the moment they fished him out. The ambulance was not going to carry him to any hospital. There was no need for a hospital. Everyone was just waiting for an unmarked, blue coroner van to get here and take him to the morgue. I was there the whole time and I watched it happen the same way you watch an episode of *CSI*.

I thought it should hit me anytime now. I was going to just collapse, cry, shake...anything. Nothing. The worst is that it didn't fuck me up. It wasn't like I was worried by my lack of reaction. I was just tense and nothing else.

"Has your brother been involved in any criminal activities," the investigator asked me after he finally walked back in. It was the same young officer who was at the canal. I expected an older cop, I don't know why, but I got stuck with the newbie.

He and some blue had taken me to headquarters in a civilian car, asked me if I'd like to stop by my house first. They asked me if I had anything I needed to pick up or something I had to do before going on with the proceedings.

"I'm good," I replied coldly. So they started the car.

They U-turned on Canal Street. The cops opened the bridge for us. We headed north, passed Basin onto Williams, took a left, then picked Ottawa at the Y intersection. Constructions sites and empty lots filled the view on my left. Soon the whole place would be filled with condos. On the other side, rows and rows of warehouses were there to remind everyone that this was still a working class part of town.

Passed the firehouse, the first few high-risers appeared. By the time we reached the underpass, we were downtown. The cop took a left on Duke and we sank into the Ville-Marie tunnel. The bright, early, sunlight made way for the narrow walls and yellow floods of the tunnel. Then the one lane we were in opened instantaneously to five for as far as the eye could see.

Traffic was light. The ride was short. A few hundred metres later, the Saint-Laurent exit appeared. We circled over the highway, headed for the main. The homeless still owned the whole of Viger Square and the Peace Park. It was too early for most commuters. The city was quiet.

Five minutes later we had reached the headquarters' parking lot. They drove up to the back door. The inspector got out with me while the blue went to park the car.

He guided me through the front desk, down to the elevator and up to the third floor. We walked through a maze of gray and dark blue cubicles, ergonomic chairs, printers, copiers, paper trays, tall recycling bins. This place could have been any fucking office, it would have looked the same. Union posters, sexual harassment awareness week. They could have been selling car insurance, it would have looked the same if you'd asked me.

The kid cop took me to one of the corner meeting rooms. It had a white board, projector, a few chairs and a small couch. He handed me coffee, told me to make myself comfortable. Said he'd be back as soon as he could and walked out the door.

A few hours later he walked back in and asked me, cold as life, "Has your brother been involved in any criminal activities?"

Cops were bastards, no news there, but most of the officers were sharp and they were out to learn what they needed to learn, you had to give them that. They'd be friendly or angry or worried, depending on the kind of vibe you were giving them. On any other day I could admire the personality type, but I wasn't in the mood and I got a terrible vibe from that guy.

His name was Louis-Philippe Bureau-Pomminville. I didn't like him one bit. He felt like a young yuppie from a young yuppie family. I could imagine his sheltered, dead-end life on the south shore. He probably hated it, too, and couldn't wait to make a name for himself in the city. His mom and dad were so insecure about making any fucking decisions, they just decided to give four names to the kid, let him deal with it later. I could imagine the discussion: "Fuck it, let's just give him four fucking names." Jesus Christ.

"Mr. Kennedy?" he insisted. It snapped me back to reality.

"No more than the rest of us," I replied.

"What do you mean by that?" he asked as he pulled himself a chair, he flipped backwards, sat in it with his forearms resting casually on the back.

Come on! "How long you been an inspector in the south-west?"

"Our unit is not specifically linked to one territory or the other. We cover the entire city."

"So you're, telling me you have no specific knowledge of the south-west district?"

"Technically speaking, from our perspective, there is no official denomination for the south-west district. That denomination changed almost a decade ago."

"See? That's the kind of thing I was worried about."

"I'm sorry. You lost me there."

"Is there any way I can speak to an old timer? Someone who still knows where Verdun ends and Pointe-Saint-Charles starts. "

"Do you think it would make any difference in the case?"

Goddamn that tone of his. What a condescending piece of shit, talking to me like I was an idiot. He could have said *fuck you* straight to my face and it would have been less insulting.

"I think it would, yeah!" He didn't seem to like that. It was the first time I had enjoyed all day. Can't lie about that. "Get me some old guy you young preppies think is washed out. Give me some guy that was there when

Matticks ran the port or when the Boucher brothers were wreaking havoc."

"That was thirty years ago."

"So? There must be some sixty-year-old cop waiting for his pension somewhere."

"You do realize that you don't really have a say into who will work the case?"

"Well, unless you're captain, I'm guessing there's a guy outranking you who will also be responsible for it. Get me that guy."

"That's not gonna happen."

"My brother got murdered. I want to talk to that guy."

He didn't like it, but then he sighed heavily and figured I was gonna make a scene if he didn't. "I'll be right back," he said as he pulled out of his chair.

Useless idiot.

He walked out the door, I could see through the open shutters that he was speaking to his superior. He was waving his arms around a lot, a sign that he was not completely in control and that he was already trying to find excuses for the upcoming failure of his investigation.

Another suit walked back in with the inspector, a better suit. I could see he was in his late-fifties, early-sixties, gray hair, light complexion, skinny as could be.

"Lieutenant Robert Langevin. How can I help you," he said with a faint francophone accent. In a second I could tell that this guy had grown up in Montreal. His English was good, better than most, but you could hear he didn't care about hiding his French roots. I liked him better than the other kid.

"D'Arcy Kennedy. You grew up around Grand Trunk and Shearer?"

"Saint-Henri. You'll have to excuse me," he said jokingly, "but we seem to be out of Pointe-Saint-Charles veterans at the moment."

"Saint-Henri's close enough."

"I hope so," he added, trying to ease off the mood. "Now, my investigator tells me you wanted to talk to someone older. I can assure you that my man is fully qualified and able to decipher what has happened to your brother."

"Oh, I'm sure he's plenty competent." He took it as an offence, I saw his face. I knew that look. *Fucking Irish.* "I'm just concerned that he doesn't know anything about how things are in the neighbourhood."

"Well, I am here now and you have me for." He looked at his watch. "Exactly forty-two minutes. Though I'd prefer you didn't take all of it. As you might be aware, your...*our* neighbourhood is, let's say, active."

"I appreciate that."

Langevin sat down in a small grey couch to my left, the inspector pulled his chair again but as he was sitting down I asked, "Is there any way I could get another cup of coffee?"

He looked at me sideways, looked at his boss. Langevin nodded quietly. I handed him my Styrofoam cup.

"No need to be wasteful," I said.

"Du sucre pis d'la crème?" he asked, trying to infuriate me because he assumed I didn't speak French or didn't want to speak French. A lot of Québécois did that when they wanted to piss off an "Anglo."

"Deux laits pis' deux sucres," I replied with my best Québécois accent. He hated that, I could tell. This was a bad time for the age-old language divide. He walked out the door sighing.

"So. What do you have against him?" Langevin asked.

"He's too blue. He's well dressed. He looks like a yuppie, he smells like a yuppie. He's the Polish kid you hated in *The Wire*. I mean, is that the kind of police we can count on these days? Probably never fought a fight in his life either if you ask me."

"He was a boxing champion in the university circuit."

"He's got four fucking names."

"Okay. Alright," he paused for half a second. "He said you mentioned your brother was involved in some criminal activities."

"Sure, I also said no more than the rest of us."

"Anything related to the Hell's or the Mafia?"

"Nah, Cillian was just your street level troublemaker. He stole a car here and there, did a few graffiti before they turned the factories into condos. I know he fucked Councilman Barreti's daughter out of a grudge fuck, but that's as far as it goes."

"What did Barreti do?"

"Nothing. I guess Cillian was just fed up seeing his face on posterboards, figured he could fuck the daughter of some rich guy just because he could."

"Was that the kind of thing he did a lot?"

"Fucking rich daughters?"

"For example."

"Oh yeah."

"Was there a reason why?"

"Simple case of class rage if you ask me."

"Simple as that?"

"Yeah. Why not? I mean."

"You think Barreti has something to do with it?"

"Oh course not. Why would he even give a fuck about us?"

"You spend a few minutes talking about it, must have meant something to you or Cillian."

"Nah. My head's not straight I guess. Barreti's just...it's nothing, trust me."

"Alright. What else?"

"I don't know. The occasional brawl."

"Bar fights?"

"Nah. Cillian didn't do bars. He trained at the gym four times a week, drank protein shakes and went to the occasional show here and there."

"So organized crime is out of the question."

"As far as I know, yes."

The inspector with the unpronounceable name walked back in with my coffee in a mug and a file in his hand.

"Styrofoam is polluting as hell, my friend. Here's a mug."

"I was done with that joke five minutes ago," I replied. But he had a smirk on his face. He had picked up on something while he was gone. He just had that feeling about him.

"Is that the toxicology report," Langevin asked.

"Indeed," the kid said as he flipped through the pages. "Blood shows elevated traces creatine, salycilin, ammoniated bleach and traces of opiates, two different kinds, Vicodin and heroin." He snapped the file close.

"What the hell are you talking about?" I shouted.

"Painkillers, for the most part. There's a clear progression in the kid of medication and drugs he's been taking. It seems that your brother has either died of drowning while intoxicated or simply died of a bad fix before he would have drowned, coroner still working on it," Pomminville said.

"My brother didn't do drugs."

"The toxicology report shows otherwise."

"You calling my brother a junkie," I said as I got up.

The lieutenant held me back, told me to calm down. "Nobody's judging anybody," he said. "Sit down."

I didn't. "Bullshit!" I replied. "Just look at the way he fucking walked in. He's fucking happy if the file says it's a bad fix, he can go back to watching internet porn and cash in his fucking pay check."

He smiled. He fucking smiled. If only I could have smashed my knuckles into those perfect fucking teeth.

"Mr. Kennedy," Langevin continued. "I have to say that a toxicology report is compelling evidence."

"What?" I shouted.

"It's nearly bulletproof in court, sir, it could be enough to close the case and I would be at ease with that."

"Fuck me!"

"Sir."

"If he died of a bad fix, how the fuck did he end up in the canal? Did you think about that?"

There was a dent in the junkie theory right there. The lieutenant seemed to be willing to roll with it if only at least for appearances. I liked him.

"Alright. Let's think about that for a second," Langevin said.

18

The kid with four names wasn't about to lose any sleep over the case. He wasn't gonna waste his time on it either. That smirk was stapled to his face like flies to a pile of shit.

"There's a den at the corner of Gill and Saint-Patrick," Pomminville said. "It's not impossible that he went there, shot up and walked out. The bad fix could have kicked in minutes afterwards. I wouldn't be surprised." I could tell he was a pro at bullshit. A fucking pro. He was talking bullshit, but it was some of the best bullshit I had ever heard. "The canal is right across the street and there's no railing around that particular area, so it's not impossible."

"It's not impossible," I said reluctantly. My brother was going to be marked "overdose" out of a technicality. I couldn't let that happen. Ma wasn't gonna bury a drug addict.

"Exactly," the kid replied. He seemed to like that expression a lot, *it's not impossible.*

"I think it's full of shit."

"Now let's all take a minute here," the lieutenant added. "Does the report indicate anything else?"

"Not much. He had a high protein content in his stomach. Given the strong muscular build of the deceased, I assume he was undergoing some sort of training?"

"Yes."

"We did find a fresh puncture mark behind his left knee. It wasn't easy to see because of all the tattoos, but there were a few bruises here and there."

"See? A few bruises," I said.

"We also found a card in his wallet saying he was a member of a fighting club."

"Yeah, he was training for MMA."

"So we can't rule out that the bruises were a result of his training. Unless there are other elements that suggest a struggle. I am really sorry for your loss, but it's not unheard of that athletes end up in drugs. A lot of them suffer from stress and especially those like your brother if I am not mistaken, who have yet to 'make it' as they say. You'd be surprised at how many of them fall into toxico-mania from the pressure to compete."

"Ah, come on!" I shouted.

"We haven't set up a full profile yet. Again," he said to his boss. "It's not unheard of. The placement of the puncture mark indicates that the deceased could have been ashamed of his drug use and used places on the body that are not as evident. The back of the knees, inner thighs, between the toes. Obviously the painkillers didn't seem like enough if he was willing to try something like heroin."

"Did your expert find any of this shit?"

"Sir," Langevin snapped at me.

"You will have me believe that a guy who trains every fucking day and lives on protein shakes, will end up using heroin?"

"I've seen similar cases, people falling down from good places. It can happen really fast. When was the last time you saw your brother?"

"I don't know, couple weeks."

"So it's not impossible he started taking drugs. It could have been his first time and he just got unlucky."

"Fucking heroin?"

"It's not unheard of." He was getting tired of saying it.

"Come on!"

"It's not unheard of."

I threw the coffee heavily into a nearby trash can. My arm just swung it. Mug or no mug, it just happened. Coffee splashed everywhere along with bits and pieces of the broken porcelain. "Well, that's a fucking lot of 'not unheard of' for one fucking case."

"Mr. Kennedy, sit down, please."

"I ain't sitting down."

The lieutenant was trying to mediate everyone. He was good at it. But I was fed up with the kid's smirk. "Your brother's social security history indicates that he owned his own business," he said.

"What about it?"

"What was the business?"

"Tattoo shop."

"Really?" Pomminville asked.

"Yeah?"

"Did they work in body piercing as well?"

"I guess so."

He wrote it down. I stared at him, my face was asking *why?*

"I need to take that into account in the report, if we are to inquire about puncture marks. It's a possibility, you know?"

Lying sack of shit, I thought.

"Do you think his death could be related to his work?" the lieutenant added. He was trying to throw me a bone.

"I don't know."

"Could you think of something?"

"I don't know," I repeated harshly. I was getting tired of saying it, too. "All I know, is that he doesn't want to work the fucking case."

"I *am* working 'the fucking case.'"

"Hey!" the lieutenant told him. "Tu surveilles s'que tu dis." I was surprised he called him out in front of me. The kid must be a fucking pain in the ass on the job.

"B'en, j'mexcuse. Mais il cours après," Pomminville replied.

"Pardon?" Langevin added.

"Rien, monsieur. Désolé, monsieur." He backed down.

"Now, Mr. Kennedy, unless you have any evidence indicating that your brother's employment could have something to do with his death, there is nothing so far, to the best of my knowledge, that indicates a violent death here."

"You mean murder."

"Violent death of any sort."

"My brother was killed, you fucking look into that."

"Do you have any evidence for me?" Pomminville asked.

"Don't play that."

"Do you?"

"Ah, come on..." I sighed.

"*DO* you have *ANY* evidence for me?" he insisted slowly.

I had to admit. "No."

"Then..."

"You work the fucking case," I shouted. "You work the fucking case or you'll fucking hear from me," I added. I was ready to bail out of there. He literally laughed at me.

"You better get yourself a lawyer then," he dared.

"I warned you once already," the lieutenant said. His eyes said *you better not fucking reply.*

I was growling inside my head. Growling hard. I wish I could have smashed my bare knuckles into his perfect, white teeth. If ONLY I could have smashed my knuckles into his perfect, white teeth.

"I'll fucking get one if I need to," I said as I stormed out the door. "But trust me. I might not even need one!"

CHAPTER 3

"Fuck you, you fucking frog," Cillian was shouting, as he was pounding the face of some kid in front of Saint-Henri High.

He must've been fifteen or so and I guess I was supposed to keep him out of trouble while Dad was on the job up north.

I wasn't doing a very good job.

Saint-Henri High was the French school at one end of Saint-Henri, James Lyng was the English school at the other end of the borough. That's where me and Cillian and pretty much every "Anglo" around who couldn't afford private schools went to. It was a '60s school built out of concrete slabs, with small windows, and a poorly maintained asphalt lot. It was stuck in the nook of the Turcot Highway Exchange. Turcot was the busiest piece of road in the whole fucking country and it was covered by support bolts and chicken wire. Not necessarily the best environment to learn.

Now, on paper at least, the English schools were nowhere near as fucked as the French schools. The French schools had the highest dropout rate in the entire developed fucking world, nothing less, but James Lyng was still shitty on all accounts. As far as I knew, it had everything we supposedly needed as young men: sports and arts and teachers to teach us. The school was probably fine as a building. I didn't know. It was probably more the poor setting and the overall condition of the neighbourhood that didn't help.

If you managed to eat right, stay out of half of the fights and dodge drunken drivers, you still had to avoid the cops, bypass the language police on whatever job you could get and dodge skinheads crews that were out to bust some heads.

One of the biggest problems, or at the time at least, was probably the age-old debate between the French and the *English*, a term that seemed to encompass everything from actual English, Scots, Irish, Jews, Italians, Greeks, Polish...everything and everyone that wasn't of French descent. Of course, not all Québécois felt that way, but enough of them did to piss us off.

The last referendum had happened only a few years earlier and *they* had lost by a very narrow margin. That sparked a wave of hard-line nationalism on both sides. That pissed me off, but I guess I was old enough to know better. We'd just have to let the whole thing blow over like it always did. But Cillian, well, he had turned to hard-line Irish nationalism. I called it his *IRA Phase.* He had gotten himself a flag from Sinn-Fein online, even tried to learn Gaelic a bit—as if Gaelic was an easy language to learn in the first place. Turned out he could manage to say "Pog Moih Hong" just fine, the rest, not so much.

It pissed him off every time the French nationalists would call him English. He wasn't from England, he was from Ireland. And so, when a bunch of kids from Saint-Henri High decided to walk half a mile on Notre-Dame Street to tag "English go home" on the front wall of James Lyng High, my brother was one among a few dozen kids who decided to take it upon themselves to defend the honour of an institution they otherwise resented.

So a bunch of burgundy shirts had suddenly appeared on the front yard of Saint-Henri and my brother was the first of them. It didn't matter if the kid in front of him had tagged his school or not, he slugged him good, followed him to the ground and pounded some more until he was unconscious.

Everyone from James Lyng pretty much did the same: pick a random guy, punch, knock out. The fight was one sided until the thugs, punks and skinheads that formed most of the French nationalists all walked out together. Some of them had knives, one had a bat, another had picked up a metal trash can on the way there. Those guys meant business.

Cillian let go of the passed out kid, jumped the guy with a bat in his hand. Typical of him. He would always pick the hard way. He would say that if you give them a single inch to move, then you are setting yourself up to lose.

The French kid swung his bat but Cillian was inside its reach *so it didn't really hurt* he told me. If he had gotten the end of it on the temple, he could have been dead right there, but instead Cillian drove his forehead in the other kid's nose. Blood spurted everywhere so Cillian did it again and once more. When something works out, why not try it again a few times, right?

When the kid stumbled backwards, my brother snatched the bat from his hand and drove it in his calf. He always claimed that's where he was aiming but I'd bet he was going for the knee and missed.

My brother fought dirty.

The French kid screamed in pain as he crashed to the ground.

"Bring a bat to a fist fight, motherfucker!" my brother shouted as he swung again. "Fuckin' pussy!"

The leg broke open and bone was sticking out. It actually made the news later that day. Nasty fucking wound. I saw the pictures in the papers. It wasn't pretty.

The brawl around turned messy with both sides suffering casualties. Some kids on the ground had burgundy shirts, some had their regular clothes on. That's how you could tell them apart. If you didn't know what language they spoke, you wouldn't be able to figure out who came from where and when. Only the shirts and their colour mattered.

One kid ended up face down, doing the sizzling like bacon on the cement. He was in physiotherapy for months because he had received brass knuckles to the back of the head. I'd a called it a cheap fucking shot if I had been there, but it wasn't like there were any rules anyways. They found the weapon in a manhole twenty yards from the school, never caught the motherfucker who did it. All we knew is that he was on *our* side.

My brother was still hell-bent over the kid with a broken leg when someone tackled him to the ground. My brother fell in a bad position, with one arm underneath him and the other still holding the bat, but as the other guy's weight sat heavily on him, he couldn't use it.

The punches started coming in one after the other and for a moment, my brother could have been just another kid on his way to rehab and speech impediments. Five or six punches landed on his face but he kept shouting, "Come on, you fucking pussy!"

That's when the police came down Notre-Dame Street. Three cars from Notre-Dame and one from Saint-Jacques to squeeze everyone in. Most of the kids scattered to the four winds but my brother was pinned and still getting pounded. The rest didn't seem to care about being arrested or anything. In fact, it's not like it was the first time the police had to go down to Saint-Henri High. Hell, the city even had their one unique intervention plan for the institution. You found everything in its four walls: prostitution, extortion, which in other schools was simply referred to as bullying. But at Saint-Henri, you had fights, drugs, drug dealers and thugs looking for a reason to live. The cops knew they were gonna have their hands full.

Some cop tackled the kid standing over my brother. The kid fought back and the cop wasn't ready for it. Knocked him right down. No shit! A fifteen-year-old knocking out a cop cold with a single punch. My brother quickly got back up. He and his opponent looked at each other in the eyes for a moment and both of them smiled. My brother threw away the bat and wiped the blood from his mouth.

Some of the kids were now taking on the cops in teams. People from James Lyng and Saint-Henri were now beating on police together like a happy fucking family. The cops traded punches and billy clubs hits, but when some sixteen-year-old kid throws trashcans and swings switchblades at you, you keep your ego in check and watch your back. They huddled together in a defensive position.

You could have expected the police to shoot one of the kids or something, but that would have sparked something worse, probably citywide havoc. In a city like Montreal, known for its many riots, the last thing the police wanted was to stir even more shit up by broadcasting dead teenagers on the evening news.

More squad cars quickly came in. My brother and his new found nemesis had scores to settle, but there was too much police for them to do it now. Hell, even the cavalry was showing up, rows of guys on their horses swinging billy clubs.

"On décriss," the French guy said to his friends. They took off on Saint-Ferdinand and escaped through some dark alley, over a fence and an abandoned lot.

Most of the kids from James Lyng had either gone back to their school or were being cuffed along with some people from Saint-Henri. A normal kid would have called it a day and be happy with the damage done. My brother was not a normal kid.

My brother started running on Saint-Ferdinand. There were two cars blocking Langevin Street so he followed the French kids down the alley. When he hopped over a fence and ended up on Saint-Philippe. Two cars at each end, no alley this time. There was an open door across the street. The French kids were nowhere in sight. Cillian wanted to keep going. So he ran across the street, jumped right into the apartment, not knowing who lived there.

"Hey!" someone shouted. But before anyone could react, my brother crossed their living room, hallway, kitchen, opened the back door and sneaked through the back lot and again on Saint-Jacques Street. He looked behind him. The cops had their hands full back at the school. He had managed to sneak through.

He took a moment to catch his breath, wipe away some more blood and smile. Cillian caught up with the French guy in the park behind the Gallerie Projects.

"Hey," my brother shouted.

"Va chier," the French kid replied.

"Call me a fucking English."

"Quoi?"

"Call me a fucking English," my brother repeated as he got close enough to punch the guy.

"Osti d'Anglais," the kid shouted, prancing about.

"Here we go!" Cillian said with a smile and he slugged the other guy with a mean hook to the jaw. The guy went down.

It could happen. Not that it necessarily did, but it could happen.

"I'm fucking Irish," my brother shouted. "Learn the fucking difference."

"Tabarnak," the French guy said. He was hazy and obviously confused. My brother then decided to serve him a bit of his own medicine.

He jumped the guy while he was down, locked his knee in the guy's ribs so he couldn't get up. He held the guy's arms down with his right hand, punched with the left.

The other fella tried to protect himself best he could but he went limp after three punches. My brother got up, kicked him in the gut one more time just because.

That's when the kid's friends came in slowly from Saint-Jacques Street. They saw there was a single burgundy shirt alone in the park. *Easy pickings.* When they saw one of their own lying bloodily on the ground, two of them started running towards Cillian while the third one got some more backup.

My brother stood his ground, thinking, *Two to one are still good odds, ain't they?* What an arrogant little fuck.

He swung at the first kid who went down but quickly got up. The second one threw his backpack at Cillian and quickly dashed to kick him. My brother took it, but a second and a third kick came in. Cillian punched back but missed, then got himself kicked again. The first kid joined in, my brother threw an elbow and opened an eyebrow but the kicks and punches didn't stop.

That's when the third kid came running with more of Saint-Henri's finest students.

"Par icitte, osti! On en a un tabarnak!"

There's only so much a single Irishman can do so my brother said, "Oh, shit!"

The two closer to Cillian turned their backs for half a second as the news of reinforcements drew smiles on their faces. Cillian took the opportunity to sucker punch the first kid to the back of the neck, threw his forehead into the second kid's nose.

"Ah! Tabarnak!" the kid shouted.

Blood splattered all over both their faces and that's when my brother bailed. There was only one entrance to the park and he wouldn't have the luck to find an open door twice in the same afternoon.

He took off and headed for the tall grass at the end of the park. He jumped the rusty fence and landed on the railroad tracks. He was out of immediate danger but the tracks didn't really head anywhere where he'd be safe.

"Yé icitte le criss," one of the kids shouted as he jumped the fence. He was first and apparently alone so my brother quickly jumped him before he could get his footing. He threw a few kicks and knees and the kid was done for. But then he received another backpack filled with books to the back of the head.

Three more faces appeared over the fence so Cillian started running down the tracks. He was probably twenty or thirty yards ahead of the other kids but an Irish guy on short legs doesn't run that fast. On his left, cops were cuffing up kids and putting them into city busses like they always did when they arrested too many people for a single wagon.

There were six or seven guys running after Cillian, some had been beaten up a bit, others were fresh out of class. A few of them were catching up to him, still Cillian had a wide smile on his face.

"Fuck you," he kept shouting again and again.

There wasn't anywhere to go but he kept shouting it. He could have gotten out at Notre-Dame but he didn't. He should have gotten out at Saint-Ambroise, but he didn't.

If you'd asked me, I think he was just coming home. Simple as that. He would have run all the way down the Pointe to Grand Trunk and Shearer. But things being what they were, that track was still a busy CN track.

My brother was almost out of steam when he got to the canal bridge. He had the French kids on his ass and what did he see coming his way? A freaking freight train. Of course, the train didn't run fast in the city, but it was still a freaking train. What was a kid to do?

"Ah, fuck me," Cillian said.

"Oh, shit!" some of the kids behind him shouted.

My brother had two choices: bail to the tall grass and get a beating or jump in the canal. He didn't think twice about it. He decided on the canal. After all, he had jumped in the canal's dirty waters plenty of times before. Why not now?

He took a few large strides on the bridge then leaped into the air over the railing and headed into the water headfirst like an Olympic fucking diver.

The French kids stopped on the bank.

"Osti, y'a sauté" they said. They couldn't believe it. "Le tabarnak, y'a sauté!"

They wouldn't follow Cillian. They didn't hate my brother that much. The next crossing was Atwater Street.

Cillian's head appeared on the surface. "Wooooooouuuuhhh!" he shouted as he gave them the middle finger. He slicked his wet hair behind his head. "Wooooooooouuuuhh!" he screamed again as loud as he could. Then he started laughing as he headed for the opposing bank, slowly, like he was doing lanes at the city pool.

I wished he hadn't done that. The adrenaline was keeping him going, but he was in real trouble. He had jumped in the canal plenty of times, alright. But it was still fucking May and the water must've been ten degrees or close enough.

I was home when all of this happened. If I remember correctly, I was doing my taxes and they were late and I needed the tax return to clear out some room on the visa.

The radio was on and they were talking about a

police intervention at Saint-Henri High. As far as I knew, shit happened all the time at Saint-Henri. The host talked about violence, riots, arrest, assaults, including at least two wounded officers, one of which had to be hospitalized on the spot. I had no reason to believe that my brother had anything to do with it. But then the radio mentioned a group of kids from James Lyng.

"Shit," I said. My brother came home a few minutes later.

The door swung open as I got up from the kitchen table. Cillian barely walked in. He was soaked wet. His black pants and burgundy shirt were sagging over his skinny legs and wide shoulders. He had his hands crossed over his chest. His blond hair slumped over his forehead. He looked bad, skin was turning pale and blue. He had a few cuts, a lot of bruises and a busted lip. His teeth literally creaked as he was shivering heavily. Still, he stood chin-up, proud like a peacock. I instantaneously knew exactly who the radio had been talking about.

"Are you okay?" I asked.

His eyes lit up with fire and adrenaline. "Any time, man!" he said as he moved his head side to side. A smile appeared on his lips. "Any fucking time!"

CHAPTER 4

The viewing was held at home. The funeral home had insisted that the viewing be at their facilities but my mother would have none of it. They would handle the "restoration" as they called it and then deliver Cillian to the house so that we could have the viewing at home.

"I'm afraid we're gonna have to charge you for this," they said.

"I don't care," I replied. That was that.

We cleared some space in my mother's tiny living room. I said we should handle the food and beverages at my place downstairs so that people could be at peace in her apartment.

"I'd like that," she said.

So me and two of my cousins tried to get a full-sized casket (with my brother in it) up the stairs of our bicentennial house in the Pointe. My friends Karl and Ryan helped a little. Ryan helped more than Karl and I. We had known each other for years. Had gone to James Lyng together but it wasn't until later that we had become friends. He was a short, wide Scotsman but not the businessman kinda Scot. "My ancestry was from the Highlands," he'd say. Not that I knew what that implied, but I knew Ryan was a tough motherfucker.

When we reached the second floor, the angle in her door didn't help things out.

"Pffff," I sighed.

"What?" The guys asked.

"It's nothing. I'm good," I said. What a horrible idea that was. Cillian wasn't a fucking couch. But then everything cleared and my brother didn't end up down the stairs so that was one less thing I had to worry about.

We had set up a nice garment arrangement over a small table. Sober greens and purple. Mom had set up an easel next to the TV with Cillian's ugly mug on it. It was a picture we had taken maybe a year ago in the backyard. I don't recall it had been a special occasion. The weather was nice. We were having a barbecue. I had just bought Mom a DSLR camera and she was learning how to use it. She held it like some fragile artifact. My mom and technology didn't exactly go well together.

She snapped a few pictures of everything and anything. Then I showed her how to zoom. "Ahhhhh," she said, all excited. "Don't move," she had told Cillian. He smiled, she snapped it and here we were ten months later, looking at that photo at my brother's funeral.

We opened the casket and he looked like he always did. Skin whiter than white, freckles here and there, neck tattoos, short trimmed beard. I was happy to see the water hadn't done too much damage. A few hours more in the canal and we probably wouldn't have gotten a last look. But we did and I was happy about that.

"We'll be downstairs. Just call when you need us, alright," Karl said.

"Thanks, you guys," I said as I shook their hand. "I mean it."

They walked out. Ma sat down next to Cillian. She hadn't shed a tear that day. Not a single yet. I didn't know if it was okay for her to bottle up so many things inside. I didn't know what to do. She had been crying herself to sleep every night since he had died but I was the one who had made the arrangements so it was the first time she actually saw him since. I was glad she didn't get to see him the way I did in the back of that coroner van. Six hours in water, the skin was already getting mushy and white. I didn't want her to see him like that. But now she wasn't moving or talking or crying. I had to do something.

"It's gonna be too warm in here soon, Ma. Can't have the AC on with the door opening up every two minutes," I said.

I had said it too loud. I said it the way you explain shit to a kid or your dog. She didn't reply. "I'll open the doors and windows, alright?" I asked looking at her. I could have just done it. I had never spoken to my Ma like she was retarded or deaf before, why was I doing it now? I didn't like it and I don't think she liked it either. I tried to change my tone. "Listen, I'm sorry."

Only then did she reach for my hand. She took it softly and looked into my eyes. "It's alright," she said. "I don't want *us* to change because of that, alright?"

"Promise."

"Now, you can open the doors, it *will* get really hot in here. It's not a bad idea. "

I walked over to her tiny kitchen, squeezed myself between her washer and her kitchen table, opened the window. I walked back around to the door, opened it and held it there with the recycling bin. The moment I did, Emma got up from the grass in the backyard with her big flappy cheeks wide open, drooling and smiling as she made her way up.

"Easy now," I said as I allowed her in. She barked a few times as she circled and jumped. "Easy, easy. Are you hungry?" I asked. She barked. "Food's downstairs, baby," I replied. She barked again. She circled around me and jumped again playfully. She had no idea what the fuck was going on.

She made her way into the living room in half a second. "Wait—" I tried to say but when I walked in she already had her front paws up on the casket, looking for Cillian, waiting for him to pet her.

"Sorry, Ma," I said as I tried to get a leash on her.

"It's okay," she said as she got next to Emma, petting her head at the same time. She looked deeply into her son's eyes. Emma did the same. She tried licking his face: no reaction. "Cillian loved that dog didn't he?" Ma added.

"I believe he did, yeah."

"Then let her have her moment as well."

Emma sniffed and licked Cillian's face, then sniffed him some more, hoping for a reaction. When she saw my brother wasn't moving she started barking and whining.

"Poor thing," my mother said.

"I'll take care of her."

"I'd like it if she stayed in the family."

"She will, Ma, of course. Now come over here, Emma, people want to come in," I said as I put her on a leash and walked her to the balcony. Ma sat back in a chair, next to the casket. There was a strange serenity to her...her black dress, her hair up in a knot, her hands resting on top of one another. She was looking out the window and the light was just right.

"You ready?" I asked her. She turned to me, slowly.

"No," she sobbed as she burst into tears. She tried to stop herself from crying, tried to smile at me. It wasn't working very well. Choked me up real good.

I didn't know how to answer to that. Part of me was happy she was crying. I guess it was healthy. It's not healthy to see your mother in such pain. That just isn't right.

Her shoulders felt heavy now, but she was hell-bent on standing straight, staying proud. Her eyes were red and you would see the freckles through her blushed cheeks. You could tell she wanted to crash and cry and beg and scream but she wouldn't. It was the Irish pride kicking in.

"I'll let the family in now," I said. She barely nodded and I finally re-opened the front door.

Karl, Phil and Ryan were the first ones at the bottom of the stairs. The walls were slanted, the wood was crooked and the ramps could have used a new coat of paint. The walls too, to be honest. Bits and pieces were missing, some more pieces were chirping off. The window over the door had not been washed in a while because my mom couldn't reach it and she wouldn't step on a ladder. The damn place was narrow. Two guys couldn't really get through it properly. We were going to have to get people to leave though the back door.

I felt ashamed of my house. We have been brought up in it and I guess we turned out alright, but for a funeral? I just didn't know.

The door downstairs was open and I could see everyone gathered in front, waiting in line. They had waited their turn so respectfully I would have never believed it.

Karl had his hands in his pockets and had unbuttoned his jacket. It was dark grey with dark grey pants. Ryan and Phil wore suits as well, hell, looking at them you'd think we were shooting a cover picture for a Pogues cover band.

I didn't say another word. I couldn't say another word. I had not cried yet but I couldn't say another word. I wasn't feeling any pain but there was plenty of rage and I wasn't about to let that out at the moment. I looked at Karl. He looked at me and knew better.

"Alright," he said as he pushed himself from the wall. "Let's get this shit over with."

I went down to the backyard after everyone had paid their respects. Ryan, Karl and Phil were sitting there under the sun umbrella. I pulled myself a plastic chair, Phil threw me a cigarette.

"Thanks," I said as I sat down. I reached for his blue Bic lighter.

"How long 'till we bring him to the cemetery?"

"We asked the priest to be there around eight-thirty for a burial at sundown."

Phil looked at his watch. "So we leave in an hour."

"Or so, yeah. Ma's gonna have her moment alone. She asked to, and then we can bring him down."

"Good."

"Most of the family said they were gonna go out to eat and meet us there," I continued. "I also got a few messages from people who couldn't make it here in time.

They promised they'd make it to the cemetery. It's going well. I'm glad. It's going good. Could have been a lot worst."

"Anyone left in there?" Phil asked.

"She kicked the last of us out," someone said from the balcony. It was Uncle Miller and his kid who were coming down ice box in their hands. "She mentioned you managed to get bagpipes for the burial?"

"Well, one guy, yeah."

"That's good. That's the only way to do it right."

"I don't get that," Karl said.

"What?"

"Bagpipes. I mean, it's Cilli's funeral, so I'm sorry to say, but that instrument has the most annoying sound I have ever heard."

Ryan replied for all of us, "You're German, Karl. What the fuck do *you* know about sorrow?"

"Alright, alright, guys," Uncle Miller said. "This is still a wake, let's keep it classy," he added as he dropped the ice box in the grass. "There are a few beers left if you want one."

"I'll have one," Karl said. He picked one up, passed it to Ryan and then one to Phil and me. Uncle Miller closed the ice box, sat on it with a beer in his hands. He popped it open and was about to drink, but then he stopped. "Here, boy, you're having one too."

"Isn't he a bit young?" Ryan asked. He was thirteen. Plenty old enough if you ask me.

"Nonsense," Uncle Miller replied. "Sit down, son. It's a hell of a day." Thomas, his kid, pulled himself a chair, sat with the beer in his hands like it was the Holy Grail.

"Don't tell your mother now, alright?" Uncle Miller

added as he pulled himself another one. Everyone laughed.

"Alright," Thomas said.

"When are you headed back to Toronto?" I asked.

"Tomorrow. We got ourselves a room at, wait, I got the paper here. The Espresso Downtown. On Dorchester. Is that good?"

"I wouldn't know."

"Probably not," Uncle Miller replied to himself. "Don't worry about us."

"Want a smoke?" Phil asked Uncle Miller.

"I quit years ago."

"Wanna start again?"

"Phil!" I said.

"Ah, why not?" Uncle Miller said. "Now's as good a time as any other." He pulled out a cigarette and the lighter. Put it between his lips the hesitated. He was looking at his son. "Don't tell your mother about this, either, alright."

"Can *I* have one?" Thomas asked.

"Don't be stupid now," Uncle Miller said as he lit it up.

"But Mom says you're not supposed to smoke anymore."

"I think you're better off if you never smoke. Shit will take the air out of your lungs, kid," Karl said.

"Listen to the man," his father added as he took a drag.

"But Mom—"

"I'm not starting again. I'm just having one, *alright?* D'Arcy—" He reached over to me, shook my hand. "I'm sorry about Cillian, man."

"Thank you."

"I guess I just don't know what else there is to say."

"It's okay."

"I mean. What *do* you say when a nephew dies. What do you say to that? He was what? Twenty-six?"

"Twenty-four."

"Twenty-four. What do you say to that?" he repeated. Then he stopped and thought about it for a moment. He raised his beer and said, "Brighter fires burn faster."

"They do," we said as we clinked our cans together.

"Hell, that boy lived a life plenty if you ask me," Uncle Miller added. "He drank some, fought some and, as far as I know, fucked more than his share of some."

"Fuck!" We laughed.

"And he wouldn't be a son of Ireland if he wasn't getting into troubles every once in a while," Uncle Miller added.

"True," I said. I raised my drink again.

"Now he might have died a young man, but I would not believe it was drugs that did it. Send me to hell if you want, I'll never believe it."

"Me neither."

"Yeah, that's bullshit. No way."

"Now it is nice to see you guys—the family—gathered here, together," Uncle Miller continued. "Because if the police don't find who'd done it, hell, someone in this family will. The devil's gonna find us in his way. Am I clear enough?"

"You didn't need to be," Ryan replied.

"Now, you see, kid," he said to his son. "That's the Irish way of doing things. The Irish never had much, but we always had friends and family to count on. We might be insane, but shoot me if we ain't all insane together. Don't ever forget that, alright."

"Alright."

"Erin go bragh," Uncle Miller said.

"Erin go bragh," I replied. Karl and Phil didn't really get it but who could blame them. Ryan knew what it was about.

"Yeah," Uncle Miller added as he fluffed up his son's hair, looking straight into his eyes.

What would he do if his own kid would get murdered, or even if he just died before his time. I knew there were some dark, dark things going through my uncle's mind right that moment. Thomas stood in silence, unsure of how to react to his father's stare. There are certain moments in life when a loved one looks at you in such a way that you feel the entire world would collapse around you if you let go of a stare for one single moment. Then he fluffed up his hair once again. "Erin go bragh," he repeated softly.

Twenty minutes later, he and Thomas walked to their car. The four of us were left behind to figure out how to get my brother out of there.

CHAPTER 5

People in Montreal had been burying their dead in the same two or three cemeteries for centuries. We looked around for a while, thought about whether we should get a more affordable spot in the east end of town, at Hawtorne-Dale or Pointe-Claire. Ma wasn't gonna ride a bus for an hour to see her kid. Our grandparents had been buried at Mont-Royal cemetery and their parents before that, I didn't know about most of the family but we did know that Grand-grand-daddy Miller had died at Cholera Bay on Grosse Ilse. He was buried there.

Now, Cillian wasn't gonna get buried on Grosse Ile, and he could have ended up in Mont-Royal. But then my mother learned that Thomas D'Arcy McGee, father of confederation and, so far, only political leader ever assassinated in Canada, was buried at Notre-Dame Cemetery. So Notre-Dame Cemetery it was going to be. Hell, I was named D'Arcy because of that guy. I guess it shouldn't be a surprise that she'd take it to heart that one of her kids could be buried there.

We got my brother a spot in one of the newer sections where there were no trees yet, where the letters dividing the lots were double digits because the rest of the place had gone through the whole alphabet more than once.

I always expected they'd dig two holes one next to the other, "But as it turned out," the guy explained to us, "caskets were piled up one on top of the other." Seemed awkward at first, but then again, why would the dead really care?

Later my mother got this idea in her head that we all die one day and that her time was coming just as well.

"I really wish we could be buried next to one another," she said. "Family's broken up enough as it is."

I didn't have the heart to tell her no so I called up the caretaker the next day; they offered financing on the spot just as if we were buying a flat-screen TV. We called the bank took a personal loan and a long-term payment plan. Thirteen and a half percent. *Shit*, I thought. *Cillian's burial is gonna be the death of me.*

But I signed the papers anyways so me, my brother and Ma would be buried together just off of Remembrance Road near the top of Mont-Royal. I guess we could do worse. My burial ground was better real estate than my apartment was. That should have been funny.

Of course, that meant I was going to have to work overtime to pay for the damn spot, but Ma had kept the house for us so I couldn't complain.

She insisted that he'd get an Irish burial the same we had the Irish wake at home. The same way that she had insisted we get baptized and get our first communion and confirmation. She also insisted that we'd get married someday. It was also her idea to get us some Gaelic names even though she never bothered to learn our ancestor's dead language.

When I was younger I'd take some mean pleasure in reminding her that Christianity really had nothing to do with Celts in the first place. She'd tell me to watch my tongue and, of course, I wouldn't and so Dad had to slap my head straight.

"You listen to your mother, D'Arcy," he'd yell.

Dad would have called us Mike and Bob if he had it his way. She wanted D'Arcy and Cillian. I never fully understood why she took it so seriously but I did remember plenty of time where she would say, "We were hungry when we came here. Can you imagine that? So hungry that there weren't even potatoes to eat anymore. And our grandparents and great-grandparents took that wretched trip so that their children could have some land and some hope. Damn, the English didn't make it easy for any of us either. And then you hear the francophones telling us to speak French only. I don't know about you, but I'm tired of people telling me what to do. Our family comes out of Griffintown and you can be proud of that. We came out of Griffintown and now we own our own piece of the land. The Irish and the Scots built half of this city with their sweat and tears..."

"Alright, alright," I'd tell her. There was only so much I could take. Irish moms seemed to be heavy on *sweat and tears.*

I called in a favour with Allan Falco, a former friend of my father who had retired from the Ceremonial Guard. He agreed to play the pipes for the funeral, didn't make a mention of any payment. I'd like to think he was happy to do it. I'd like to think he was happy just to play to any audience anymore.

We rented a Chrysler for the occasion. I was driving. Mom was in the back with her sister Addie. The hearse lead the way. A few friends and family members were following right behind us. We came up Côte-des-Neiges after leaving the Pointe and soon we say the castle-like building of the CDN Armoury. A hundred yards after that, the thick, dense buildings of the city made way for the seemingly endless green pastures of the cemeteries that flanked Mont-Royal Park.

The hearse turned right, passed the iron gates, headed slowly into the sinuous roads up the hill. The cemetery was so green and quiet that you'd have a hard time believing you were at the heart of a major Canadian city.

When we reached section FT, way up on the hill, I could see Mr. Falco was already set near the grave. He saw us coming in the distance, picked up his pipes and stood at the ready. He wore his kilt, knee-high white socks, had an olive wool coat on. He couldn't wear his military uniform. It would have been disrespectful to the military because Cillian had never served, but he looked like a million dollars.

The hearse stopped maybe fifty yards short of Cillian's grave. Father Normandeau walked out of his car across the field. He set his white collar straight, wiped away some summer dust from his garment. He took his Bible the way you'd hold a young child and started to walk towards the freshly dug grave.

The pallbearers gathered at the hearse, in the shade of a tall oak. There was Ryan, Karl, Phil plus Thomas, Uncle Miller and me. We pulled out Cillian from there but it was not until we all held the casket properly that we were not all ready to walk, that Mr. Falco started to play.

He took the blowpipe to his lips, placed his fingers over the chanter. The notes started to carry across the mountain, as if they were riding on the winds to the skies. It felt like everyone in Montreal was meant to know that we were resting the soul of our Irish brother today. If the winds were strong enough, they could have heard it all the way to the RDP if I had it my way.

Mr. Falco opened with "Flowers of the Forest," played Glengarry's "Lament, When Irish Eyes are Smiling." I loved "When Irish Eyes are Smiling." We stepped into the sun with Cillian. People behind us were walking out of cars, joining in line behind us. We rested Cillian next to the grave. I asked Mr. Falco about the "Amazing Grace." He agreed to it even though I'd swear he sighed at the idea of playing that song for the millionth time.

I looked around. Only closer friends and family had been at the wake, now the entire extended family had shown up for the burial. My mother had six brothers and sisters, some of whom I had only met a handful of times in my life. Each came with their sons and daughters, two or three of them each with their husbands and sometimes, young children as well.

Everyone lined up with the sun in their back. The warm summer weather did not stop them from wearing their finest of black garments. I noticed Aunt Addie's two daughters. They had made the trip from Belleville and were probably headed back right afterwards, a five-hour drive.

There were two of my cousins Eric and Matthieu who had gotten jobs in the videogame industry. Their grandmother had changed her name from Miller to Milaire sixty years ago and jumped into the French Wagon.

Another cousin, Dylan Miller, spoke perfect English

but he was an overly intellectual snob who I didn't like very much. His dad had made money in construction and he went to college and that made him arrogant for some reason. He was there with his wife and his two-year-old son he had insisted be named Emile after some Montreal poet who had died decades ago. Emile Miller, goddamnit! He was that kind of guy.

A few people from school and the Pointe had shown up. Mam' Carla from the diner over on Wellington had come. She was a friend of Ma and we had been eating at her place for as long as I can remember. She wore a light flower dress with a dark ribbon in her head. I had known the lady probably for twenty years and I had never seen her without her diner's outfit. There must've been something to that.

Patricia McCready was there too, coming out of a cab. She walked over to us, dark eyeliner underneath her eyes, white flowers in her hands, her curves looking marvellous under her black dress. She looked good, no way to lie about that. I liked to think she wasn't there for Cillian. She knew him, of course, we all shared the same back alley, but I liked to think she was there for me. I looked at her and smiled, her eyes spoke to me a genuine compassion. She took a hand to her heart. I nodded.

Then the pipes came to an end and it felt like the loudest silence you would ever hear.

Father Normandeau started the eulogy in French, then moved to a broken English. I didn't really know what a funeral was supposed to sound like. I had been to a wake or two, but that was the first burial I had ever been to. It felt alright. It felt appropriate.

I stopped listening a few moments later. It's not that I was bored or that I couldn't bear it. It was probably worst in fact. Another taxi came around the curve, stopped in front of the rented Chrysler. Could have been any member of the family, but it wasn't. It had been ten years at least since I had seen him.

My dad, our dad, had just shown up to Cillian's funeral and I didn't know if I was to be happy about that or not. On one hand at least he had made the effort. On the other hand, there was a second spot available down that fucking hole in the ground and he would fit right in if you asked me.

Dad had bailed the week before Cillian had turned thirteen and I wasn't in the mood to deal with him.

He got out of the taxi, looked our way. He was a short man, large shoulders, larger hands, wide chest. You could see it ran in the family. He was tan and his skin had gone a lot more rugged than I remember. His hair had receded back an inch and had turned to gray. Otherwise he seemed to be in fair shape and the clothes he had on told me he had not spent the last decade in a ditch somewhere.

When the priest was done and my brother was in the dirt, the family started to spread to the four winds. We all gave each other a few handshakes, kisses and pats in the back. For most of us, it would be *See ya' when the next one caves in.* And it wasn't a joke.

My mother left right away with Uncle Miller. She didn't have the heart to speak to Dad and I guess no one could have blamed her.

I waited by Cillian's headstone. He would have preferred if I had walked to the shade he was standing under. He probably would have preferred if I made the effort and not him. He probably felt like jumping on a plane and paying cab fare from the airport to the grave was effort enough. That's what I thought anyways. I wasn't going to give it to him.

"You made it this far," I shouted, "aren't you gonna walk the last thirty yards?"

He didn't answer. He paid his cabbie, waved him away. He picked up his duffle bag and started walking. I stood to one side of the headstone. He stopped when he reached the other. He dropped his bag, stood and looked at me through his shades. I remembered the last words he had said to me: "Tell your brother I love him, alright?"

I hated the man.

"Your mother called," he said. "I came in as fast as I could."

"Did you take the time to finish your shift?" I replied bitterly.

He smiled half a smile, finally took off his glasses and took a deep breath.

"Fort Mc to Edmonton, Edmonton to Toronto, Toronto to Montreal."

"So you finished your shift?"

"D'Arcy..."

"You still a rig pig?" I asked. Man, was I bitter.

"I have the right to be here too," he said.

"To call it a right is a bit of a stretch."

He swallowed it. I could give him that much. He swallowed it, nodded silently, then said, "You look good."

I took a breath myself. I looked to the side then swallowed enough of my pride to say, "Yeah, so do you, I guess."

"Your mother said something about drugs or maybe even murder? Now, what's up with that exactly?"

"It sure as shit wasn't drugs."

"Can you be sure of that?"

"Cillian trained twenty hours a week, worked the other fifty and that was that. He was on creatine, protein shakes and wasn't even allowed to drink by his coach. It wasn't drugs or at least it wouldn't have been heroin. None of that."

He nodded. "I'm glad to hear that."

"Well. He's still dead, you know?" That pissed him off—finally.

"Do you doubt for a second that I don't know that?"

"I didn't think you doubted it. I just thought you didn't give a shit."

"I always cared, D'Arcy, always cared."

"You weren't home often enough to care."

"You were sixteen."

"He wasn't."

"I had a good reason."

"A fucking job?"

"A good fucking job. You know I asked your mother to come with me, bring the family to Alberta."

"And she said no."

"Of course she said no. She'd rather be stuck in the Pointe the rest of her life. The way she clings to that neighbourhood, you'd think she believes the world ends at the goddamn river. What was I gonna do? Work a job eighteen hours away from my house for the rest of my life?"

"I got a job in Montreal."

"At what? Fourteen, fifteen bucks an hour?" He had me there. "Don't make it seem like I'm the bad guy here. I offered to pay for the trip, to bring you and your brother over. Anytime you wanted."

"We're not the ones who moved three thousand miles away. You could have come home every once in a while."

"There was nothing in this city for me back then. I don't see what's in it for me now."

"There was us, sir. There was your family."

"Ah, D'Arcy. You're a grown man. You were a grown man back then, and you're old enough to know better." He looked down for a moment. I could see he was looking for a way out. He wasn't too good with people so he just said it. "Listen, I can't stay in Montreal too long. I have other obligations too. I'm sure you understand."

"How's the wife and kid?"

"They're alright. Healthy and strong."

"Good," I said. I wasn't sure if I meant it. "How old are they, now?"

"Three years and eight months."

"Nice."

"Yeah," he replied. He put on his glasses again then looked at me as he picked up his duffle bag. We were done with small talk.

"Like it or not, I was always looking out for you," he said. He rested the bag on top of Cillian's stone. "I had set aside a college fund for the both of you. But since you never went and he was murdered, I guess you're not gonna need it for school anytime soon."

"We never asked you to—"

"I know," he said. "Now there's thirty thousand dollars in there. And some change."

"What?"

"Thirty thousand dollars."

"How did you come up with thirty thousand dollars?"

"I might *just* be a rig pig, but the money's that good if you don't spend it all. It should cover the burial and give you enough money to do what you have to do now."

"Meaning?"

"You said yourself it wasn't drugs and I don't believe in suicide. I saw that kid fight his way through karate championships. I don't believe it one bit."

"So you are implying—"

"I don't need to imply anything. You know very well what I'm expecting of you now." He paused, I didn't reply. "You find that son of a bitch, D'Arcy. You find him and by the grace of God, you make that bastard pay."

CHAPTER 6

Me and the guys went to the canal later that night, on Griffintown's side. The city had recently green lit some billion dollar redevelopment complex in that semi-vacant lot. Soon it would be home to thousands of single, young professionals or all shapes, colours, creeds and kinds—so long as they were rich.

The place was vacant, noisy as hell, sequestrated and stuck between Wellington Bridge and the tracks. It's why we liked it so much.

For us, it was simply the place where we drank beer, got into fights or even fucked every once in a while, at least when we were teenagers. I did it once, myself. I was in eleventh grade or something and her name was Hellen Aubry. We walked up to the edge of the canal with a fifth of whiskey. She could have fallen into the water at any time and I'm still amazed she didn't the way she pranced around.

It wasn't like the cement walls weren't all that comfortable, but I guess it was my ass that was rubbing against it. Why the fuck do we do these things when we're freaking kids? I didn't know. The canal's no place to have sex, goddamnit. But we did, we fucked for all the city to see and when we were done we threw the fifth and the condom in the water. There were a few others down there anyways.

But times changed, the way they always do. They

already set up a sales office with this tiny, minuscule demo apartment that could be yours, starting at three hundred grand (plus taxes). Five hundred thirty-four square feet. *No shit!* Five hundred thirty-four square feet between Wellington Bridge and the tracks.

The crane was up with a large, red banner from the construction company hovering on its side. *SaleCon*, it said, lit up by two gigantic floodlights. Some of the steel columns were pinned halfway into the ground with some sort of two stories tall jack hammer hovering above them, ready to start pounding again the following morning.

"What the fuck now?" I said. A fence had been set up around our spot.

"What do you mean? What's up?" Ryan asked. Then he saw. "Ah, goddamnit!"

"They fenced the park off, too."

"I don't think that park's gonna stay a park for long," Karl said.

"Y' peuvent pas faire ça, osti!" Phil said.

"Man, they can do whatever the fuck they want," I said.

"S't'un parc fédéral, osti," Phil replied.

"I'd believe it."

"Tabarnak."

Of course, we probably could have gone around to Peel, see if there was a way inside from there, but why would we do that, right?

"You want to jump it?" I asked.

"I'm too old and fat to jump it," Ryan replied. He started looking for a weak spot in the fence, the place where the roll came to an end or something.

Phil had his face plastered against the sales booth window. "The place advertises a den for you to work in. It's not a fucking office. It's a fucking den." He looked our way, pointing inside the demo unit. "I think my dick is bigger than the damn thing. You can barely fit a laptop in there."

"And some guy's gonna lose his life savings in that shit." Karl said.

"Maybe it will gain some value." I said.

"At three hundred thousand?"

"It's a fucking bubble," Ryan shouted from afar.

"How do you know?" Karl asked.

"The economy's crashed in the states," Ryan said as he drove his foot into the fence. "It crashed in Argentina. It crashed In Ireland, in Spain, in Greece. It's about to fucking crash in France and in Italy too." He banged and banged his heavy boots into the fence. "Why wouldn't it crash here just the fucking same?" he said as he had finally kicked a whole into the fence. He pried it open and added, "I know *I'm* sitting tight with twelve thousand dollars in my bank account. When the market goes south, I'm a swoop me a nice little house at a very fair price while these motherfuckers will still be paying for that overpriced baby room over there."

Ryan talked a lot of sense every once in a while. It scared me a little. Big tough guy that looked like a fucking idiot but who was actually as smart as any motherfucker at McGill. He picked up his six pack, got through the hole, I followed in behind him.

"You know these towers will be here before that happens," Phil said. "Soon we won't be able to come here to drink anymore."

"Horse shit," Ryan said as he opened his first can. "I'll fucking come and drink on their balconies if I have to. They'll fucking get to know who Ryan Duncan Scott is."

"Ha!" I laughed.

"I'm serious."

"I know you are."

"I swear to fucking God. I'll walk right through here in my fucking boxers with a six fucking pack. I'm a sit my ass right on their balconies and get pissed drunk just like back in the days."

"Are you gonna fuck the misses too?" Karl asked.

"It would do her some good, wouldn't it?"

I laughed again, louder this time. It felt good. My friends were completely insane, the way I liked them to be.

We circled around the construction site, headed for the abandoned three-story warehouse by the tracks. There was a section of railing missing near the pier. A small bush grew there, holding on to the cracks in the cement for its dear life. Ryan stomped it out of the way, cleared enough room for the four of us to sit there. He picked up the bush, threw it in the canal, then he drained his beer, threw it in the canal as well and picked himself another one.

A gray Yaris appeared over on Wellington Bridge. It was some security car with a little red logo on the doors and yellow lights on top, trying to emulate a police cruiser. I guessed he was here for us. There was no one else around. That meant we had triggered some silent alarm or something.

"Well, guys. I guess the party's about to be over," Phil said.

Ryan laughed at the idea that some security guard could convince him to leave.

"Is he even coming over here?" Karl asked.

"Probably."

"Maybe there was another rape in Wellington Tunnel?" Phil said.

"Wouldn't they send the cops for that?"

"Well, I ain't moving until they kick me out," I added.

"You got that right," Ryan said as we clanked our drinks together.

"What about you, Karl? You want to defy authority with us?"

"What authority? He's a fucking security guard. When the cops show up, then *maybe* we'll talk. Until then he can eat his minimum wage and head the fuck back home."

A few minutes later, we could see his shape as a shadow coming our way. You could see he was walking with way, way too much care.

"Ah! Criss, appelle les cops si t'es pour etre cave demême!" Phil yelled at the security guard.

He drove his flashlight our way, said, "You can't be here." I could hear he was Arab. He walked through the empty lot, got closer. I could see he was Arab.

"You leave or I will call the police."

"You ain't gonna do shit," I replied.

"I will."

I nodded sideways once or twice. *Is he gonna do it, is he not gonna do it. What would it matter anyways?*

"What's your name?" I asked.

"You don't need to know my name. You need to leave—please."

"Hey, if we're trespassing, why the fuck are you saying please?" Ryan shouted.

"Leave the terrorist alone," Karl said.

"Shut up a minute," I replied, then to the security guard, "I asked you a simple fucking question. What's your fucking name?"

He sighed heavily.

"Osama."

Ryan laughed.

"Told you," Karl added.

"Ciboire!" Phil said, laughing. I gotta admit, I couldn't help but to smile myself.

"Alright, alright. And I'm right to assume that you're an immigrant, aren't you?"

"So what if I am?" he replied, the question made him angry.

"Good. We're all immigrants here," I said as I slapped my hand on my thighs. "I'm Irish, he's German, he's French and the big scary guy here's Scottish."

"I ain't Scottish," Ryan replied.

I popped open another can. "Really? Ryan Duncan Scott ain't Scottish."

"Maybe it used to be."

"Then which one are you?" I said as I took a sip.

"I'm Canadian."

"Alright. You're a Canadian nationalist of Scottish heritage."

"Yeah, I like that better."

"Sounds like a fucking title," Phil replied.

"Eat shit, PQ," Ryan said harshly. Ryan was a mean drunk.

"Heille! J'ai jamais vote PQ d'ma vie moé, criss."

"So you say."

"Ne-Ver."

"Bullshit. You're like all the rest of the fucking frogs. The moment something doesn't go your way, you go straight back to the separatists."

"Ah pis va donc chier," Phil replied. "The French dumped us here, same as the Irish, alright, so eat shit."

"Can't argue with that," Ryan added.

"Misters," Osama shouted. We seemed to have forgotten about the security guard. "So you're all immigrants, you still need to leave."

"You want a beer?" I asked him.

"Hey, oh, wait a fucking minute," Karl replied. "He's a fucking raghead."

"You shut the hell up," I snapped. "They used to be called the white niggers of America," I said, pointing to Phil. "And we were the first wetbacks on the fucking continent. I say he's gonna sit his ass down and have a beer."

Karl looked at Ryan and Phil for some support. They raised their shoulders. They didn't really care either way.

"He's got a point," Phil said.

"Alright, alright," Ryan added.

"It's my job to get you guys out of here. So go!"

"Heille, laisse faire ta job pis éffouare, ca va t'faire du bien," Phil replied.

"He's not gonna drink. It's in his fucking religion." Karl asked.

"Well, seeing that it's Saturday night and that it's,

oh..." I looked at my watch. "Three...something in the morning, I'd say you'd be better off without it."

"The job or the religion?" Phil joked.

"Both," I replied.

"This is the best I could find," Osama admitted.

"The job or the religion?" Phil joked again. It was getting a bit old. "Alright, alright." He threw a can to Osama. He caught it and finally agreed to sit down next to us, squeezed himself between the railing and what was left of the bush.

There you had it, one French, one Scot, One Irish, one German, one Arab. If you had an Italian, a Jew, a Haitian and a Chinese kid, then you had one representative of every major group in the city. Sure, there were arguably a few "first nations" left on the island and there was also the British, but I hated the Brits, so did Ryan, Phil and probably Karl too just because he hated everyone.

Osama didn't open his beer. He rested it next to him as his feet were dangling above the water. "So this is what Canadians do?" he asked.

"Well. I don't know about Canadians, but it's what *we* are doing at the moment, yeah."

He didn't reply. He was just waiting and staring. He was getting the hang of it.

"You're not gonna drink that?" I asked.

"No."

"Is it Ramadan?"

"No."

"Then you're having that beer, sir."

He opened it but didn't drink yet.

"So, where you from? Afghanistan? Pakistan? Iraq?" Karl asked.

"Tunisia," Osama replied. Pissed him off, too. "You know? Why would I be from Iraq or Afghanistan? There's like three thousand kilometres between Afghanistan and Algeria. You expected what? Some allahhhhayaiiiiahhha freak with a bomb over his chest? I'm twenty-six years old. I was protesting in 2012, I was right there when CNN showed up and everything."

"There you go," Ryan said. "Guy's got some teeth after all."

"So let me guess," I said. "The immigration officers or the publicities or whatever the fuck got you convinced to come over here, they promised you it was gonna be easy. They said that you'd get an IT job at fifty K a year to start with and a good stay-at-home-wife with a mortgage so low you wouldn't believe it?"

He finally took a sip. "Something like that, yes."

"Well, you've been conned my friend."

"Works every time," Phil said. "Don't be mad at yourself. The French, you know who they sent when they colonized the place?"

"No."

"Criminals and prostitutes. I'm not shitting you. The courts would tell them *It's Canada or prison.* I still think most people took prison."

"So you know what a fucking winter is like here. Can you imagine that shit with no gas, no food, no electricity? No wonder the only ones who'd come here were either crazy or desperate."

"I'd drink to that," I said. Well, at that point I'd drink to anything, really.

"And then there was the Irish," Phil continued, "who were so fucking hungry that they'd jump on any boat with a promise of food at the other end."

"They told us we could get any piece of land, work it and it would be ours," I added.

"That doesn't sound like a bad deal," Osama said.

"Fuck! Ninety percent of this fucking country is pure rock. The French and the Brits already had most of the good land. Shit!"

"And then it was the Germans," Karl continued. "And the Italians and the Jews—and the Poles, who were fleeing the war. We all worked the shit jobs, the textile mills and the lumber mills and the grain elevators. All the shit jobs until we got our heads out of water. And I ain't shitting ya, the fucking mill's right there across the canal."

"They said my diploma would be fine," Osama said. He sighed, took a sip.

"And is it?"

"No."

"Nobody will hire you because your name's Osama."

"I don't know if it's that. They'll hire me in telemarketing, but that's it."

"I guess telemarketing will be the shit job of your people." Phil said.

"It's a really bad job."

"Well," I said as I drank the rest of my beer. "Shit flows downhill and you're as low as it goes." I threw yet another can in the water. "Fucking Murphy's Law if you ask me."

"Whose law?" Osama asked.

"Okay. You're here now, you're gonna have to read a

fucking book or something. Because we ain't got time for *that* much theory." I could see he didn't like my tone. I gave in. "Alright, Murphy's Law is the *law* that if something shitty can happen, then it will definitely and inevitably happen."

"Amen," Ryan said. We all drank up, except Osama.

"Did Murphy's Law have anything to do with you guys being here tonight?" he asked.

"Oh yeah," Ryan said.

"My brother died," I said. Pissed me off when I said it. "Was killed, died. We don't know yet. They found his body a few hundred yards back there."

"Are you serious?"

"Yep. Right there under the bridge. Shit, you can still see some yellow tape dangling on the side there."

"That's horrible."

"Yeah, I guess. I got a question for you," I said. "How did you know we were here?"

"Cameras on the constructions sites."

"Just this one here or elsewhere too?"

"Seven construction sites from here to Chateau Saint-Ambroise."

I looked at Karl. He looked at me. We were going to need to see that footage one day, one way or the other.

"I'm sorry about your brother," Osama said. "I didn't think things like that happened here too."

"No? What did you expect then?"

"Big houses, healthcare, freedom, everybody's equal."

"Is that how the rest of the world sees us?" Ryan asked. "Like it's one big, endless barbecue party and you get to fuck the blonde at the end?"

"Well...Yes."

"Yeah, well, my friend," I raised my drink, "welcome to the fine lie that really is North America."

CHAPTER 7

I walked home from my guy's night out. I guess it must've been four, four-thirty in the morning or something. I didn't dare to look at my watch. Ryan, Philippe and Karl had gone home, so did the Arab guy we had just met. He got in his security car and headed back to his dead-end job.

I walked over the bridge they had fished my brother from on Des Seigneurs. There was no other way around it and I guess it pissed me off that unless I moved, I would have to take that bridge nearly every goddamned day for the rest of my life. I guessed I was going to be pissed a lot in the coming years.

I waited there for a minute, thinking about Cillian and what a shame it was. I was also thinking about what a load of crap it was that he had either been killed here or that he had OD'd, whatever the police said. The mob no longer took their business to the canal. It was way too crowded for that now.

"Ugghh,"I growled alone on my bridge. It was too late or too early for this shit. It was really time to get the fuck home. I rubbed my hands together as I was hanging back against the railing. "Come on," I said out loud to myself, "time to go."

I headed south and soon I was at my corner. For some reason, I stood and looked at the street sign. How many times in my life had I seen the words *Grand Trunk* and

Shearer? How many times was I going to see them again?

Shit.

I took a left, took my keys out, but when I reached my door, I could see that it wasn't locked and there was light inside. My mother didn't come down anymore, especially at that hour. As far as I knew, she was spending the night at Uncle Shan's house anyway. The only other person who had the key was Cillian and I couldn't remember if the police had handed them back to me or not.

I was better sober up, and fast. I ran every possible scenario in my mind about what Cillian or I could have done to piss someone off that bad. Not much. Could have been anything from a simple Pointe home invasion to Uncle Miller being too drunk to find his hotel. Was it someone trying to steal from me? But then again, nothing in my kitchen was worth the trouble. The most expensive thing in there was the freaking microwave and I had bought it at goodwill for twenty bucks.

What the fuck was really going on? I didn't know.

I didn't know a lot of things, but I knew I wasn't expecting company, that was for sure. I hid against the wall, trying to look through my own damn curtains. The kitchen lights were on, the rest seemed to be as I left it. Why would someone want to hurt me or kill me or steal from me and leave the lights on? Who would be stupid enough? I mean, there were plenty of dumb fucking criminals in the world and the Pointe was no exception.

I was just being drunk and paranoid. That a few beers and a murder would do that to a guy; that I should just walk home like any other day. I went around anyways. I tried to be subtle, looked through my kitchen window. No one in sight. Was I that drunk and had just forgotten to close the lights?

Big old fucking idiot, I thought.

I walked across the backyard. I took out my key, walked into my home.

The kitchen was wiped clean. Wiped fucking clean. And I didn't mean as in all my shit got stolen. I meant it as everything was sparkling. The dishes were done and lined up in a sort of plastic rack I didn't own that morning. The smell of old, forgotten garbage had made way for fresh, orange cleaner. The table was not littered with ashtrays and cigarette butts or dead soldiers or, well, anything in fact.

"Just who's in the house?" I yelled.

"I'm over here," I heard from my room in the front.

I walked to the living room, same clean environment, same fresh scent and then Patricia McCready walked out of my room with fresh towels folded in her arms.

I had never fucked Patricia McCready. I had never kissed Patricia McCready. As far as I could remember we had never even been on a date. I started thinking maybe we should have.

She lived a few houses down the backyard. I'd check her out from my balcony when I was a kid. Sometimes we'd jump the fences and have a beer or smoke a joint and that was it.

She was a good-looking woman. Maybe five-six. She wasn't small but she kept herself in shape. As other people our age were pushing through their thirties with shitty backs and beer guts, she was perfectly at ease with herself. She had a good smile and curves in the right places, plus she was a tough little gal with the right attitude and family values.

"I asked your mother for a key after the funeral," she said. "I figured that picking up after yourself wasn't gonna be a priority right now."

"You didn't have to do this."

"I know," she said with a smile as she put the towels back inside my tiny, tiny closet. She was still wearing the three shades of black she had worn at the funeral. Probably hadn't gone home yet. She had taken off her high heels and was walking around in her stockings. Feet must have been hurting like hell.

Poor girl. I appreciated the gesture.

The truth was that I had sorta been taking care of Patricia in the last two years. Not like I was macho about it or anything. It was nothing like that. Patricia had the unfortunate stigma of being a twenty-eight-year-old widow. She had met her husband at twenty and they had gotten married at twenty-two, something rare in this day and age. They didn't have children because he didn't really want to and she wasn't too sure about the money and the life she could give them.

"What's the point of making twelve babies like our grandparents used to do if you can't fucking take care of them or even send them to school?" she'd say. I couldn't argue with that. Neither did her man, apparently.

The husband, I didn't know him except that his name was Thierry Perno, a French-Canadian mixed with some Italian and something else from Lasalle who had been working odd jobs most of his life. He wasn't rich or well-connected but I guessed they loved each other. He wasn't good looking either, nobody would argue with that, but after an IED blew up his *un*armoured transport vehicle on a road in Kandahar, well...let's just say the funeral was a closed casket.

What was sad was that it wasn't about the Taliban or freedom or 9/11, hell, we're Canadians. And he wasn't even there to please our American allies in the south. As far as I knew, no one around cared too much about that. They had joined for the pay and maybe the thrills. Probably more for the thrills. The army paid well enough, but far from extraordinary.

Patricia could live with that. She could live with being alone a few months at a time. I wouldn't even think she was fucking around. She wasn't that kind of girl.

It was a statistical anomaly that Perno's unit was sent to that province at that moment. And it was a statistical anomaly that he was killed on that particular road on that particular day. Hell, there were a hundred and twenty Canadians killed in Afghanistan over a ten-year period. What were the odds of that? It was just the luck of the Irish, or the luck of the French-Canadian, I guess. Their luck was just as bad as ours was anyways.

Ever since she had been a widow, I had sorta been looking out for her in my own way. I helped her move when she wanted out of her apartment. I rented the truck and straps, found some help. I'd never imply that she couldn't have done it on her own. It wasn't like that. I just *wanted* to help.

I didn't ask for nothing in return. I never asked for money, I never tried to fuck her. We'd still have a beer or smoke a joint and that was that. It wasn't that I didn't want to "upset" the army or the memory of her former husband. I didn't care one bit about him. It wasn't that I didn't find her attractive either, she was a *fine* woman you make plenty of Irish babies with...Come to think of it, I didn't know why I hadn't tried to fuck her yet. It felt weird all of a sudden. I should have dated that chick and here she was folding my laundry.

"I don't know if I'm comfortable with all of this," I admitted.

"With what? Me cleaning up your mess?"

"I guess, yeah."

"Don't be silly, you're just the type of guy who won't let anyone help them," she said as she headed for the kitchen again.

"I—" I said as I ran after her. She was already at the fridge, door wide open. "Don't look in there, it's a mess."

"Not anymore it ain't," she said smiling. "Oh, and by the way, three old boxes of pizza is a little sad."

"They were for the wake."

"No they weren't. I threw them out anyway."

"Listen. It's way, way too late for house cleaning."

"And you're exactly right," she said as she closed the door with her foot. She had two bottles in her hand: a fifteen ounce of whiskey in one and a bottle of red wine in the other. One for me, one for her. She stooped a little, with her killer smile and that look in her eyes. "Pick two glasses, I'll be waiting in the living room."

We sat there in my old burgundy couch. I had picked up a beer along with a shooter and a wine glass for the lady. The heat was heavy. I felt my own sweat run down the middle of my back but I didn't want to let it get to me. I sat at my end and she sat at hers, one arm leaning towards me. Her fingers were half an inch away from my shoulder and I could almost feel them but I'd like to think she kept the distance on purpose.

She was wearing one of those shirts, I didn't know how to call them, that was loose and leaning over the side of her shoulder, halfway down her arm and I could see plenty of skin. She poured herself some wine but not too much because she wanted to have a drink with me, not get wasted.

She looked at me peacefully. Her eyes were walnut. I hadn't noticed that before but I wasn't about to forget it now. She had good legs, black pants served her well. Her breasts were impressive. I couldn't find another word to describe them. Or at least they seemed that way from where I was sitting, really full, perfect curves, perfect size for a woman like her.

Her shoulders were round but fair, her neck was beautiful. Thin and beautiful. It was weird somehow, but it was nice. You can go a long way if your neck is beautiful. She wasn't heavyset, she just wasn't deadly skinny like all the models they threw in the magazines all over town. She was just a *fine*, curved woman, the kind that takes you to a game. The kind you take to a tattoo parlour on a third date.

I didn't know what to say. I didn't want to start some sob story about Cillian. Luckily for me, she spoke first.

"I'm not gonna say shit like 'I'm here for you' or 'sorry for your loss.' That goes without saying," she said. "I mean, don't get me wrong. I loved Cillian. I'm gonna miss him like hell. But you don't need that. I don't think you need that. Not right now."

"I don't know what I need."

"I do. Don't worry."

That surprised me. I looked at her and somehow she was right. "I know you do," I admitted. I took a sip, so did she. She took a sip, took a breath. She placed a flock of her hair behind her ear. It was in the middle of her face but I didn't dare to say I liked how it looked right there.

"You know, when Thierry died," she continued. "Everybody was *there* to support me when all I really needed was someone to cuddle with. When his jeep got blown up, I had been sleeping alone for ten months already. Ten months sleeping alone. He barely skyped anymore in the end anyways." She took another sip. "So when he died, I felt that I just needed someone to grab when I was trying to sleep at night. I needed that warmth and, well, just spooning I guess."

"You got yourself a cat?"

She smiled, shyly and confessed, "I bought myself one of these body pillows."

"Nah," I said, laughing.

"Don't laugh," she said, slapping me gently.

"Like, a long, big pillow."

"Big blue one," she smiled. Goddamn, that smile.

"Well there you go," I said. "You don't need a man. You got a large pillow."

"No, D'Arcy. You see, I need someone just now. You need someone right now. And I don't mean your mother or your friends or uncles. I'm not sleeping alone tonight and you're not sleeping alone either. Hell, if I'm lucky, I won't sleep another night alone for the rest of my life. See, when he died, I needed somebody close to me and I couldn't get that because it was my husband who had just died and it took me a while to figure that out. But I did. I figured it out so you don't have to now. I know that tonight is no time for you to be alone, and hell, I think you've been nice to me long enough for one of us to make a move."

"Wait," I replied, putting away my drink. I wanted everything to be clear. "I never did anything just—"

"I know," she said and then she climbed on to me, legs both sides of my lap. She put her hands on the back of my shoulders. I put my hands on her thighs. With a swirl of her head, she sent her long dark hair to the back of her shoulders. She had a long skinny neck, a beautiful neck. She took my face into her palms. She had this look about her, like love and despair all mixed in the haze of summer heat. She looked at me, straight into me and said, "Don't you tell me you don't need me tonight. Don't you *dare* tell me you don't need me tonight."

She said it and I knew she was right. I took a deep breath and accept her truth as my truth. I looked at her and it was like the alcohol was drained out of me. I didn't feel drunk, I didn't feel drunk at all. I just looked at her. I was at peace for a moment.

It wasn't like this was just sex either. I didn't know what it was yet, but it wasn't just sex. We had been having a beer together for a decade now. We had gotten high in my backyard, in her backyard, at the canal, even on Mont-Royal once or twice. I had watched her marry another man then bury him and again, today, we were together at a funeral.

Life was short and life was shitty. At least it seemed that way when you spent half the week alone in your own filth.

I reached further, one hand grabbing her lower back,

the other one grabbing her thigh right above her knee. She kissed me and I kissed her back.

I was gonna marry that chick one day. I was gonna marry that chick and fall asleep next to her for the rest of my days if I was lucky.

She moved closer still, made herself at ease and pushed her hands underneath my shirt. I grabbed her by the waist, pinned her down by pulling on her belt. I could feel her full, firm breast against me, her lips against my ear as she kissed it. The first rays of light were showing up in the east. I hadn't had sex that late or that early in years.

She dug her nails into my back; I dug my teeth into her neck. She seemed to like that.

"You got a hell of a good neck," I said when I was done.

"I know, right?" she replied. Walnut eyes were smiling at me.

I liked that. I liked that a lot. You can go a long way with a good neck.

CHAPTER 8

"What the fuck is this shit?" Were the first words that ran out of my mouth when I heard him pick up the phone.

I had received the police report by some FedEx guy. It was a load of bullshit 'cause the motherfucker who wrote it didn't have the guts to call me and let me know in person what he was thinking about the case.

Instead I was left opening a little manila envelope, pulling out a goddamned file and the first words that popped up were "accidental death while intoxicated."

"Goddamnit!" I started reading.

Time of death is estimated between 02:00 AM and 04:00 AM. While suicide was considered as a possibility in the early stages of this analysis, in the absence of prior hospitalization due to mental illness, the absence of prior depression diagnosis, combined with the absence of notes, warnings or other recent incidents in the deceased's life, we are ruling out suicide in this case.

I skipped a few lines, flipped a page and kept reading.

In regards to the drugs found in the deceased's bloodstream, while the time of death stands between 02:00 and 04:00, the amount of opiates, specifically heroin, still in the deceased's system during analysis suggests intoxication took place minutes to an hour before drowning occurred. The toxicity levels of the opiates were not, in our opinion, lethal in nature. There were, however, significant amounts of bleaching agent. The deceased seemed to have been the victim of what is commonly known as a "bad fix," injecting a heavy dose of poorly diluted drugs, mixed with bleaching agents.

We requested a consultation with a specialist from the anti-drug department, Agent Yannick Séguin (matr. 6897) provided us with the following professional commentary: "While it is rare that the resellers would dilute heroin in such a poor fashion (he mentions the awkward nature of the cutting agent) he mentioned that certain low-level resellers, especially those in poorer neighbourhoods of the city, do not have the knowledge or equipment that more powerful groups have, so in his professional opinion, it is 'not unheard of at all."

That bullshit was starting to get the best of me. It felt like the entire fucking police force had found themselves a loophole they could use any time and place they didn't want to do actual police work.

We believe that the nature of the injected compound sent the deceased in shock, which could have happened anywhere between time of injection and several minutes after injection. The presence of a known narcotics den upstream from the canal coincides both with the nature of the injectable drugs and the deceased's drowning. We believe that the state of shock in which the deceased found himself rendered him unable to swim or otherwise escape the water once he fell into the canal.

Furthermore, while the deceased has died of drowning, we have little doubt that without swift hospitalization, the injected compound would have been fatal to Mr. Kennedy in a matter of several minutes to half an hour at most.

In regards to possible criminal accusations regarding this case, the laboratory unit believes that conclusions regarding possible accusations of involuntary manslaughter or attempted murder or murder (though unlikely) on behalf of the alleged substance reseller fall beyond the mandate of this unit at this time. Further testing is to be postponed until the lead inspector on the case sees fit to require so.

And so, in a little over a page and a half, the government of Canada, through its police department of this great fucking city of Montreal, believed the death of Cillian Kennedy to be accidental. The murder rates didn't go up, the property values would keep on rising. It was just one more case of white trash *finally* clearing some space for the new-rich to move in the Pointe.

"Goddamnit," I said to myself. First thing I did is punch in the idiot's number, that Bureau-Pomminville guy and when I heard him pick up, it just got out: "What the fuck is this shit?"

"I'm sorry what?" he replied.

"You're closing the fucking case?"

"Who is this?"

"Kennedy. It ain't hard. Like the president. They didn't fucking do their job on that one either, did they?"

"Okay. Mr. Kennedy. First of all, I'm gonna have to ask you to calm down. Second of all, I'm afraid there really was no case to start with." Good thing he was on the phone, I could have slugged him right there.

"What do you mean there was no case to start with. A guy is found floating in the canal, an Irish kid floating in the canal, and you're telling me there's no case."

"Just the fact that he was Irish and that he was found

in the canal is no substantial proof of criminal activity. This isn't the nineteen-seventies, Mr. Kennedy. I mean, unless you have something to say that I am not aware of, Cillian was not on records for significant criminal activities. Now if you need to vent your anger, the only people you could file a complaint to, in this case, is to Parks Canada for not putting a railing there and to the Montreal historical society for petitioning to keep the canal 'as is' in the first place."

"My brother was killed, you Franco piece of shit. Don't talk to me about railings and historical societies."

"Hey, hey, there's really no need to start calling names over this. Now, I understand you are still mourning, I'm willing to let it slide, but as far as police work is concerned, we are writing this one off as a drowning while intoxicated."

"Is that what the lab told you?"

"It is, actually, to the very word. Don't pretend you don't know. I shipped that report to you myself two days ago and with your phone call, I can only assume that you received it. You are reading the same pages I am, Mr. Kennedy. The very same pages."

I started pacing in my kitchen, my tiny fucking kitchen. Even after Patricia had cleaned it up, everything felt like it was in the way. The chairs were pissing me off, wouldn't go far enough under the table. The trashcan was pissing me off 'cause it still was in the way of the door. I ran my foot into the recycling bin as I tried to reach for the file, fucking everything was in the fucking way.

"Well, maybe they missed something. Maybe they should have looked for hair or something," I said as I started flipping through the pages once again.

"This isn't Hollywood, Mr. Kennedy. It's not like there's a gigantic conspiracy where our lab specialists are covering up for something."

"Yeah? What about those condos that are freaking popping up everywhere, there's big money in that. What if there's something to it?" I replied as I slammed the file on the table.

"I refuse to get into that, sir. I absolutely refuse to get into that. It's not healthy, sir. It's not what you need right now."

"Don't fucking tell me what I need right now." I punched the fridge. It was never a good sign when you're using your fridge as a punching bag. It breaks your knuckles and it chips off the paint. The metal starts to rust.

"I'm sorry, maybe..." he tried to say.

"Don't fucking tell me what I need right now."

"Okay, I won't. Please, calm down."

"Don't tell me to calm down either." He got fed up with me. Right there. I had reached his limit. Good to see he wasn't all that frigid after all.

"Mr. Kennedy," he shouted. "As far as I am concerned, I have fulfilled my duties and communicated the report to you. If you insist on being harsh with me, I don't feel obligated to keep this conversation going. You understand me? Other cases require my attention as well." He pause then insisted, "Do you understand me?"

"Yeah, I understand plenty. Câliss!" I shouted.

I hung up. The motherfucker had some nerve, as I bailed out of the kitchen. I paced back and forth between my living room and my kitchen table. The apartment felt small. There was only twelve feet to pace on and it wasn't enough.

I was pissed. I swore to all the saints of the world in three different languages that I'd rip the eyes out of his fucking preppy head if I could only get my hands on the son of a bitch. I was gonna walk into that tiny, fucking cubicle of his, smash his head on that melamine fucking desk of his, cave in that thick fucking skull of his and turn myself in right there on the spot.

I swore to God I would. But then I hit my leg in the living room table again. I kicked it out of the way. "Goddamnit!" The couch got in the way I kicked that too, then I kicked it again and punched it and kicked it and punched it and punched it and kicked it, yelling "Fuck" every single time. The couch didn't feel anything so fuck the goddamn couch.

When I had gotten the anger out of me, I turned and saw that Emma had been watching from the kitchen. She seemed weary and nervous, shaking her skinny little legs because of me. I hated the way she was looking sideways at me, head leaning downwards, tail between her legs. I didn't know if Cillian used to scorn her that way or not, but I felt bad. You don't do that to a dog.

I was out of breath, let myself crash down on the floor, pouting my breath away like an ageing, fat Irish man who was living the last of his good days. That reminded me that the few times a year I dared to show up at the gym really did nothing to help my failing health. I was gonna have to do something about that.

"Fuck my life," I said. I looked over to the dog without getting up. "Come here, Emma," I added. She didn't move. I snapped my finger, slapped my thigh twice. "Come here, girl, I'm sorry, alright?" Still no movement. "Ah, come on. Don't do that to a sorry old fart. Come on. Come on!" She finally came over, jumped onto my stomach.

"There you go," I said. "I'm not angry at you, alright?" She licked my face. I was nailed to the floor so she had the advantage, started slobbering all over me as I was playing around with her cheeks, stretching them like flaps. A minute or so of that and I was covered in dog drool but that didn't bother me. I sat up said *come here* one more time and gave her a kiss on the snout. She didn't like that.

"You miss him, don't you?" I asked while giving her two little love taps in the ribs. She didn't understand what I meant. As far as she knew, I was feeding her now, I was walking her now, picking up her shit. She might have loved Cillian still, but she had no way to say it and as far as she was concerned, I owned her now. "I know I do," I added as I gave her one last tap. "*I* fucking do."

Cillian was dead, the cops had no fucking clue and what else was new in the world? I needed some information from him, that idiot cop, more than what was in the report. I needed to poke around and get a feeling for the case, maybe see something he didn't think about. I needed to feel like every stone around the canal had been turned, if not by the police, then by me and my peers. I needed that.

Ten minutes later, I had calmed myself down and I was on the phone again, calling *Officer* Bureau-Pomminville, expecting to behave properly this time.

"I'm sorry," I said up front before he even said *Hello.* That seemed to have worked.

"It's okay. It comes with the territory," he said. "You got it out of your system?"

"The couch got a beating, if that's what you're asking."

"Better the couch than your wife," he joked. That would have been funny, but I wasn't in the mood to laugh.

"Last I checked, it was doctors and lawyers who beat up their wives the most."

"Or cops."

"Well, if you say so, I wouldn't dare to imply you guys have problems at home."

"You'd be surprised," he admitted. I wouldn't be but I kept quiet about that.

"How's the murder rate?" I joked.

"Surprisingly low in fact," he replied. "Very, very low."

"Good. I guess. Though if it keeps up you might be out of a job."

"Not that low," he added.

"I guess." It was getting awkward, *Stick to the plan,* I reminding myself. "Anyhow, thanks for taking my call. Given...my tone, it's only fair to say you don't owe me anything but I'm just gonna say there are a few things I'd like more details about."

"I don't really think there's any more I could add, Mr. Kennedy. You did receive a referral to psychological support, I believe. Maybe the social worker or a therapist could help you though the grieving process."

"Please."

"Mr..."

"Please," I insisted again.

"Alright," he sighed. I could hear him drop some files on his desk over the phone. Then he asked straight up if I had anything more to say about my brother's death. If anything came to mind, or any sort of situation had come up since. The tone was mellow enough. I didn't think he expected any development but he wasn't mean about it. I played my cards better this time. I was gonna let him take the floor, have his moment in the spotlight. He seemed to like that. If I poked around too hard he might get suspicious, so first I said, "No. No. Nothing new. And I really want to say, sorry for the temper."

He said it was alright. I blamed it on the Irish blood. Then I admitted I really didn't know anything about police work. So I asked, "What exactly *is* a police investigation? Just so I can get a feel for the job, a feel for what you guys did for my brother. I'm just trying to understand things here."

He seemed to like that. I was rubbing him the right way. He started to open up about the job, first in general terms, about the precincts and how the city divided the territory in local police hubs, "community policing" it was called. "When you get a call and get to a scene, the most important thing is to keep everyone at bay. Not so much so they don't see what's happening, but more because you don't want them messing up your crime scene."

He kept talking and talking, feeling good about being revered once and for all I was felt amazed at the vanity of mankind. So far, nothing really good came up. Everything he was saying could have been copy-pasted from a *CSI* episode, didn't help me much. The only piece of information I could actually use was when he mentioned Cillian's financial inquiry.

"In your brother's case there was nothing out of the ordinary. There were regular deposits of seven hundred to twelve hundred dollars from his job as a tattoo artist, and one deposit of six hundred from his fight purse a few weeks ago. There probably was a case of mild tax evasion, as it is often the case in that profession, but nothing to be concerned about as far as homicide goes."

"Six hundred bucks?"

"Yes."

"Wow, you'd think people would ask for more to get your face pounded in."

"Most people do it for their own egos," he replied.

"So he didn't get rich or poor all of a sudden.

"It does not appear so."

"So there would be no motive?"

"None that we could see, no. Usually it's about money or love."

"I'd doubt love was involved."

"Well, I'm glad to hear you say that. It means you're starting to accept it, I guess. You know? We don't always get the answers we'd like to hear. It's not always easy. I mean, it's not that different from my end, you understand? If a case turns up, you want to get to the bottom of it. If someone had killed someone, you don't want that guy out there on the streets. You want him in jail and you want to be the one who puts him there. The job's not so much about statistics and paperwork than it is about you trying to figure out what happened."

"Yeah," I replied. "I guess you're right."

"You have the report, Mr. Kennedy. Everything you

need to know is in there. Your brother wasn't killed. You can have some closure on that. Listen, I'd like to have more time, but the reality is that I don't and I really have to get back."

"Of course," I replied. He said take care, I said take care. Neither of us meant a word of it. We hung up.

I was standing there in my kitchen, thinking about Cillian's financials, where they found him, when they found him, how they found him...Everyone expected that much of me. Shit, Dad had flown three thousand miles to tell me so. If the cops weren't gonna do it, I was going to have to do it.

The next thing I did was call Phil, Ryan and Karl. I was going to need their help. *Not about statistics and paperwork. What a load of shit.*

CHAPTER 9

I was back at work the next day. The bosses told me they were glad to see me. There was the whole *sorry for your loss* bullshit, but then they hit me with a stack of mistakes the guy replacing me had done and I was gonna have to fix them. I hadn't even made it to my desk yet.

I was a team leader, some new term for foreman, working the receiving department in a small warehouse on Ottawa Street. It wasn't fancy but it paid enough and it was better than what most people in the Pointe got. The "old" Pointe anyways.

The building had seen better days. It was a one story, red brick-painted-blue building with one large garage door and that was it. One year we had set up some sort of open shed over the door to keep the rain and the snow out, but as it turned out, this was still Montreal, homeless people started sleeping underneath it every night. It was not that they wouldn't move when you asked them too, most of the time they saw me coming and got up on their own and made no fuss about it. Sometimes I'd bring them coffee and bagels, if the pay had gotten in and I was in the mood. But that all stopped last spring when, one night, one of them had set up a fire under it and nearly set the whole door in flames. Since then the bosses have been nervous about putting so much as a tarp outside for the smokers to cuddle under when it rained.

My office was right inside the door. I had three windows, a few hooks for the winter jackets, flannel shirts and rain coats the company provided for the workers if the weather was bad. We had no real loading dock to speak of and most of the work was done by hand or with that one forklift. It wasn't like the place was well equipped to actually do what we did, but we had no money to move so we lived with it.

I was listening to the news on the radio. It was six forty-five. I took a sip. The coffee was perfect. I flipped the pages trying to get some work done to keep my mind off things. I needed to.

Me, Phil, Karl and Ryan had gone to bed late last night after ending up in one big online session, chatting about who was gonna do what and where. Phil was gonna poke around the southern edge of the city, looking into the tapes the security guard told us may or may not exist. Ryan teamed up with Karl because they were headed to the north end of Montreal ask around some bouncers they knew if the mobs were at each other's throats again.

At around one PM, Ryan and Karl texted me saying they were just around the corner. I had not expected to hear from them that early, especially if they were gonna drive to Montreal-Nord, RDP and maybe even Laval. But they were back and that could have been good news or bad news as far as I knew.

One of the company's trucks was getting out of the warehouse. I looked at the plate number and knew that it was headed out to Ville Saint-Laurent. They all looked the same, the trucks, but just the plate number was enough for me to know who was in and what was headed where.

Ryan appeared right behind it, slapped the back tail of it as he and Karl were crossing the loading area. It had rained a little the night before and the tires splashed in a puddle as the truck took a right. The guys working the lift didn't pay my friends any attention so long as they kept out of the way.

I waved them in, they opened the door. "Hey, guys, come on in."

"So this is where you work?" Ryan said.

"Yeah."

"I think I prefer being a bouncer."

"And you're probably right," I replied. "You get to see a lot more women than me. Good-looking women, I man."

"You think?"

"Yeah! The last one that came into this office fucking looked like...fucking Marlon Brando."

"No shit," Ryan said.

"There's a cute saleswoman from Equitex that comes around every now and then, that's about it."

"You mean to tell me there is not one single good-looking woman in this entire place," Ryan said. "What? Broads don't look for jobs these days? I thought we were supposed to be all equal and shit."

"Broads don't want to work in warehouses. Not good looking broads...Well, okay, there's this one girl but I can't talk about her 'cause I'm her boss."

"Maybe you'd get to fuck her."

"Hey, hey, hey. That's exactly the kind of shit that could get me fired."

Karl didn't really do small talk or girl talk. Karl was more of a *do it or shut the fuck up* kind of guy. While Ryan and I were male bonding, he was snooping around, reading the safety posters and all the other shit I had on my walls. Shit like what to do if battery acid got into your eyes or if a forklift's fork ended up lodging itself into your tibia. Then he walked slowly to my other wall.

He stopped to look at one little thing I had framed a few months earlier.

"So, D'Arcy, what's up with that?" he asked as he pointed at it.

It was a written warning I had received about a year ago saying I had neglected my procedures during work hours. It was bullshit about one, single power cable I kept forgetting. I wrote a big, big "DON'T FORGET" in red caps on it. I still didn't know if I wrote that to remind me it was either time for me to get a better job or to do the one I had right.

"That's nothing. Don't worry about it."

They slumped into the chairs in front of me. I rolled mine to a small side table that had my coffee machine and a tiny fridge.

"You guys want some?"

"I'm good," Ryan said as he pulled out a can of Kilkenny from his pocket.

"I'll have one," Karl said.

I served his cup of joe, refilled mine. Ryan started drinking his beer. He shook it to hear the plastic ball that was in there and said, "One day I'll fucking get it out of there."

"Why?" Karl replied.

"Just to look at it."

Made sense enough.

"So, the cops have closed the case?" Karl asked. It wasn't a question so much as he was just stating a fact.

"That thing is closed and it's not coming back. Nothing I can do about it."

"Fuck?"

"I know. It's bullshit. They're ready to mark it as a drowning."

"Didn't he OD?"

"He drowned before he OD'd, so drowning it is."

"Well, the drowning I could have swallowed," Ryan said. "It's the drugs I don't buy. Why would they mark it as a drowning if the guy was supposedly high?"

"Statistics," Karl replied. "It looks better for the city if someone drowned than if someone OD'd."

"So if I see some junkie having seizures, and I stab the guy, they'll write it down as a stabbing?"

"Nah, an overdose sounds better than a stabbing. The same way drowning sounds better than murder."

"Man, everything is such bullshit," Ryan added. He was right. "If it had been a pretty rich girl from Westmount, the fucking RCMP would have come down here in a helicopter to bust some heads. But us? They won't care. That little fucking yuppie they got working the case didn't work the case at all because we're not important. We're not high profile. We're not pretty and we're not right."

I picked up right where he stopped, said, "The report's vague in certain places, precise in others. It's like they know how to do paperwork that won't get back at them. There's nothing else to it."

Everyone was the same when you really thought

about it, me, the guys who worked under me, the cops. Everyone was just shovelling shit forwards, hoping the report was good enough not to come back, good enough so the job was marked, *done*. Just so we can go back to sitting our asses somewhere, every single one of us, waiting for anything to happen. But when anything *did* happen, then we were eager to get rid of it ASAP and so the world turned.

Shit.

"You know what the idiot told me," I said. "He tries that compassionate tone and says, 'If you have information that you are holding back on me, then you are just as guilty as the guy who supposedly did it.'"

"Nah."

"I couldn't tell the little fucker to fuck off, you know?"

"Why not?"

"That's true, I guess. How about you guys?"

"We're not exactly done," Ryan said, finishing his beer. He burped and threw the can in the corner of my office.

"You gonna pick that up?" I said.

He looked at it, wondering if there was any reason I would mind the empty can sitting there in my corner. "Nah," he said. He wasn't gonna pick it up.

Karl continued, "We heard this and that, but nothing that would mean Cillian got killed. Or if he did, then it probably wasn't someone from the city."

"Heard back from Phil?"

"Not yet. He's trying to *charm* his way into letting SaleCon give us the security footage from their constructions sites."

"Yeah, that'll happen," I said.

"What," Ryan added. "You don't believe in his suave French demeanour?"

I laughed. Couldn't help but picture Phil in a sexy-ish pose trying to flirt with some secretary: *Come on! Give me the tapes!*

"D'Arcy. Hey, D'Arcy," somebody shouted at me from the warehouse. Work was catching up to me when I least wanted it too.

"Shit, gimme a minute," I said as I walked to the door, I just got my head out. The noise of forklifts, jiggers and plastic wrapping machines filled my office. Guys were loading and unloading trucks, filling orders. The wheels of metal carts and dollies made enough noise to remind me it was time to buy some WD-40. I had too much on my mind to be at work, but then again, I couldn't afford not to so I shouted, "What?"

"We found Martin asleep in the corner again."

"So?"

"Well—"

"Is Gilles around?"

"No."

"Alright. You know what? Let him sleep and when he wakes up, have him wash the fucking fridge in the kitchen. That'll teach him. There are lunches in there that have been lying around since before I got into this fucking job."

"Woah, you're mean today."

"You want to do it?" I asked. "He's sleeping on the job."

"Alright, alright," he said as he turned away.

"And make sure the Ingram skids are done otherwise I'll hear about it tomorrow."

"I'll put Patrick on it."

"Don't put Patrick on it. I need him for the Randmar. Ingram's easier so put the new kid on it."

"Alright."

"Sorry about that," I said to the guys as I closed the door. The noise in the warehouse felt like a bomb or at least a grinder. The silence in my office suddenly felt weird to me.

"Hey, man, we're the ones walking in at your job," Karl said.

"Are you gonna take some time off?" Ryan asked.

I slumped back into my chair. "I took my 'legal' days already. I have a week's vacation, but the boss would rather have me work because nobody else can do my job."

"Fuck your boss then."

"He ain't that sexy."

"Ha."

"But brother dead or not, I still need to pay the bills, take care of my mom, you know?"

"Didn't your dad clear the building?"

"Yeah, but taxes, repairs, hydro, food, medication—shit adds up. I mean. She's not paying a cent. I don't want her paying a cent. My boss will come around in the end. I'll give him a few good days here and he'll let me take my leave. But that also depends on what you heard. There's really no reason for me to miss work until we know what we're doing or where we're going to do it."

"We asked up north, RDP, Laval. Talked to a few fellow bouncers who run the clubs around there, asked about the mafia wars, see if Cillian or any other Irish got caught up in a cross fire."

"The Italians?"

"Yeah."

"Why would my brother have anything to do with the Italians?"

"Well, it's not so much about what your brother had to do with the Italians rather than it is about who's killing who these days."

"And."

"Nothing," Karl said. "As far as we know the war is strictly in the north. Italians, Haitians, that's it. The Jews, the bikers, the Irish, nobody else seems to be targeted at this point. So I think we can write off the war."

"Then we went to see Hugo from the shop," Ryan said.

"He was up?" I asked.

"He's got a kid man."

"Really?"

"Baby daughter, cute as hell."

"I didn't know that."

"You know, he's up to the neck in diapers and shit. I'm not sorry for him. The only thing he could remember was that Cillian had hid a dick in some jock's tattoo a few weeks ago but apparently that's common practice in Montreal these days."

"It keeps the douchebags at bay," Karl added.

"He hid a dick?"

"Yeah. A nice little shaft and two tasty testicles," Ryan said. "Apparently the guy deserved it. According to Hugo, the guy walked in, acting all tough and shit. He had the wife beater gene, Hugo said but that was as far as it went. He said it would be a stretch for the guy to A) even notice the dick and B) come around to kill the artist who did it."

"Well, would you admit publicly that you have a dick tattooed on you?" I asked.

"Only if that was the idea in the first place." Ryan would do that and probably never regret it. That's what was most troublesome.

"In this case, it wasn't," Karl added. "Aside from that, it's the usual. Tribal tattoos are dead and gone, most people want cheap Asian shit. Chicks with red hair want sailor tattoos, hipsters want some line art shit that I can't even figure out, a few blonde preppies want a slut stamp here and there to show off at the gym."

"They're referred to as *ass antlers* apparently," Ryan said.

"Oh yeah?" I asked.

"Yip."

"Could it be another shop trying to run a hostile takeover?"

"The market's pretty mellow these days. There's plenty of money for everyone and waiting lists everywhere, even in the shitty parlours on Ontario East. So no one's really hostile."

"So it's not work related."

"As far as tattooing is concerned, nope."

That was one dead end I would have liked to keep open. If Cillian had been killed because of his job, then Hugo could have been of some help. The guy was ancestry in the city as far as tattoos were concerned and he could have asked in a few favours for me. I probably could have asked him for help, but seeing he was a dad now and he had to provide for a full shop's rent with half its income missing. It would have been a stretch and Hugo, although I loved the guy, was not a guy I wanted to owe something too. Shit, I already had Karl to worry about when everything was over, I didn't want to add to that.

"You know," Ryan said. "If the body got caught up at Des-Seigneurs, that *does* mean he was dumped up river."

"Yeah, I figured the cops at least had that part right."

"Which means it happened up river," he added.

His conclusion was evident. I shook my head twice, agreeing with him. "That means he could have *fallen* at the Pitt house."

"Or dumped," Karl said. "Did they even go to Pitt house to ask around?"

"I'd be surprised if they did. The report doesn't mention they actually did. It says the Pitt house is a well-known *resale point* but as far as actually *going there*, nah. Too lazy."

"That means we need to check it out," Karl replied.

"I still don't see what business Cillian would have had there."

"Maybe he was there, but for other reasons," Ryan added. "Maybe he got himself a job."

"Tattoo artist not paying enough?" I asked.

"Well, it pays enough. But if he spends more than he makes, then he'd still be short."

I thought about it for a minute. I didn't see Cillian as a pusher. Not at the Pitt house. He was too clean for that. But then again, maybe Ryan was right. If Emma was any indication of how Cillian was spending his money, it wouldn't be far-fetched that he'd be hired as a collector or maybe even an enforcer. The cops said there was nothing unusual with Cillian's financials but what did that really mean?

In the grand schemes of things, I was ready to believe the most unlikely of scenarios at this point. Anything that pointed away from drowning or drug use. Maybe Cillian wasn't making enough money at the shop and he mismanaged his money enough to end up in debt but managed to deposit only what *made sense* in his account and kept everything else as cash. Every other tattoo artists on the planet did it, why not Cillian? That didn't mean he didn't owe someone money, that just meant it was off the radar for now.

So in all the possibilities, Cillian could have been hired to collect the Pitt house and some junkie jumped him, stabbed him with the bad fix he was about to shoot himself with. Cillian could have passed out before getting so much as a bruise that was unexplainable to a coroner and then the junkie could have dumped him in the canal where no one would have seen him before he died of the fix.

It was a lot to swallow, that much was true. But given the luck of the Irish and the Kennedy's strong sense of Murphy's Law, the idea of Cillian getting killed on his first mob job, shit, I'd believe it.

Karl looked at his phone, said, "Phil's on his way."

"So you guys are gonna head to the Pitt house?" I said. They didn't move, looked at each other. They had watched me process everything in my head and now they looked like there was something they weren't telling me. "What?"

"We'd appreciate if you'd come."

"But I'm at work."

"I called in sick," Karl said.

"I'm skipping sleep for this," Ryan added.

"I don't know."

"This could actually be it. And if not, that's something else we scratch of our list."

"I know, but—"

"It'll do you good."

"How could it do me good?" I asked.

"Junkies," Ryan replied, smile stamped on his face. I looked at him, my eyes asking, *So.* "I got my baseball bat in the car," he added.

I sighed at first but then I was surprised that I was even surprised. It was Ryan and Karl we were talking about. I felt a lot safer with those two guys on my side but still, I asked Karl, "You let him bring a bat into your car?"

"Only because he doesn't own a gun," he replied. He was probably serious.

Holy fuck! "I think it'll be better if I'm there."

CHAPTER 10

"Come here, girl," Cillian said. I remembered he was eighteen, maybe nineteen and I hadn't seen him in a while. He had left home at seventeen, not because we were getting on his nerves, but Dad had left in a shitty way and Cillian never felt quite at home after that. He didn't have the heart to stick around so he found himself a place in Verdun at first, then NDG and then Verdun again. At barely nineteen, my brother had already moved around a lot. I didn't remember where he lived that one time but he dropped by often enough so that we didn't have to worry about him.

"You got yourself a dog?" I asked.

"Yeah, will you look at her," he said, "She's fucking awesome."

He started playing around with her. It was an American Pitbull, big one, but not mean looking, not the *fighting* dog that most kids used as if it was a weapon. She was gray with some white stripes here and there, flappy cheeks but skinny, skinny legs. I could see why he loved her.

"But how are you gonna pay for her?"

"I got her for free, man. The guy who had her couldn't take care of her anymore. He lost his apartment."

I got on my knee, let her sniff my hand. Then I petted the side of her face and her head. Within three seconds, we were friends.

"Alright, but I mean, is she vaccinated? Is she neutered?"

"I don't know. I don't think so."

"Well," I said as I got up. "You'd better get her neutered unless you want to have like, six dogs to take care of."

"Are you gonna be whoring around," he told the dog on a playful tone. She smiled and wiggled her tail. "Yes, you are. Yes, you're gonna whore around. No, you won't?" She barked happily, started panting. "Yes, you would, wouldn't you?" he tapped her twice in the sides. "She would, right?" He looked at me. I nodded yes. "Shit. I better get her fixed then. How much does it cost?"

"I think it's pretty expensive. Like, you need to get her vaccinated first or the vet won't operate on her."

"So what? A few hundred bucks?"

"Yeah, I guess."

"Alright, I can come up with that."

"You working these days?"

"Yeah, I finally got a job as a full-time artist."

"Oh yeah?"

"Yeah. There's Hugo's shop that just opened in NDG. Man, those rich kids have so much money to waste, it's fucking insulting."

"NDG's rich?"

"Well, richer than the Pointe."

"If you want money you need to go to Westmount?"

"Westmount won't allow tattoo parlours on their territory. But I mean, it's cool. The guy who owns the shop, Hugo, said he was thinking about moving closer to it though. NDG but east of Décarie. It looks like West-mount, it feels like Westmount but it's still Montreal so there's nothing they could do. I mean, we'd have to look into that. Hugo says he's been thinking about it but nothing's for sure yet."

I was impressed. "That would actually be pretty fucking smart. Want a beer?"

"Nah, man, I'm good."

"You sure?" I replied as I opened my fridge.

"Training, man. And, I mean, I don't want to diss, but, I mean, you look like, well..."

"Hey, be careful what you're about to say. These paws could hurt you just fine," I said as I waved a fist his way.

"I'm not saying otherwise, just as long as you don't fall on me afterwards."

I laughed, little prick. "What are you saying?" I added, opening up my beer.

"Well, I mean. You could lose a few, just saying."

He dared.

I scratched my head, pinched my lips, swallowing my pride.

"Wanna use me as a test subject?"

"Sure. What are you looking for?"

"I don't know. Anything."

"Celtic cross?"

"I'm an atheist."

"You're still Irish."

"And I'm still an atheist."

"Anchor and a banner?"

"I have never set foot on a boat in my entire life."

"Grandparents came in on a sail boat."

"I have never set foot on a boat," I repeated.

"Alright."

"You know I was thinking it would be very sexy?" I turned around and pulled up my shirt, belt buckle was loose, pants were dangling from my "overweight" behind, old boxer shorts not helping anything, with the crack in plain sight. "If you would draw me a large tribal, right here right over my sexy ass. That would do just right."

He laughed.

"No?"

"No, not unless you expect to go flirting in Laval or some shit."

"Nah," I replied. "I don't do Laval." The dog invited herself into the conversation, put her head on my foot. She was cute. So I said, "You know what? Let's just walk the dog for now."

"Alright," he said as he put on her leash. I opened the door, we headed out.

"What are you gonna call her?"

"How about Emma."

"Emma?" I asked. The dog barked. "Well, what do you know? She's already used to it." I crouched to pet her again. "You like Emma?" She barked and wiggles her tail, licked my face a few times with quick, short snaps of the tongue. "Okay, don't neuter her just yet. I might want one of them someday."

"We'll see," he said he pulled on her leash. "We'll see."

* * *

A few days later I saw him and Emma again. Emma had a large plastic collar around her neck. Poor Girl. They were walking down the street with this gorgeous twenty-something girl, classy look, sunglasses, expensive jeans, loose tank top—designer shit—and a fresh tattoo on the back of her arm.

I figured Cillian had done it. It was a pair of sparrows with a banner underneath it that said, "free spirit." That kind of bullshit. The lines and the colour scheme were his, I was sure of it, but it was an otherwise ordinary piece. She could have fucking picked something more original than a pair of fucking Sparrows. Next thing you know, she would get a set of praying hands that said, "Only God can judge me."

She looked good, though. No matter what you said about the kid, you had to give it to Cillian. He knew how to pick them.

I tried to figure out when or where I could have met her before. I tried to remember if we ever went to school together or if she worked any of the suppliers we had at work—nothing came to mind. I would have remembered someone that hot, I knew that much.

"Hey, D'Arcy," my brother shouted. He let Emma drag him up to me. She jumped into my waist "This is my brother D'Arcy," he said to his date.

"Hi," I replied we shook hands.

"This is Elizabeth," my brother said.

"Nice to meet you," she said with a thick Francophone accent.

"Vous vous connaissez depuis longtemps?" I replied with my shitty Anglo accent.

"Pas vraiment," she admitted. Cillian looked guilty,

like he had been busted or something.

"Oh," he said, "did I tell you she's a veterinarian?"

I smiled, laughing my ass off inside my head. "No. No, you haven't," I replied. Little bastard. He had managed to nail himself a gorgeous, most likely well off, veterinarian.

Later that week we had coffee at the diner and I asked him about it.

"So how did you guys meet? You got Emma fixed she was the vet?"

"Nah, man. You know I got no money for a vet."

"Oh," I said, surprised. "Then how?"

"You know Sean the loan shark?"

"Of course."

"Well, he was organizing this party for the graduating class at UdeM. Veterinarian Science graduating class."

I couldn't believe it. "You've got to be shitting me," I said, took a sip of Coke.

"So I asked him if he could get me in or something."

"He says, 'Sorry, they ask for ID's and shit. But I can put you on the staff if you want to work.' So I figure I load up a few crates and some gear and I'm in, you know?" He chewed down a bite. "And you know what? University is like, nothing but *women* now. It's like, there's no more guys going there anymore."

"And the guys who do—"

"Well, let's just say I was the manliest shit in there."

"Except for Sean."

"Well, of course. Sean is definitely the alpha male. I mean...you know? Everyone feels like a pussy next to Sean." Cillian said. He reached in his pocket and took out a bottle of pills, he opened it and took one. They

looked like prescription but they could have been anything, really. I didn't like it. It wasn't like him to take
pills, even prescription drugs.

I stared at him a growled a bit. The way the Irish
think that it's gonna change something in the behaviour
of a sibling. It didn't. It never did. That time was no
different. He put the bottle away and just kept talking.

"So I'm walking in there, there are *so* many chicks,
you wouldn't believe it." I would have believed it. I
started eating again. He shoved down nearly half his
club. "So I'm done packing crates," he continues, mouth
full of food, "and he pays me cash for my work, so now
I got twenties I'm willing to spend and a good place to
do it."

"Where was the party?"

"I don't know. Up on Côte-des-Neiges. Sean drove—
some college bar or some shit. But the place is full. Full,
man! If Dad would have told me all the women were in
college, I might have worked harder in high school."

"Yeah."

"I've got this one and that one looking my way and it
feels good but I'm just not sure, you know? Mind you I
also gots to make sure she's a veterinarian. 'Cause I ain't
just looking for a booty call, you know? Emma needs to
get snipped."

"So, of course, you went for the ordinary girl, asked if
she was graduating," I said as I took a sip.

"Fuck no! I went for the supermodel."

I couldn't help but to smile. My brother was a dick,
sure, but I could safely say he was the most honest
person on the entire fucking island.

"What then? I can't imagine *are you a veterinarian?* to be a good pick-up line."

"That's the beauty of it. I didn't need to ask. Some other guy pays a round and I reach for a shooter, he shouts, 'Sorry, friend, graduates only.' But then she picks one and he lets her pick one. So now I know, you know?" he took a sip of water. "So I order myself a beer and I walk back there and say, 'Hey.'"

"That's, it?"

"What?"

"So you just say, 'Hey.' and that's it."

"Yeah."

"So she was hot *and* easy?"

"Ah, don't say that. Come on. You'd be surprised how often just *hey* said properly works. She wasn't easy."

"You fucked her yet?"

"Of course. But I don't want to say she was easy. I don't want to think that. She was really nice, you know?"

"Well, if you say so, I guess she is. Your French not getting in the way too much?"

"Are you crazy? Sometimes I think they want to fuck me just because I'm an Anglo."

"Is that true?"

"Yeah. I mean, you pull out three sentences in French, they think you're making an effort and boom! You're in."

"Yeah?"

"Absolutely. And, yo, she's a rich girl too."

"Of course she is," I said as I poured more salt and vinegar on my fries. "So you scored big time."

"I don't know, man."

"Do her parents know you *defiled* their daughter?"

"Hey, man, it was just sex. I mean it's not like—"

"I was talking about the tattoo."

"Oh, *that.*" He smiled. "I don't know. I don't think so. I haven't met them yet."

I could see he was getting shy or something. I could tell he liked her. I could tell he didn't want me to know he liked her but I knew. He was laughing more than usual, smiling more than usual. Maybe he just wanted to keep his options open, as he was still a young man. I fucking knew he liked her and so I wanted to bust his balls about it.

So I asked, "Are you gonna marry her?"

"What?" he said. He smiled again. "Nah, don't be stupid. I know what this is. I mean, she lives on fucking Doctor-Penfield. The minute I take her down to Shearer she gets like, turned on and she wants to fuck. But she'd never *move* there or some shit. I mean. I know what *this* is. I ain't stupid."

"You could move to Doctor-Penfield. You already live halfway up the hill."

He hesitated. "Yeah, maybe." Then he thought about it for a second. "Nah, man, it's never gonna happen."

"Hey, it's not like you didn't call each other back. You were walking Emma around in a bright sunny afternoon so—maybe."

"You know what?" he asked, as if his confidence had just grown a spine again. "You ain't wrong. She's nice. I'm alright. Or at least I think I'm alright. Why wouldn't it work out?"

It was weird somehow. Cillian could pretty much lay

any girl he wanted, but the minute he actually liked someone, he felt inadequate. I never understood that. Maybe it wasn't just him. Maybe it was the whole world. I didn't know "You'll never know if you don't try."

"Yeah," he replied as he took a bite out of his sandwich.

I could tell he wasn't sure. I could also tell he'd give it a shot. I wanted to believe that she could have been into him for more than just the sex, for more than *just fucking a bum* or *slumming it out while in college*. I would have liked to think that someone from up on the hill could be in for the long run with someone from "down here." I really wished that.

It didn't happen.

I didn't know if it was Cillian who broke it off or the girl. I didn't know if he felt inadequate in such a luxurious environment as Doctor-Penfield. I didn't know if the sex got old and they realized they had nothing much to talk about once they were done fucking each other.

I didn't know if she got tired of his poor Irish ass and wanted to go on vacation in Israel or Manhattan or fucking Thaïti if she cared for it.

All I know is that three weeks later, Cillian was telling me they were going through a rough patch.

"I don't know, man. It just got weird," he told me over the phone. I heard the pop of a bottle and him swallowing something. I didn't like it. I didn't like it one bit. A few more days and Emma's collar was off—they were officially done with one another.

CHAPTER 11

The Pitt Street crack house was named as such, originally enough, because it stood at the corner of Pitt Street and it was a crack house. It had been a crack den for as long as I had been alive. Twenty-eight years now. We'd take out bikes there when we were kids, threw rocks at the broken windows and lean in to hear if we had hit anyone.

It was a few thousand feet south of Atwater Boulevard, down a stretch of land destined to forever be in shambles. On the northern end of the canal, all you could see were newly built condos for the young urban rich. Pitt Street would never see such development for the simple fact that it was poorly placed. It was cursed for being a fifty yards wide stretch of land stuck between the canal, the 20 Highway and the Aqueduct. The only thing that anyone would imagine being built there were housing projects, and that would hardly improve the condition of the strip now, would it?

The "house" itself used to be a three-story loading dock/warehouse right next to what used to be a military factory in WWII. The whole place was red brick, square industrial windows, all of them shattered. The neighbouring building across the street was a former art-deco textile mill. One factory made bullets, mortars and bombs, the other one made clothes, boots and tents.

The women of the Pointe worked fourteen-hour shifts

there and were paid very little to make sure that England would be safe. Kids from the Pointe would drive trucks filled with gear up the hill to the Bonaventure station where more kids from the Pointe, or from Hochelaga, Tetreaultville, Verdun, Pointe-Claire, Greenfield Park— all the poor places in the city—would pick up the gear and get on board to be shipped off to the war. Most of the Brits who lived in Canada were cozy higher on the hill in their Westmount houses, far from the mud and the lice or any actual work.

We drove on Saint-Patrick in Karl's twelve-year-old BMW, went all the way to Angers and circled back to the other end of Pitt. You could still see the old water tower in the back, the green paint falling apart in strips ten inches long.

There was a trucking yard a hundred feet away, maybe the factory next to it had reopened. It was hard to tell but the few people we saw around were poor factory workers and immigrants stuck in what was probably an illegal shop.

No one was going to call the cops unless something incredibly big happened, like an explosion or a terrorist attack or some shit. A simple fight wouldn't do it. A simple murder probably wouldn't do it either. Hell, if fire caught up to the place, and I was always amazed it didn't already, then the fire department would probably just hose down the building around so the fire wouldn't spread. They'd let the place burn to the ground and that would be one less problem for the city to deal with.

Even I had to admit I was surprised the drug addicts of Pointe-Saint-Charles made such an effort to walk all the way down there for their fix. There were probably plenty of other apartments they could do drugs in. The Pitt house was just one of many in the end, but still, felt like a stretch to walk. I didn't know, maybe the exterior was just a front. Maybe they were handing out clean needles in perfectly clean beds where the "guests" could shower and be served toast in the morning. Wouldn't that be a sight, right? But then again.

"What is it that we're expecting to find anyways?" Phil asked.

"I don't know exactly," I said. "Maybe get to talk to the pusher, see if one of the junkies was around when my brother was killed?"

"So what are we waiting for?"

"I'm looking for the back door."

"Why not go up front?"

Ryan answered. "I don't know. Think about it. You're a drug dealer in a dilapidated warehouse and you see four sturdy, young gentlemen such as ourselves walking in the front door. Your first reflex ain't gonna be, *Good day to you, sirs. How may I help you?*"

"It might."

"It won't."

"They're Canadian."

"No one's *that* Canadian."

"Shut up," I said I was trying not to shout. "If they killed Cillian, they might as well kill us too. I ain't walking in there in the front door, plain and simple. Maybe the front door's booby trapped."

"I don't know, if I was to booby trap something, it would be the backdoor." That was true.

"Alright, alright. That's enough."

Karl put his foot on the ground. "We're going through the back."

"How come?" Phil objected.

"Just to contradict you," Karl replied. "Now, I can't expect any of you guys to be pussies in there, alright? If shit goes bad, we need to be sure we'll react properly. "

"That's insulting," Ryan said. Karl looked straight at him. He meant business.

"Phil?"

"Why are you singling me out?"

"You're not the most serious of people."

"Shit. *You're* so serious it's fucking insulting. You need to get the Germany out of your ass someday, man. It's not good for your health."

"What did you say?"

"Enough," I said as I started tightening my work boots. "We're about to bust a bunch of junkies, maybe the pusher, maybe not. But there's probably glass and piss or worse in there. They got needles and AIDS and shit. I don't want to get stabbed by a needle or step on a needle or slide on a needle."

"That's a good fucking point," Ryan said. "Now I don't fucking want to go."

"You're going," Karl said sharply.

"I know I'm fucking going. I just don't want a fucking needle stuck in my calf or something."

"What are we gonna do?" Phil added. "I mean, if a guy shows up, can I punch the guy? If I do and I open my knuckles and his blood falls in the wound? What if he spits on me?"

"You can't catch AIDS with spit," Karl said.

"How do you know?"

"Jesus Christ! I read it in a book."

"Use your crowbar to defend yourself and then throw it away afterwards."

"I paid forty bucks for it," Phil replied.

"Phil!" I shouted. "We stick to the plan. Walk in from the back, take them by surprise and see who would talk." I opened my door, got out of the car.

"There was a plan?" Ryan asked.

"I guess so," Phil added.

They walked out after me. Phil grabbed his forty dollar crowbar. Ryan got his baseball bat from the trunk. I was more of a brass knuckles kind of guy. It was there in my pocket. I reached down just to touch it, just to feel it. I wanted to make sure it was still there even if I already knew it was there. The cold touch of the metal felt reassuring at the tips of my fingers. I pictured myself holding the bastard who had killed my brother, driving the four points of my knuckles into his skull, sending his brains and blood everywhere around.

We jumped the fence at the old water tower, climbed a rusty old rig that looked like it was going to collapse under our weight. Karl wore work gloves and that looked like a great idea all of a sudden. I didn't know if he had a weapon. He didn't look like he had one. He was a firearms specialist and none of us really thought about bringing guns. We weren't those kinds of guys. But now what we were climbing this rig and heading towards the squat, I felt like I would've liked for Karl to have a pistol or something.

"We should have brought a gun," I admitted.

"Probably," Karl replied coldly.

"We could come back," I said

116

"Quit finding excuses," he replied. We were on the roof of some garage extension. He just kept walking towards the nearest window, probably to see if we could get in from there.

Phil and Ryan caught up to us. Phil wasn't the most agile. None of us were really in climbing shape, but he looked pathetic. I would have bet he was gonna fall off the damned ledge. His one hand was holding to the edge of the roof for his dear life. He threw his crowbar ahead, leaned dangerously over the gap between the old rig and the wall. Some of the brick was chirped off and slippery, there were fresh bird droppings all around and, of course, he put his hand right into it.

He grunted as he wiped it off his pants. He was having a shitty time. I would have helped him but now, with the bird shit and all, he was on his own. He swung once, then twice and after much effort, finally managed to swing a leg over.

"Jesus Christ," Ryan said. "Why did we bring you along if you can't even get on a roof?"

"Pourquoi on a pas pris l'osti de porte?" he started panting. "J'voulais juste basher une osti de porte, pas aller faire de l'escalade."

"They wouldn't expect that, would they?"

"Moi j'pense pas," Phil replied, catching up his breath. "I think we'd have the element of surprise." The four of us probably had a collective IQ of sixty, tops. What the hell were we doing here?

"Now that is some bullshit," Ryan replied.

"Why? You think everyone's just gonna bust in through the front door? Nobody does that. It's the unexpected-expected."

"And you've worked that into a theory?"

"Yeah. You want to hear about it?"

"If the both of you don't shut up right now, they're gonna know we're coming regardless of which way we enter," Karl said.

"Alright! Alright! S'correct," Phil said. He paused to catch his breath, again. then added, "Hey, it's like two in the afternoon."

"So?"

"Well, what kind of self-respecting drug dealer sells heroin at two in the afternoon."

"He's maybe got a point there," Ryan added, looking at Phil.

We had never actually set foot in there and only knew the reputation of the place by friends of friends and rocks thrown from afar...Ryan and Phil could be right. If we were to trust the Pointe's gossip, we were exactly in the right spot, but none of us knew if it was open 24/7 or not.

"Two ain't that early," I said. We looked at each other, clueless.

"Well, would you shoot up at two?" Phil asked.

"I would if I was a junkie," Ryan replied. "Junkies need their fix whenever they need their fix, two in the afternoon or not. I mean, don't you ever jerk off in the afternoon?"

"Good point," Phil said.

"You guys are idiots," Karl added.

Of course, getting in was not going to be as easy as we would have expected. The windows were still six feet above us and were barred with plywood and metal with broken glass still jagged around the edges. The few holes here and there weren't big enough to climb through.

"If we break it, they're gonna hear us."

"What do we do?"

"Wait here," I said. I walked over to the other end of the garage's roof. There was an access ladder to the building's main roof. I didn't know it if was going to hold my weight. I didn't know if anything was up there but it was worth a look.

I stepped on the first step, rattled the cage. It seemed strong enough. I decided to take my chances. *Don't look down.* I didn't. Instead I started looking at every rickety anchor, rusted screw and missing piece of mortar in front of me. That wasn't good. But one rung after the other and there you had it. Twenty-five feet higher, I had reached the roof.

A few pigeons were having a break there. The entire place was covered with their shit, cooked and burnt by the sun. There were a few weeds growing through cracks in the tar. I pictured the roof collapsing under me every step I took. The birds went flying at the sight of my fat Irish ass. They flew north towards downtown and I couldn't help but to notice how beautiful the skyline really was.

Beyond the rusted shed in front of me and the old WWII alarm tower from the canal park, the city was truly breathtaking. Mont-Royal was right ahead and the towers of downtown were to the right. The canal stretched both ways too far for me to see the end of it. Trees had managed to grow through the pavement in the former parking lot. Leaves were slowly dancing in the warm wind. If I wasn't out there to look into my brother's death, I could have made this a new drinking spot for me and the guys. Climbing up turned out to be easy enough. How hard could it be with a few beers down the throat?

Then I had a flash of Phil's sorry excuse for a climb back at the old rig and suddenly, our spot back at the Atwater Bridge felt exactly like what we needed.

I gave up on the sights, turned my back to it and walked to the hatch. I didn't have the pry bar on me and the hinges on the door looked rusted as shit but the lock was suspiciously new. It was no more than a few years old, stainless steel still sparkling in the sun.

I tried to pull it, wobble it, banged it. Some rust came down from the door but the lock held tight. The whole door was a mess so I was better off bashing at the rusty hinges. The bar we got should do it.

I walked back to the ledge, looked down. Karl seemed pissed, as usual. Ryan and Philippe were arguing again.

"You know they're gonna turn this into condominiums," Phil was saying.

"Nobody's gonna buy a condo in this piece of shit."

"I swear. They announced it. The city promised services and a new bus line. They're talking about redevelopment."

"You've read that where?"

"On the internet."

"Guys," I hissed.

"And you trust the internet?"

"Why not?" Phil asked then he looked at me. I waved them towards the ladder, signalled them to come up. "Looks like we're going up," he added.

"You can't trust anything that's on the internet," Ryan continued.

"J'vois pas pourquoi pas," Phil replied as he started climbing.

"Because the internet is full of crap—like penis enlargement ads, Russian brides, online gambling, jailbait dating sites, nine-eleven conspiracies," he started losing it, "and ideas like turning this piece of shit into condos."

They were talking too loud and it was getting on my nerves. "Guys," I said, trying not to shout. "Goddamnit, you two get married and fuck and buy a condo if you fucking want. For now, would you shut the fuck up already?"

Karl reached the top. I helped him up. "I'm giving up," he said.

"Hey, what's up with the homo implications," Phil shouted at me.

"You two sound like a fucking couple."

"Well, its homosocial, not homoerotic, alright," Phil said.

"Homo-*what?*" Ryan replied.

"Homosocial. An harmonious, non-sexual social gathering between people of the same sex. Homosocial."

"We're gonna get killed," Karl said as, arms shouting to the skies.

"What the fuck's up with him?" Phil asked.

"I say its hemorrhoids," Ryan answered.

"Heille. Laisse faire le cave," Phil replied.

The two idiots finally made it up.

"View's nice enough," Ryan said.

"I wish we had brought beer. Come look at this."

"Give me the bar," I said. He gave it to me then went to the ledge, sat on the edge of it, feet dangling four stories above ground.

I placed the tip next to the rusty edge of the hinges. I grabbed it tight, ready to push it in. I held it like a battering ram. One swift strike at the right spot could hurt the screws. The frame was wooden anyways, maybe we wouldn't even need a crowbar.

"You know, next time we need to be better prepared," Karl said. "Maybe leave the two kids at home with a babysitter."

I looked at him, looked at them. "I know, I know," I said. "It's not like any of us are career criminals or anything."

Karl didn't reply. He just stared at me like he does sometimes. We were not career criminals, but Karl's face said *speak for yourself.* He probably had jobs on the side we didn't want to know about. The guy scared the shit out of me sometimes.

I nodded sideways twice, took a swing as hard as I could. I hoped that the wood would cave-in just enough for us to pry open the door. The first hit lodged itself between the wood and the metal, gave me a quarter inch to work with. I took another swing. A loud crack was heard along with the *bang* the bar was set in deep enough. It wasn't as strong as I expected it to be.

"That's good, keep it up," Ryan said sarcastically.

"Hey, I thought we were supposed to be silent about this shit."

"We were."

"That's not silent."

"Give me a break," I replied. I was fed up with them, turning red from the heat and the sun. I was struggling with the pry bar...to hell with fucking silent.

"I think you're being hypocritical, that's all," Phil added.

"Shut up," I said as I pulled on the bar once more.

I expected the hinge or the wood to give in, then I would work on the second hinge and squeeze myself in whatever space I'd free up. But who the fuck could know? The wooden frame didn't give in. The hinge didn't give in. Nope. The whole damn thing literally detached itself from the cement wall around it.

Ahhhhh, shit! What else could I do?

The *whole* door frame fell backwards, cement blocks breaking down under the pull of it. It went down with the pry bar still fucking stuck in it, stout like a good little soldier at *Atten-sion.* I tried to hold it back, but that was just stupid. It was a full-metal door and I was holding it by the tip of a crowbar. Then I prayed it would fall silently but that was just stupid too. The whole thing was heavier than I was.

The door finally crashed inside, going down sideways inside the staircase. It made the loudest noise we have ever heard. Bits and pieces of concrete fell into the rusty metallic staircase.

Fuck!

Phil just started laughing. There was nothing else to do. He just started laughing. I had never heard someone laugh so honestly in my entire life.

"We might as well call it quits and come back another time," Ryan said. "I ain't walking in there right now. It's not very SWAT team now, is it?"

I just sighed, couldn't speak a word. I waited a moment, looked inside the staircase to see if anyone was coming up towards us. No one.

"Check the door," I said to Karl. I went to the edge of the roof next to Phil. Two guys had been scared off by the noise.

"I told you this shit was going to collapse," one of them was shouting to the other. The second one was just saying, "Shit, shit, shit, shit, shit..." on repeat. They looked like crap, walked crooked. I could *imagine* the smell all the way up to here. Definitely squatters.

After a few moments, no one had shot at us, came out the door or through the staircase. I didn't really know what to make of it. Was this really a crack den? Was there really someone in this piece of shit who would dare to kill my brother? To kill anyone? Why would the cops even mention this place in the first place if there was nothing to it, then?

Either way I had to get in, if only to scratch it off my list. Maybe I was a shitty criminal, but one thing I knew for sure, I was a good brother so I said, "Fuck it, I'm going in."

CHAPTER 12

The air was humid and thick, and reeked of moisture and sawdust; rust and lead. The scent of sewers was powerful enough to remind me that some things in this world were worth gagging for. I fought it, swallowed my own disgust and looked back in.

I shook the entire structure, just to see if I would fall down with it. It seemed to be strong enough. I wondered how long it had been since anyone had been here. Since the lock had been changed recently, then I guess the whole staircase could still support a grown man.

"You coming?" I asked.

"Sure," Phil said. "Smells like shit, but sure. Whatever."

"It smells better than your apartment," Ryan replied.

"Hey, that was uncalled for."

"Alright, your apartment reeks of shit, this is more like mould and stale water," Ryan replied.

"Smells like lung cancer," Karl added.

"You're probably right about that."

I didn't wait for the boys. They seemed to busy socializing anyways. I stepped in over the collapsed door.

There was a single lightbulb still on, dangling from its own cord from the very top of the hatch. I made my way down slowly, the guys were six feet behind me.

"Go back a few feet more," I said.

It wasn't that I expected anyone to come out and bash my head in at this point. With all the noise we had made a few minutes earlier, if they wanted us dead, we would have been dead already. No, I was just scared the stairs would give in if we all stepped on the same flight. I just wanted to be on point. If the whole thing collapsed, then I would have my own soul to carry to hell with me.

There was only one way to go when I reached the ground level. I stood against another rusted, metallic door. This one didn't have a brand new handle, didn't have a handle at all. Only a hole where the handle should have been, rusted edges, some sort of brown slime oozing out of it. It was very dark down here. The dim light three stories above us didn't do much good for me.

"Fuck it," I told myself. I opened it and the smell of death added itself to the fine mix filling up my nostrils. There was blood and feces, chemicals and burnt candles. It was truly un-breathable in there.

"Ahhh, God," I said, covering up my mouth and nose with my hand. No way anyone's hanging around here just for the fuck of it. But then I was proven wrong, a human being in despair will fucking resort to anything.

Someone in there moved alright. It was hard to see, even coming from the staircase. All the windows had been barred and you could only see small rays of light coming in through the cracks. There was electricity in there, two or three lightbulbs still in roof sockets, but no one seemed eager to let the sun light in. I saw the front door swing open and then close. Whoever had just left didn't want to be in trouble, didn't want to get found and didn't want to fight about it.

I stepped in, trying to scan the ground for glass, nails, debris and, mostly, needles. Ryan was the first down.

"Jesus Christ," he said as he covered his mouth. "And I thought the toilets at Foufs were bad."

He stepped in as I reached the first junkie—a young woman—she seemed like a teenager. Hell, she probably was a teenager and the drugs just fucked her face up. My eyes were accustomed to the darkness now and I could see her very well, sleeping on a mattress I wouldn't take a piss on.

There was a bottle of vodka next to it. There was also and a spoon and a small candle to prep the drugs. I didn't see a needle. I could've been stepping on it because I didn't check properly enough. I lifted both my boots to see if it was there, waiting to infect me with hepatitis or some shit. Nothing.

I looked back at her, crouched next to her. I expected a disgruntled, crusty punk but she was rather wearing Joshua Perrets pants, some high-end brand from up on the hill. She had a designer T-shirt that was probably worth more than any clothes I owned. Everything was dirty as it could be. That meant she hadn't been home in days or weeks and that was probably as bad as it sounded.

I didn't know what to think. I didn't know what to feel. You can't be happy about this. There's no way to be happy about this, regardless where you're from. No one wants to see their daughter end up in a place like this. I couldn't hate her just because she wandered down from the hill, could I?

I decided not to wake her up, couldn't bring myself to it.

Phil walked in. He didn't say a word, didn't complain about the smell or the needles or the shit. He just kept walking with a sense of purpose, headed straight for the front of the building, looking for something and when he found it, he shouted, "There!" He opened the front door, proud like a goddamned peacock. "No traps, no nails, no guns or knives. Nothing." He swivelled the door around twice, looked up and down at it. "No lock either. Hell, this door is better than the one my landlord fucking put on my apartment."

"Alright," I said.

"I climbed up and down three stories for sweet fuckall, moé, tabarnak!"

"What do you want me to say? Sorry for being cautious?"

"Pour commencer, ouin."

"I'll buy you a beer if you hush about it."

"Good."

"Leave it open," Ryan said. He walked into the light, trying to place himself in the stream of fresh air coming into the room.

"What do we do now?" Karl asked. He looked as troubled by the place as I was. We all had seen some shitty places in the Pointe, some shitty families in the city. I had known this woman, we called her "The Whale." Wasn't nice, but there was no other way I could've described her. She had five welfare kids that played badminton over a chainlink fence with barbwires on top of it that acted as a net. She'd sit in that couch that had spent seven million winters outside. She'd sit there, her fat guts dangling on both sides of her legs, old flannel robe didn't help at all. Sometimes a tit would stick out and she'd try to place it back in and fail.

She was a mess and so were her kids. She'd poke them with a broom stick if they'd be fucking around too much. She'd poke them with it if they were too loud or if they weren't loud enough. She'd poke them around if she wanted them to stop doing something or if she wanted them to get her a beer or a Coke and her cigarettes. Compared to this place, The Whale now felt like a goddamned beauty queen.

The Pitt house had officially just topped everything I had ever seen as the nastiest place in this city. Even that shithole place we used to play music up in Mile End felt like a decent home. Hell, my apartment felt like the fucking Ritz now. I'd never look at my dirty sink the same way again.

I looked at Karl, he knew how I felt about the place just with that look in my eyes. He agreed with a nod, lifted his hands in recognition that there was nothing we would do about it.

"Alright," I said. "Ask around, see if anyone is awake. Let the girl sleep."

"Okay."

We counted three people in the house. I picked the one closest to me. He was sleeping too. He was a young guy. I slapped him in the face.

"Wake up," I said.

He mumbled something, then drooled a little.

"He seems sober enough," Ryan said. Rough him up a little.

"How do you know he's sober enough?" I replied. "He's either asleep or passed out."

"Hey there, fella," Ryan as he kicked the junkie in the ribs.

"I didn't do nothing," the junkie shouted the second he woke up. I had to snatch him and pin him down by his shirt.

"Who says you did?" I said, trying to stop him from wiggling around.

He had panic in his bloodshot, crystal eyes. His breath was heavy, heart beat was through the roof. He started mumbling *Man, man, man, man* really fast, almost sounded like a dog panting. I checked both his hands: empty. Checked around the ground if there was something he could grab and stab me with. Nothing I had to fear. He was wearing track pants that didn't have pockets. I could start asking questions.

"You know a guy named Cillian?"

"What?"

"Cillian. It's not like there's a hundred of them around here," Karl said.

"Cillian? No, no. I don't know anybody. I'm just a junkie man. I'm just a piece of shit."

"A bunch of junkies and no pusher."

"*Is* there a pusher around here?" Karl smirked.

"What do you think? Of course there is."

"What's his name?" Ryan asked.

"I don't know."

"Don't fuck with me right now." Ryan raised his big ass paw in the air. The junkie cringed just thinking about how much it would hurt.

"I swear. I don't know his *real* name."

"That makes sense," Karl told me. It kinda did.

"Alright. *Who* sells here then?"

"What do you mean, who?"

"Are they black, white, Latino?"

"White."

"But you don't have a name?"

"I don't know. I just know his face is enough for me."

"Any Irish come here?"

"I don't know."

I raised my voice, "Don't..."

He shouted back, "It's not like they're walking around waving flags, yo."

"Where are they right now?"

"There's no *they*! There's one guy, sometimes two, but only one come in and he doesn't stay here all the time..."

"Can't blame him," Karl said.

The junkie continued, "They just show up once or twice, man. They let us hang around as long as we want if we buy something."

"Like a fucking coffee shop?" I asked.

"I don't know."

I didn't think he was lying. He had no reason to lie and everything he said made sense. I looked at him straight in the eyes. Straight in his blue eyes. Didn't see much but I saw fear and I didn't know what that meant except that he was a waste of my time.

"Few days ago, an Irish man died right outside this door. Look at my face," I said. He looked away. I pulled him closer. "Look at my fucking face," I repeated. "You sleep here often?"

"What?"

"Answer me. Do you sleep here often?"

"Yes," he shouted. "Yes."

"Then look at my face. You see it clear?"

"Yes."

"A guy that had a face a lot like this died around these parts. That guy was my brother. You get that?"

"Sure, yeah. I didn't do..."

"The cops seem to think he was in here the night of his death, that he then somehow fell into the canal across the street. Did you ever, *ever* see my brother in here?"

"I don't remember."

"Don't fucking play with me."

"I don't remember. I don't think so. I don't remember," he repeated and he meant it.

One side of me was happy to confirm that my brother had not OD'd in here. That much was good to know. I don't think I could have remembered him the same if he did. It still didn't explain the dope in his system the cops said they found, but he never got as low as the Pitt house.

"What do you think?" I asked Karl.

"Dead end."

"Yeah, feels like it."

I let go of the junkie. The moment my grip was loose, he bolted out of there. It startled the shit out of me. He grabbed some old plastic bag with his belongings in there, and took off to the door. I never would have believed a junkie, or anyone in fact, but especially a junkie, could move so fast.

He literally jumped in front of Phil, kissing the opposite wall just in case Phil would have tried to catch him. Phil didn't move and started laughing.

"Damn," Ryan said. Every single one of us was impressed. "Want us to chase him?"

I got up, looked out the door, looked at Ryan and dared, "The way he's running now, I don't think you could."

He laughed.

That was one down; there were two other people in the place we'd get to choose from. Our argument had woken up the young girl. She got up from her mattress. Her pants were loose from her famished hips but still hanging on to her large ass. She probably hadn't worn a bra in weeks and her breasts we saggy. Her hair was dirty and full of stains. Her face pretty much looked the same.

She was not a bad-looking girl. She had just spent too much time down here with the rats. If you threw her in the canal and shook her around like in a washing machine, then maybe you could slap the cute back into her. Not yet though. At that moment, I wouldn't poke her with a stick.

"Are you guys here for the delivery," she simply asked. She was ready to pay or ready to fuck for her drugs, that much I would believe. I didn't reply right away. I simply looked at her, trying to figure out why any normal young girl would fall that low.

"Well," she said with a dash of sassiness that didn't fit her anymore.

"No. We're not here for the delivery," I replied. She got defensive, crossed her arms together over her chest, her head felt like it sunk into her neck as she looked sideways.

"Well, what are you doing here then?" she tried to snap back at us.

I got up, looked straight at her eyes until she forced herself to look at me the same way. There was pain in there alright, but I had to stay focused on what I was here to do, so I said, "Looking for a guy who could find a guy."

Her hand started shivering and she dug it under her ditch to try and hide it. She had probably been beaten more than once, raped maybe and there I was, big Irish guy trying to push my shit on her. Her face said *not this again*. No. It said *I'm fucking dead this time*.

"Cillian Kennedy ring a bell?" I tried to say, a bit softer.

"No."

"Any young Irish guys?" Karl asked.

"Looked a lot like me," I added.

"No."

"Anything unusual lately?"

She looked at me, eyes asking *Are you fucking serious?* I was, so she said, "Just this guy over there."

I signalled Karl and Ryan to check him out, then said, "What about him?"

"I don't know. Skin is peeling and shit. He mixes his drugs with gasoline or something."

"You mean Krokodil?" Ryan asked.

"I don't know," she answered.

Phil got excited, "Yo, I heard about that shit in Vice. Can I see?" He started walking towards the guy but Karl was already there.

"He's dead," he said.

"Ahhhh." Phil was disappointed.

"Looks like shit," Ryan said.

"Smells like it too."

Phil lifted the guy's shirt. I couldn't help but look at it. The girl held back a gag.

His skin was like scales, large crevasses all around, rotten, blackened flesh in odd spots with large chunks peeling off. You could see muscles and bones where it was the worse and for the first time in a long time, my mind was absolutely clear. It was that bad. There's nothing you can fucking think about watching something like this.

"Duuuuuuude! This is fucked up," Phil said. He snapped a picture.

"Let him be," I said.

"Yo, I mean, would you believe the shit this drug does to you?"

"He's dead. You're taking pictures of a dead guy. What are you gonna do with them anyways?"

"Rotten dot com."

"That would be a public service announcement if you ask me," Karl added.

The girl had turned catatonic or something. She had dropped into a stared at the sight of the dead guy. Her eyes were blank, one hand still in front of her mouth to hold back a gag that the brain wasn't gonna send anymore. She looked livid.

"Lady," I said, snapping my fingers twice in her face. I had to push a bit more. "Lady."

"What?"

"I think you're gonna want to get the fuck out of here."

"Where to?"

"Got family somewhere?"

"What is it to you?"

"Whatever got you down here, home can't be worse than having a dead zombie in the corner."

Karl grabbed her gently by the shoulders, walked her to the front door. I was surprised he did that. "Here's twenty," he said. "Get home somehow."

"My bag," she replied as she pointed back in.

"Here's forty. Whatever is in there, buy something new." She allowed him to push her out. He did it with care. She cringed like she hadn't seen the sun in days, started walking westward.

We all got out and stood there in the door of the dilapidated factory that once helped defeat the Germans. When she was thirty or forty yards away, I said. "That was nice of you, Karl." It really was. It didn't feel like something Karl would do. Maybe the guy had more good in him that what I usually gave him credit for. That was nice to know.

"I guess," he replied.

"It's not like you, is all."

"Well," he sighed, "forty bucks didn't seem like much to finally get her out of my face. Hopefully it will be enough for her to overdose on her next fix." He stretched his arms out and yawned. "Come on, car's over there."

Turned out I wasn't wrong and Karl was still Karl.

CHAPTER 13

So the cops had their heads up their asses just as I suspected. The Pitt house was a dead end.

We made our way to a deli in Saint-Henri, Notre-Dame Street. It wasn't like the fancy places that kept opening through the southwest these days. No ethnic-jazz and indie-rock there. The radio played CHOM, place was old but it felt like everything was paid for. *Opened in 1979* the sign read. Seeing as it had survived two economic collapses and a recent, relentless wave of gentrification, it would still be open a decade after the fancy place across the street was gone.

"So what now?" Karl asked.

Phil was reading the papers, Ryan was having a bagel.

"I don't know," he said, chewing on it. "What do we know?"

"Well, it wasn't' drugs," Karl said.

"So the cops got it wrong." Phil said.

"Are you surprised?"

"Not really."

"But they can't be *all* wrong," Ryan added. "I mean, if Cillian was killed and then dumped in the canal, it had to be upstream. So that means we at least have some-where to start with."

"The cops said he had been in the water for five hours before they got the call. How do they figure out the drop point?" I asked.

"Current speed, wind, obstacles," Karl replied.

"You're the sniper here, where do you think he was dropped?" Phil said.

"I'm not a sniper," Karl replied. "Snipers takes classes, have training, combat experience. I'm just a really good shot."

What Phil had just said got me thinking about the kind of guys I had around me and how lucky I was to have them. Karl *was* a fucking marksman. Not a military guy, but Karl Anderson, had learned to shoot at the age of twelve. His father being a fan of all things firearm had managed to hand down to his son an amazing talent with handguns, short weapons, rifles...anything that shot a bullet.

The word was that Karl had managed to cut a nail at a hundred yards with a 30-06 at the age of fourteen. By the time he was sixteen, he managed the same shot with a 9mm at twenty metres. The achievement might not sound as impressive, but it caught the attention of certain scouts with the Shooting Federation of Canada. Two years later Karl Anderson, a young man from NDG, Montreal, whose total family revenue was around twenty-two thousand a year, was endorsed by Remington, Home Depot and Gillette. Karl Anderson hated construction work, kept a full beard throughout his endorsement and used a Ruger. He didn't like any of these companies, but he happily took their money. Karl Anderson was a hustler. Any of us would have done the same.

"I can hit a target," Karl continued, "that doesn't mean I can figure this out."

"Take a guess."

"I guess the cops probably were in the ball park when they mentioned the Pitt house."

"You think?" I asked.

"Well, what about you? You're the fucking genius here..." Karl said to Ryan.

Ryan was in many ways, a genuine fucking genius. We had met at a Death Threat concert in one of the ramshackle squats that used to plague Saint-Henri.

That's where my face became acquainted with Ryan Duncan Scott's incredibly smooth and soft elbows. The song went in a breakdown and I guess he just felt like hitting whatever was in front of him.

I was in front of him.

Wrong place, wrong time. There was nothing more to it. "Just a guy in a mosh pit," he'd say. I wasn't prepared for it, knocked me out enough that I stumbled on the floor.

That was something you'd expect from a guy who looked like Ryan. But then the weirdest thing happened. You usually take care of your own wounds in shows like these, but as I was standing outside the pit, I guessed he felt I was *off limits* in a weird sense of honour. After knocking me down, he picked me up from the middle of the pit, walked me backstage, sat me down in one of the chairs. The other bands looked at us sideways. We had no reason to be backstage, but Ryan looked like a guy you didn't argue with, even if your band's name is Death Threat. He got me some ice from the band's cooler and said, "Sorry about that."

We started talking.

He was not as strange as I had originally believed him to be. In fact, he was a lot stranger than I'd expect. He had punched me, he said, because of some incredible urge he felt every now and then.

"It's just, *in* me," he said. He started explaining that he tried to live his life by the teachings of Friedrich Nietzsche. "The only guy worth reading." He said that when this *primal urge* takes him over, he allows himself to give into it, which doesn't mean that he loses his ability to use reason the moment afterwards, thus, the apology and the ice pack.

We became friends after that and years later we were in some deli trying to help me solve the murder of my brother.

Phil flipped another page of the Pointe's paper. He was in his own bubble and didn't say a word for a while.

"But we went to the Pitt crack house, it wasn't there." I said.

"Well, the house had nothing to do with it. Maybe that's still where they dropped him."

"Okay. So we look around the Pitt crack house. We look for tire tracks, skid marks, ask regular joggers. I mean, it's not like there are any security cameras around, right? It's just a federal park. So our best guess is still the SaleCon cameras. We really just need to pay off *one* guy, don't we?"

We looked at each other. It was probably hopeless but it was something.

"I got something better," Phil said without raising his head from his article.

"Like what?"

"There are cameras around I can have access to?"

Phil flipped back a few pages.

"Well, What? Where? Who?"

"There's a crime spree in Saint-Henri. Home invasions, theft, property crimes."

"What the fuck is there to steal in Saint-Henri?" Karl smirked.

"Well, they say most of the crimes target the new condos on the edge of the canal. They're rich so that's where the local trash go to get their TV's and shit. So, the condo towers started installing gates and cameras."

"So there might be footage?"

"Maybe," Phil replied. "And guess who's on the fucking picture installing one of those security systems?"

"Who?"

"Matthieu Saint-Louis," Phil said, "from the shop, here on Notre-Dame."

"Never heard of him?" I said.

"Me neither," Ryan admitted.

Karl shook his head.

"That's because you all went to James Lyng. I went to Saint-Henri."

It lit up in my head like fucking fireworks. Crossing the language barrier of this goddamned city might actually help us solve this fucking thing.

"Shit!" we all said.

"Let's go pay Matthieu a visit."

We tipped the waitress, and headed out the door. The locksmith/camera dealer was three blocks from the coffee place we were in. We didn't even have to take the car.

We headed west, past the old pawn shop, the pharmacy and the new grocery store. People were walking around on the sidewalks. The new rich collided with the old poor. Different kinds of baby strollers were telling a lot about what kind of families were raising what kind of kids. The yuppies had McLaren designed baby carriages. The families that had worked and bred in Saint-Henri for seventeen generations still carried used stroller from the Renaissance centre.

We walked in front of the old theatre that had turned into a church that had turned into a squat. It was a beautiful building, probably one of the nicest ones on the strip in fact. When they'd be done pushing the working class out of the neighbourhood, I would bet that whoever took over the theatre would get the city to invest in it, make it a beacon for culture that the rest of us didn't deserve.

Notre-Dame was known downtown to be a beautiful street, home to the Provincial courthouse, a bunch of big old buildings that were now tourist attractions and fancy hotels.

The reality was that the overwhelming majority of Notre-Dame Street serviced some of the poorest of shittiest parts of the city, from Saint-Henri to the Molson Brewery, Hochelaga, the Longue-Pointe Army base, city port, Tétreaultville, the refineries, Montreal-East...It wasn't 'till it reached the very end of Pointe-aux-Trembles that it got any better, and even then, you were so far out in the suburbs, you could hardly call it Montreal anymore.

That's where Phil spent most of his youth, the working East End of the city.

"It's worse than you'd think," he'd say. "It's like this one time, I was living way deep in Hochelaga, like in the few blocks between Sainte-Catherine and Notre-Dame and the guy upstairs always hired hookers and shit. So, like, every month or so we would hear the banging and spanking and slapping among other things, plus what we could only imagine were a pair of sexy male-fuck-me-boots stomping on his floor-slash-my roof. That said, I'm fucking broke and I'm living in Hochelaga, what else do you expect? Right? I mean, I ain't stupid. I knew where I lived. But there was this one, faithful night, when at three in the morning they fucking start going at it and I hear what I could only describe as pig noises and a few minutes after that, what I (again) could only describe as litres and litres of liquid being spread out on the floor like he just gutter the damn animal, or the prostitute, who fucking knows?

Now the police never investigated so I figure everything was within *legal boundaries* or he was just a very good serial killer (in both cases, I ain't asking questions). I moved out of there anyways. You had the creep and the Portorican pushers in a turf war with the Québécois pushers over on Vimont, plus the hookers and the junkies and the Nazis and shit, this wasn't HOMA, you know, it was still fucking Hochelaga back then. The only cool thing I miss is the Latino family on the corner who always took out their fooseball table and played outside on the sidewalk—every fucking night. They'd buy themselves a few cigars at the corner store and fucking play fooseball on the sidewalk all night. Now that was cool...the rest...not so much.

Every time I heard those kinds of stories, I said to myself the Pointe wasn't so bad, even though we knew better.

The locksmith was right across from the underpass, on the road to Chateau Saint-Ambroise, also one of the nicest buildings in the city. You could see its six story, redbrick edge at the end of the street. They called it a castle, but it was just another old factory, it just looked like a castle and was advertised as such with tall billboards.

The locksmith was open so we walked in.

"Bonjour, hi," the guy said from his counter.

"Hey, Matthieu," Phil said. "Ça fait un boutte."

"Hey, Phil, quoi de neuf?"

"Pas grand chose. Pas grand chose. Écoute, j'te mentirais si j'te disait pas qu'on est ici pour une bonne raison. Tu sais le gars qui à été retrouvé dans l'canal?"

"Ouais."

"C'est son frère," Phil said as he pointed to me. The locksmith looked at me but he wasn't surprised. It felt like the glasses he wore were permanently stuck to the tip of his nose. He had a skinny, famished face, tiny arms and an expression in his stare: that guy had seen and heard absolutely everything.

In the next half hour or so, we explained the whole thing to him. Still, he didn't really have a clue—or gave a fuck—as to why we were in his shop, talking about Cillian. We mentioned the cops, the Pitt house, how the date and place of death sorta made sense, but not how or why.

"This is where you come in," I said. "We've been told you were handling the security units for those condominiums."

"Pis l'à j'assume que vous aimeriez voir les enregistrements," he said and smiled. *Shit's gonna cost me.*

"That would be worth way more than a favour."

"Oh! Y'aura pas de frais."

"Are you serious?" I asked. He nodded yes. It wasn't gonna cost me a fucking dime? "Why?" I asked.

"Just to see where this goes."

"Le temps est long?" Phil asked him.

"Vraiment!" the locksmith replied.

"So which way to the tapes?" I asked.

"Tapes?" he said, laughing. "Messieurs, this is the twenty-first century. Laissez-moi barrer la porte."

He took us in the back. I felt a little stupid about the whole *tapes* thing. I imagined some '80s set up with rows and rows of gray VCRs lined up as an entire archive of tapes. When we got to his office, and that's all it was, there was simply a laptop there connected to a box. Not even a big box, maybe one-square-foot.

"That's it?"

"Sixteen gigabytes of data in compressed video. Je peux archiver deux ans de film la dedans."

"Wow," I said.

"I know."

"So you can trace it back to five days ago, say midnight to four AM."

"Sure! Quelle unitée?"

"We didn't take the time to write it down."

"That's not a problem."

He opened Google, typed *Montreal*, zoomed on the Pitt warehouse. He then went across the canal, zoomed to street view. I felt tech illiterate. Even with all the social media accounts I had opened over the years—even if I didn't use them—even after working ten-hour shifts on a computer, I felt tech illiterate.

"Voilà," he said.

He switched programs, typed in the address. A pop menu of all the security archives appeared.

"We're looking for a view of the canal. Maybe if you have something that can see across from there," Karl said.

"We have three cameras in the back. La plupart des voleurs entrent par l'arrière."

"It this legal?"

"Breaking in?"

"No, you showing us those tapes?"

"Probablement pas. Mais regarde," he added as he leaned towards a key cabinet. "We have the keys to all the apartments right there."

"Is that legal?" I asked again.

He gave me a look, *don't ask, won't tell.* I couldn't help but start laughing. I smiled, shook my head and got back the laptop's screen.

He opened one of the security feeds. Four camera views popped on screen. He fast forwarded at four times. Nothing happened for a while. I had my eye across the canal. You could only see so much of the Pitt House, but that was the best shot we had. If the cops were right, we should see something happening any minute now. With some luck, my brother would have been dropped inside the angles of those cameras.

"We got something, maybe," Ryan said. Matthieu slowed down the video.

"I don't see nothing," I said.

"Not across the canal, but on this side, here."

We could see the hood of a white Econoline. Only the hood.

"Well, that's definitely suspect. Is there a better angle?" I asked.

"Not on this one, I'm sorry."

The van didn't move for a minute or so. Seventy-four seconds to be exact. We timed it. Then in took off in a hurry. All we could see was half of the top and the tinted windows. No licence plate. That was definitely more than suspicious.

I could picture the events perfectly in my head. The guy or guys opening the sliding door, dragging a doped up or passed out Cillian, dragging his ass over to the canal and dumping him in the dark waters where they knew he would drown. They probably didn't even care to look twice and hurried back to the van, took off as fast as they could.

"Should we go to the cops with this?"

"Bien techniquement, you were never allowed to see it, alors, comment auriez-vous su? Et c'est pas comme si j'allais avouer que je vous ai laissé regarder le feed."

He was smart enough to hide or delete the feed if ever he was suspicious that we'd go to the police. The only thing they would find was an empty recording, probably copied from a day earlier that week.

"The cops never showed up here and asked to see this?" I asked.

"Non."

"So we have a van," Karl said. "A white van. That's not a great lead."

"I know," I said.

"That street circles around?" Ryan asked. "Right?"

"Oui."

"Est-ce que y'aurait un autre angle de vue?" Phil asked.

"Peut-être."

"Please try."

He switched buildings, looked at the time stamp on the recordings. We saw the van coming on from the other condo building's angle.

It took a left the street right after that. There wasn't much to go on. We had a few good frames of the side, but that was it. No licence plates.

"Can you zoom there?" Karl said.

"Sure."

Matthieu took the frame out of the video, imported it to Photoshop. The quality was surprisingly good.

We didn't have much, but it was something, a small logo that looked like a metal band's name or something. It said "FIH" and it had sort of a reverse peace symbol without the circle. Everything was inside a black shield and that was it.

"What the fuck is that peace symbol? Hippies killed Cillian?" Phil asked.

"That's a white supremacist symbol." Karl said.

"It's a fucking peace symbol," Phil replied.

Karl explained, "Upside down, broken arms."

"Ahhhhh..."

"What? They killed Cillian because he was Irish?"

"Did Cillian have anything to do with Nazis?"

"Nah. He even joined the ARA for a while some years ago when he was sixteen or something."

"So, the *whites* killed him because he was in ARA?"

"That would be a stretch. I mean. They had a few fist fights here and there. I never heard about anyone getting killed over this shit."

"Google it," I said to Matthieu. He did.

Google gave us two point five million hits on "FIH," none of them useful. The first one was the French International Hockey association. Some hockey league didn't kill my brother. Then there was Foxconn International Holding, some hospital Federation and a website that was called "Forward Into Health."

"Deux secondes," the locksmith said.

He typed in "FIH white supremacist."

It gave us a few sites like the Aryan resistance movement, the eco-fascists of the world *because the superior race needs a green earth to thrive*, there was a page form Rock Against Communism, an anti-racist watch dog group called "The Sisterhood" and right underneath it there was an old MySpace page for a band called "Faith in Hate."

"Faith in Hate," I said. "Shit!"

We clicked on the page. No recent activity. There were a bunch of pictures of boneheads in front of swastika flags. They all had beers opened and tried to act tough. Another picture showed them in the van we had seen on the security footage. They had a few of their songs online. The titles were not so subtle: "Fuck off," "Black Pigs," "Pure Blood," and a cover of Screwdriver's "Smash the IRA."

"So Nazis killed my brother."

"We don't know for sure. But it's a decent lead if you ask me," Karl said.

"Where are they from?" I asked.

"Ça le dit pas."
It didn't say.
What was I thinking? Of course it didn't say. Shit.

CHAPTER 14

Next we were headed for the office of some semi-legal skinhead group Ryan knew about from a bouncer he used to work with at Katacomes Club. They operated out of a small building in the former red-light district on the lower main.

Next to it was a vacant lot, a rarity in this city. The office was in a former triple-decker converted into commercial units. It must have been two hundred years old if I was to trust the full-stone front of the building. The rest belonged to the glory days of the '90s: twenty-year-old mural on the side of it, paint faded by the sun, bricks falling on the edges, crooked stairway and barred windows in the bookstore downstairs, L7 poster washed out by the sun.

We made our way up, banged on the heavy metal door on the second floor. A sort of improvised vent had been cut four inches by two in the middle of the door. The guys had done the job themselves it seemed, as there were still jagged edges to that thing. If they had been left there on purpose or not, I couldn't figure, but you could cut yourself easy enough to be careful.

A slider opened and you could see some sort of hammered grid, battered and bruised inside. I figured someone had once banged on the door, waited for someone to open and tried to poke an eye with a stick. Either that or he had straight up shot the man and they put up the grid so that you couldn't aim right once the slider opened.

"T'é qui toé?" the guy said from the other side of the door.

"Je m'appelle D'Arcy Kennedy," I tried in French but as it always happened, I went right back to English. "I'm here because I could use your help."

"Is Etienne around?"Ryan asked.

"He's not here. What do you want?"

"Well, gentlemen," I said. "We're looking for information on a bonehead crew called Faith in Hate."

The slider closed down. There was a pause. We didn't know if the guy was going to open or if he just decided to ignore us all. Then we heard the noise of at least three locks being opened but the door still didn't move.

"You got weapons?"

"No."

"Anything. Baseball bats?"

"No."

"Crow bars, tools? There's a camera in the corner, look at it, open your arms." I did.

"See. Nothing, sir."

Then the door opened a few inches with two chains still holding it tight. The guy was standing against the door, ready to close it if need be, standing out of harm's way. I started wondering if I had missed some sort of wave of Nazi-related crimes in the city that we should have known about.

"Screwdrivers?" the guy added.

The hole in the grid.

"I can strip naked right here if it makes you feel better."

"It won't."

"Glad to hear it."

He closed the door, unhooked the last two chains and finally opened up. "The Black Dot" was on a huge tag on the wall across the room. We walked inside, the place was vacant but still smelled of last night's sweat and blood. The guy who opened the door was busy cleaning the floor and the stage. The bar was full of empty bottles, two trash cans were by the door. The place was small, maybe big enough for forty or fifty people jammed in tight. One skinhead was sleeping behind the sound booth, still drunk or so it seemed.

The roof was decorated with the red and black flag of the Spanish Revolutionary War. The walls were covered with posters from punk shows and protests against police brutality. If I was to trust a blackboard calendar on the wall, the place was used as a venue for Oi! shows and punk shows, as well as a rally point for a bunch of anarchists, revolutionaries, RASH skinheads, the Montreal Sisterhood...Pretty much anyone who wanted to beat down Nazi scum, capitalists or cops. We started walking around.

"Selling beer," Ryan said. "Probably illegal."

"And I would bet they weren't compliant with fire safety," Karl tossed out.

"When you chose that lifestyle, fire regulations probably aren't your biggest concern," I added.

A large punching bag was resting in the corner, you could see traces of dried blood in the middle of it and it's got me wanting to punch it. Maybe it was the smell in the air or the weird silence in the place. It gave me that itch to destroy something and make noise out of it. I didn't care if it was a punching bag or a wall or some guy's face...silence was just heavy. I started stretching my hands, cracked my neck, wiggled my fingers as if I was about to do a workout. I probably could've used a visit to the guy or a date with a punching bag.

"What about Faith in Hate?" the skinhead asked.

"We have reasons to believe that they are involved in the murder of my brother."

"Is that so?" he was suddenly interested. "We had problems with boneheads in the past, but it would be the first time we heard FIH would have anything to do with it."

"You mean you had *murder* problems with boneheads in the past?"

He got defensive. "I wouldn't have those kinds of details," he said simply, trying to be as unemotional about is as he could. The guy had been to court more than his fair share, I could tell you that with certainty. I liked him.

"Fair enough," I said.

He relaxed a bit. We weren't cops or *the enemy*. The guy had seen plenty of bullshit and once he had figured we weren't a threat, he had no reason to keep the tough front attitude. When that wall came down, I could see he was someone I could have actually worked with at the warehouse or in the Pointe. He had a Social Distortion T-shirt, not arguably the toughest band out there and you could see his neck tattoo actually read *maman* which was both cheesy and sweet.

The only difference between me and him was that his shaved head was shaved shorter than mine. He also liked his Dickies tight and high, I preferred mine loose and saggy.

We told him about Cillian, about the police thinking it had something to do with drugs and the Pitt house. He laughed when he heard that and said it didn't surprise him about the cops. We told him about the people waiting for deliveries inside and about the cameras in the condos across the canal. We showed him the picture of the van and he agreed, it was, indeed, a Faith in Hate logo.

"Karl here said you might know about the band's movements and time in Montreal."

"I'd have to ask Marie-Ève." He headed to the door, stuck his head out in the stairway. "Marie-Ève," he shouted upstairs. The door opened, a short, strongly built girl opened the door. She had half her head shaved and the other half was dangling on the side of her head in various shades of green, pink and faded purple.

"What's up?" she said.

"I got guys looking for Faith in Hate here, you know about their whereabouts?"

"We have a file, yeah,"

"She has a *file?*" Phil whispered, surprised to Ryan. He just raised his shoulders. *I don't know.*

"We'd appreciate any information you could provide," I said.

"Well, it's a white power band from Ontario and they're affiliated with the Heritage Front as far as we know. The last time they played a show in Montreal was maybe eight months ago."

"Are you sure?"

"We keep tracks of the three or four bookers that set

155

up shows with Neo-Nazis, we haven't seen any posters or anything lately."

"Are you sure?" I repeated.

"Well, come up. We'll see what we can find."

We all got up to the third floor. We expected some dilapidated office or a squat much like the Pitt house or another mosh pit friendly room like the one downstairs. Boy, were we wrong. The third floor was still an apartment that the anarchists had converted into some kind of library.

The place felt like a hippie commune: plants everywhere, two couches, a hamac, smelled of incense. There were some posters in Spanish about a labour strike in Chile several years ago, a bunch of shit about feminism, leaflets that mentioned Anarcho-Syndicalism. If the place had played Janis Joplin instead of the Circle Jerks, I would have said Ryan's friends' leads were bullshit but seeing the whole place organized as it was, I was willing to give them a few minutes of my time.

There were books everywhere and a large round table at the centre of it. It was full of 'zines and small leaflets for various political causes. The books were organized by themes: feminism, anarchism, communism, capitalism, social science, poetry, fiction, drama, engineering, agriculture...The place was as tidy as a hospital. *No Smoking Allowed* a sign stated.

The back balcony had been converted into an urban garden. I looked out the window. Three stories below, a village of hobos living in tents and cardboard boxes down in was set-up in a hidden backyard. There were four or five large, blue tarps set up between the building and a tree. Up here they had peppers, tomatoes, salads, even a grapefruit vine on the wall.

"We try to plant seeds that will grow vertically in order to save on space," she said to me. "One day we hope to have enough resources to make a full rooftop garden."

"Impressive."

"Thanks. But that's not why you're here for, is it? Sit down."

Each of us took a seat around the table. The girl sat back at her desk. Phil picked up one of the leaflets on the table, didn't really read it and said, "So you keep tabs on Nazis in the city?"

"Not just me, there's a bunch of us."

"But why?"

"Because they're Nazis."

"You Jewish or something?" Karl asked.

"I consider myself an atheist. A few of our members are of Jewish origin but we're all anti-racists, that should be enough."

"There can't be that many Nazis in town," I said.

"Thanks to us."

"Really?" I asked. That sounded like a load of shit and I started wondering if she wasn't so full of herself to actually help us.

"Well, they call themselves nationalists, the heritage front," she said, "white supremacists, in French, they use the term *identitaire* to hide their true philosophy."

"You have a lot of spare time on your hands," Ryan said. It pissed her off. Instantaneous backfire. She turned to him and that look on her face told me that punk/hippie, whatever she was, could in fact turn into one of the nastiest, angriest person I ever met.

"September 8, 2004," she started, "four Nazi skin heads single out a militant by the name of Asif Patel. He was a community organizer and had managed to start reinsertion programs for opiate users as well as shutting down Kosta, Inc. from spilling known pollutants in the Saint Lawrence. Why did he get beat down? Not because of drugs or Kosta, because he was an anti-racist militant and he was Indian. That was enough for the boneheads. They beat him up with pipes and chains, when he was on the ground they started kicking him even though he was unconscious and they left him there for dead. He woke up three weeks later in the hospital."

Ryan didn't reply but you could see in his face *Alright already*. But it was too little, too late. She was on a mission.

"Want another example?" she continued. "Two years later, a young up-and-coming white supremacist from the South Shore named Frankie Beliveau. He tried to run his car into a crowd full of young punks that were waiting in line to see a Jeunesse Apatride show. If he hadn't run the car into a pole, he probably would have killed six kids. A year later, he beat up a Hatian corner store clerk in Hochelaga just because, no accusations. He probably thought, 'one nigger in Hochelaga is one nigger too many.' A month after that, he went down to Yermad's bar downtown and decided to beat up a black man sitting at the bar, just because. Too bad for Frankie, the black man was a cop with friends in the army. The RASH wanted to kill Frankie, we wanted to kill him, the Hatians wanted to kill him, the cops were gonna look away. I don't know who did it, all I know is we haven't heard from that guy ever since. Do you know how many firebombs have been thrown at this building over the years?"

Ryan was pissed. He wasn't the kind of guy who'd allow himself to be talked down by some borderline-homeless French-Canadian chick, especially not over this kind of shit. He snapped back at her, "I guess not that many 'cause the building's still up. Maybe I'll thrown in the next one and let them build condos over your little hippie commune."

"That's enough, both of ya," I said. It pissed her off, but she swallowed it. I took a deep breath, looked at the girl. "What about Faith in Hate?"

"Well, as I said," she pulled out a file from a drawer, threw it on the table, "Faith in Hate are from Ontario. They're an Oi! band doubling as a white power crew. As far as we know, they operate out of Hamilton."

"Hamilton?" I said as I opened the file.

There were photographs of the band, some of them standing in front of swastikas, others with the iron cross. You could see, in one of them, a poster of some slave hanging, in the old south. One picture was live, with the whole band and crowd doing hail Hitler salutes. They had accumulated flyers, posters from past shows, CD leaflets. Some of the lyrics had been highlighted to note the racist content.

I didn't know who that chick was, but they did have too much time on their hands. There couldn't be enough Nazis in Canada to warrant that kind of surveillance.

Most of the photographs were of poor quality, printed on a black and white laser printer. One of them had the *believed* names of band members. The back of the photo had handwritten notes about what the band had been up to the last time they had been in Montreal.

One of them mentioned *most likely false licence plates* noting a Manitoba place while the band was known to be from Southern Ontario. It all looked pretty impressive when it fell into your lap, but once you started to really look at the information, there wasn't much to help us in there.

"They used to be in Toronto," the girl said when I finally looked up. "A lot of Nazis were, but as the city gentrified, they moved south."

"I know the feeling," Phil said. "If prices keep going up, maybe we're gonna have to move south too."

"But Hamilton is still pretty big," Karl said.

"That's true," I added. "It's not likely we can just go down there and stumble on them by mistake, Hamilton's what? Half a million."

"Six hundred fifty thousand or so," Ryan replied.

"Don't you have an address or something," I asked her.

"I can give you the name and where to find a guy who knows where to find the crew who booked them the last time they were in the city. It's a long shot but maybe. He's a busboy in a gay bar now but he used to be a total gay basher only a few years ago. Push enough and he'll tell you what you need."

"Former gay basher?" I looked at her, not convinced.

"Total white supremacist," she replied.

"That's the best you've got? Aren't there people like you in Hamilton?"

"I'm afraid we only keep tabs on what happens in Montreal, I can't guarantee what information we have on groups elsewhere. What I can do is send an e-mail to

RASH groups in Ontario, see what comes back. But there are odds those groups have been infiltrated by white supremacist just to get information."

"You'd believe that?"

"Absolutely."

That one was way over the top. That chick believed she lived in a fucking cold war spy novel. White supremacists infiltrating anti-racist movements. *Come on!* I was better off doing my own work than to trust the local psycho-paranoid-anti-racist-anarchist. I wrote down the address of the gay-basher-turned-gay.

"Don't e-mail Hamilton. We'll look into it ourselves." I got up, headed for the door. "Thank you for your time. It's appreciated."

"Can I ask why you are looking into FIH?"

I put on my poor boy hat and replied, "Lady, I'm pretty damn sure they killed my brother."

CHAPTER 15

The address she gave us was in the east end of the village; the shitty end of the village. A place where gentrification seemed to crash against the pillars of the Jacques-Cartier Bridge and failed to push into the Centre-Sud district. I had seen places in this city that I couldn't believe were being rehabilitated, but the whole economy was going to collapse before they could do anything decent with Centre-Sud.

The bar was called The Studded and it looked a lot more like a biker bar than what you'd expect a gay bar to look like. It was miles away from the flamboyant Chez Mado or the luxurious Drugstore. Then again, you could just happen to be working class *and* gay and need a watering hole just like anybody else. Who the fuck was I to know?

We walked in. The Alouettes were playing on TV. The place was nearly empty. There were ads for Carlsberg, the upcoming Euro and Montreal Impact games. There were two pool tables, sparkling new, and a sketchy ATM next to the bathrooms.

There was this one guy on a stool by the bar. Huge man, at least two-eighty and not a fat two-eighty. He had arms like tree trunks, shoulder plates as wide as a truck, calves that could lift a thug boat. He had a shaved head, white goatee, "Sons of Anarchy" shirt on. He looked like he could have been a bouncer or a roadie for Black Label Society.

"I thought this was supposed to be a gay bar?" Phil asked.

The caveman heard him. "It *is* a gay bar," he said and took a sip.

Phil walked over, helped himself to some peanuts resting in a basket.

"It don't feel like a gay bar?"

"What? You toured all of them to compare?" the guy replied.

Phil laughed an honest laugh. "I don't know. I don't think so."

"Do I look gay?" the caveman said, looking straight at him? He was a little drunk.

"I don't know. Are you gay?"

"Are you asking because you want to fuck me?" the caveman said.

Phil laughed again. "Good one," he said then he pulled himself a stool. "I'm, Phil."

"Michel," the other guy replied. "Can I buy you a drink?"

Phil was pleased. "I'll take a beer?"

What a fucking idiot. "I don't know if we got time for this," I said.

"This your boyfriend?" Michel replied.

Phil shouted in laughter again. A few beers in and he'd be man-hugging papa bear over there like he was his mother.

"Seems uptight," Michel said.

"Nah, his brother got killed, give him a break. I'll have a Molson Ex," Phil added as he turned towards the

TV. "So, who's winning?"

"Ti-Cats."

"Ah câliss."

"Francophone?" Michel asked Phil.

"Ouais."

"Moé aussi!"

"Ah ben criss. J'aurais pas su."

"J'ai fait quinze ans su'a ligne à Oshawa."

"S'pas pire, ça..." Phil continued.

The barman came around with Phil's beer. Michel paid for it. I couldn't bring myself to tell Phil that *that* made it, officially, a date. They kept chatting. I looked at the barman, asked, "Simon Boucher?"

"En avant au bar d'la terrasse," he replied.

Who knew? Maybe Phil could become friends with a gay man and it not mean a thing. That could happen. We made our way to the front, leaving Phil to his new best friend. In the side door, one guy was loading empties on a dolly. The beer delivery guy was unloading a skid from his truck on a lift. Except for these two, there was no one else in there.

I crossed the sliding doors, there was a large terrasse on Sainte-Catherine. A dozen tables or so. The bar was inside but when they opened the doors, it was like it was live on the street. It was one of these things I couldn't imagine anywhere else than in Montreal.

But then again, not everything was tip top in the city of sin. Across the street was an abandoned church that still had a sing on it that read *the fruit of your homosexuality is eternal damnation*, with a bunch of tags on the bottom of it and a few holes in the sings from rocks people had been throwing at it over the years.

With all of our good intentions, there were still zealots and idiots everywhere. What a weird fucking city we live in. Then I said, "Why are you guys leaving that fucking sign up? The place looks like it's been abandoned for ten, fifteen years?"

"What do you mean, you guys?" the barman replied with a thick Franco accent.

"Gay guys," Ryan said.

"See? We're not gay," Karl said.

"Yeah, I can see that," the barman replied.

"Pheeeuuw," Ryan said. "I'm fucking glad."

"One of you ought to have a ladder or something?" I added. The barman got defensive.

"You want a ladder? I'll go get it and you can tear it down if you want."

"Nah, that's not gonna happen."

"That's what I thought. The whole place's gonna be gone soon anyways," he said, nodding towards a large sign across the street. It advertised condos for sale, soon, right here in the village. "Bon débaras, criss," he added.

Those fucking things were everywhere. Only difference was that these ones had two good-looking guys having coffee together on the balcony instead of a family running around with their latest offspring. No matter who you fucked in life, the banks were out to get every single one of us.

"You guys want a beer?" the barman continued. "Because something tells me you're not here to cruise."

Karl looked at Ryan, blew him a kiss. "Want to fuck the superior race?" he said. Ryan played aroused.

"Only if you can handle a Northlander," he replied.

"If you guys are here for gay bashing, I can tell you right now this shit don't fly here. So I'm gonna have to ask you to leave or I'll do it with a baseball bat."

"Ah, come on, can't you fags take a joke?" Ryan added, adding salt to the wound. And in a second, a baseball bat appeared from behind the bar. I raised my hand calmly, signalled him to put it down. I leaned against the bar.

"Speaking of gay bashing," I said softly. "I was wondering if you'd be Simon Boucher?" That seemed to startle him.

"Who wants to know?"

"I don't know. But I have it on good authority that you, yourself, have done quite a bit of gay bashing in your time. I heard stories of a few hospitalizations, some broken jaws, even pissed on a guy, if I'm to believe my sources."

"I don't know what the fuck you're talking about," Simon tried, but he knew what the fuck I was talking about. We had just gotten the upper hand on this piece of shit. I looked inside the bar, hoping no one would come out and give him a chance to get out of this. I had him in a corner, I wanted him to stay there.

"Really?" I replied. "Because I'd like to know what your friends inside the bar would think if I was to walk over there and tell them you used to be a fucking Nazi, beating down on gay guys just for kicks."

"Do you still do that?" Karl added. "Do you still beat up your boyfriends after fucking them?"

"Hey, fuck you," Simon replied. "You don't know shit. Whatever the fuck you think you know, you don't know shit. You think it's easy being gay? It's not easy. They know, alright? The guys inside, they fucking know. You don't know anything, fucking asshole, now get the fuck out of here."

"I don't know, man, that's a pretty big fucking skeleton in the closet," Ryan added. He flipped one of the chairs by the street, sat in it with his arms open wide against the railing. He looked arrogant as fuck.

"They fucking know. Want me to get them? I can do that right now."

"You're staying right here," I said.

That's when Ryan pulled out his iPhone and snapped a shot of the guy. "And what about your former Nazi friends? They know you turned gay? Because I'm sure that the right hashtags will send them right back to you."

"You see the bar's name right?" Karl asked Ryan.

"Oh yeah, right in the middle, can't mistake it."

"Trust me. I'm yesterday's news to these guys," Boucher replied.

"The old ones, maybe, but you know how it is. I know how it is. There's always a new guy out there who's looking to make a name for himself."

"Tabarnak," Simon said, now resigned to deal with our bullshit. "But one day, I'm gonna have you guys fucking killed for this."

"Not when you hear why we're here," I said, trying to calm everyone down a little. "The name Faith to Hate ring a bell?"

"Of course."

"They played a show here a few weeks or maybe a month back."

"I wouldn't know anything about that. I'm out of that whole scene, man. I've been out for a while and I still get bullshit from you guys."

"Well, we were told that you knew where the guys who booked them lived."

"Told? Told by who?"

"I don't think that's of your concern right now," Ryan said.

"Fuck you and my concern," Simon replied.

"RASH sent us your way," Karl said.

"Tabarnak," he swore again.

"Yes, tabarnak," I added. "Now, I don't care much about you, but I care about finding that band, Faith to Hate."

"They're from Ontario. You're looking in the wrong fucking place, man. A gay bar in Montreal? You're in the wrong fucking place."

"We already figured they were from Ontario, but it's not like they're handing out their home or work address online, now do they?"

"Unlike you," Ryan added, showing up his phone again.

"Ontario's a big fucking place," Karl added.

"Okay," Simon replied. "First, that is unnecessary. I've said I'd help you already. So fuck you. And second of all, I know Ontario's a big fucking place."

"Thirteen million people," I said.

"Needle in a haystack," Karl added. He came up to the bar, leaned against it like I did. I felt like we were good cop bad cop for a moment. Can't say I didn't like it.

"So why don't you point us in the right direction and

you can get back to whatever it is that you were doing."

"Like sucking dick," Ryan said.

That pissed *me* off. "You're gonna have to shut up right now," I snapped at Ryan. "If you're not helping, you're in the way."

I didn't like the gay bashing. I hated the barman 'cause he was a piece of shit who used to be a fucking Nazi, but I wasn't about to let one of my friends get on the bandwagon just 'cause he felt like being an ass for a minute. It pissed Ryan off to be talked back at, but at least that seemed to get me some leeway with the barman.

"Please excuse my colleague. He seems to have issues with the idea of male genitalia colliding together," I said.

"I know the feeling," the barman joked.

"Hey, don't you even..." Ryan tried to say. I hushed him with the raising of my hand. Didn't even turn to look at him.

"So," I continued, "if you can't tell us about FIH directly, tell us about those guys who booked the band. Where do they live?"

"I don't know for sure," he admitted. "As I said, I haven't been in that scene for six or seven years."

"Well, what do you know?"

"We used to get together in this apartment on Sicard Street. The owner's a racist, won't rent to any immigrants, not even European immigrants, no poles, no Jews. He'd do a background check on anything that wasn't straightforward Québécois. That's where we used to hang out, two guys rented the place but there was always a few more boneheads hanging around."

"You'd think they'd still be around?"

"I'd think so. The owner's a hardline nationalist. He believes that selling would mean giving 'them' the neighbourhood. He wasn't gonna give them an inch back then, why would that change, you know?"

"What's the address?"

"1640 Sicard. Around Adam. Right across the park."

"Alright, it's worth a look," I said.

"I'd say so," Karl added.

I believed the guy didn't know about FIH. Why would he? I didn't know where the bands I liked lived. Why would a former gay basher have that knowledge? What he told us about the owner and the apartment also made sense. Sure he had been out of the scene for six years, but racist landlords didn't' sell their blocks, no matter how crappy they may be. They kept them 'till they died and *then* their kids would sell them for the money.

I liked to believe that we would find at least a few answers by going to the apartment. It was three-thirty, the address was maybe twenty blocks away from us. We could be there in ten fucking minutes if we wanted to.

"Want to go right now?" I asked Karl.

"It's not like I'm gonna take fifty days off to settle this shit," he replied and then headed for the door.

"You didn't hear it from me, alright." Simon said. "I know what I used to do, alright. I don't like it, man. I got beat up plenty of times over this shit already, alright?"

"I don't give enough of a fuck about you to spread the word around. As far as I'm concerned, you were a pit stop and nothing else."

"I'm serious. This shit can't come back to me, man. If word gets out, man..."

"Then you should have kept your mouth shut in the first place, right," Ryan said.

"Can you delete the picture," he insisted. "Come on!" He looked plenty nervous about that picture.

"What? Why?"

I looked at Ryan, my face said *why not*. So he said, "Alright." And he showed the barman that he had deleted it.

"Happy now?"

"Thank you, guys. Thank you so much."

"You're still a gay basher," I said as we got in. *So, fuck you.*

We met Phil back at the bar who was already on his second beer with big papa bear over there. There were plenty of peanut shells in front of them, they seemed to be talking and getting along, felt like they were bonding.

"Ah, man, we leaving already," Phil said when we walked by. "The *Als* are back by six in the third."

"Two-point conversion," the caveman said.

"Yeah! Two point conversion, come on guys."

"You're welcome to stay if you want," Karl said.

The big guy looked at Phil with a spark in the eyes. "He's right. You're welcome to stay." He sounded so incredibly calm and mild. Love was in the air.

That's the moment Phil *kinda, sorta, coulda* figured out the guy who had been buying him beers was maybe, you know, gay. Phil got really ill at ease for a minute.

"No, I think I'm gonna have to leave," he said. "Thank you, though. I mean. I can pay you back for those if you want? You know, just to be fair." The other guy seemed to be more disappointed than pissed. I felt bad for him. "I mean, I'm sorry..."

"Phil, don't hurt yourself," I said, cutting the conversation short. He smiled half-a-smile, walked out with Karl. I stood there in the door.

"I'm sorry my friends are such idiots," I said to the caveman.

He started sipping on his beer, said, "Just get the fuck out of here."

So I did. I stepped into the sun. Ryan was waiting for me. Phil and Karl were by his BMW a block south.

The streets were filled with rainbow flags waving in the wind. The banks were open for business, coffee shops were at full capacity. You'd see young gay couples passing by or older guys in their sixties, holding each other the way only old lovers can hold each other. People seemed happy there. Of course, you could never really know just by taking a snapshot during a nice summer afternoon, but still.

"Did you really delete the picture," I asked Ryan. It didn't feel like Ryan to be compassionate like that.

"Of course I did," he said. I looked surprised. Ryan, doing the right thing. That didn't sit right. "But don't worry. That thing's been online ever since I took it." He looked at his phone. "It's already got seventeen shares."

That sounded a lot more like Ryan. Poor barman was probably gonna get a serious beating in the next few days. It was going to be another spark of violence the whole village could probably live without but then again.

The guy reaped what he sowed, right?

CHAPTER 16

"Ah, fuck," the Nazi said when Ryan drove his fist into his nose. I knew Ryan loved to fight, but I don't think I've ever seen him that happy to bust someone's face.

"Gawd, that felt good," he said.

Ryan was completely insane, no doubt about that, but he was a libertarian and well, fascism was the exact opposite of that so he was *motivated* about our next assignment.

As planned, we found the apartment across from the small park right where the barman said it would be. The park was a piece of trash, maybe twenty-four feet by twenty-four feet and I wouldn't let any kid play in it. There were a few benches, tagged and burnt out in the edges. There was one beaten up trash can and a single, three step slide in the middle of it. Even the slide's rickets had started giving in. Long live the East End.

The apartment was a mess too. You couldn't miss it. The ground floor still had all five "oui" poster boards from the last referendum, twenty years ago. The upper left window had a patriot's flag and I could see a bunch of stickers on the door: Screwdriver, Stars and Stripes, Hang Mumia and Hatebreed.

I liked Hatebreed. Hatebreed wasn't a racist band, they were just a heavy band but it was true they attracted everything and anything in the underground world of *extreme* scenes. Guess you couldn't blame the band for being liked by fucking Nazis.

There was a stand of papers. One of them was *Maîtres chez nous*, which was classic Quebec nationalistic bullshit and one from England called *Strong Again*. Both of them had front pages indulging in Muslim bashing of some sort.

The door was barred, and it looked pretty strong. I started wondering if we were gonna need to get the crowbar again, but when we reached the balcony, I just pressed the bell like I was visiting a friend. It happened mechanically and it felt weird for a second. I didn't expect it to work, but then it did. One idiot on the other side just fucking opened it. I didn't expect it to be so easy. I expected them to be careful, like the crazies at the black dot or something.

Ding Dong.

Hello.

Punch.

Blood splattered over the Nazi's face and we were in. The guy stumbled three steps back as Ryan pushed him in. Ryan had a mean right hand. I had gotten hit with one of those punches every now and then and I knew how much it hurt.

Phil got in next, then me. Karl was as casual as a motherfucker. He picked up one of the *Strong Again* papers, walked in, closed the door behind him as if he had just picked up his morning paper and he was headed for his cup of joe.

As things were with most Montreal apartments, most old ones anyways, the place was basically one long hallway close to the centre of the building, with a double room on the left. Then there was the bathroom and the hallway skewed left after, with a window in the angle of the wall for the kitchen and probably one other bedroom near the alley in the back.

We were ten feet inside when two other guys appeared in the kitchen. Two skinheads in Doc Marteens, blue jeans, black shirt. One was fat, the other was built like an MMA fighter. They saw their friend's bloodied face, Ryan holding him like a puppet.

"What the fuck!" they were shouting. "Pogne le bat! Pogne le bat Criss! On va leur câlisser une volée."

The fat one ran, the other one took a bat. So far it was going a lot better than I expected.

Ryan dragged his guy to the living room. There was an old couch there, a swastika ridden flag on the ceiling. Someone's bedroom was in the other half of the double room. The walls were covered in poorly written tags: white power, Supremacy, Burzum and White Aryan Resistance.

The first kid *finally* punched Ryan back. It startled him but he was just sort of surprised. The kid punched him again. Didn't hurt much. Ryan, in his short lifetime as a bouncer, had been stabbed more than once, hit with bottles, broken bottles, metal bars, been on the receiving end of a thrown keg at and had a gun pulled on him. He didn't even count the brawls anymore. Ryan just started laughing at the kid's petty attempt to strike back. He threw him over the table and into the couch then he kicked the table into his calves. The kid screamed in pain.

"Oh, don't be a pussy," Ryan said as he rested a foot on the table, pushing it further in the kid's legs. "This

shit would have been candy in the SS," he added as he
leaned forward. He looked back at us to see if we were
alright. We were in a stalemate in the hallway. He sighed
a bit, turned back to the kid and asked, "Do you think I
look Jewish?"

"Quoi?" the kid replied.

"Est-ce que j'ai l'air Juif?" Ryan asked again.

The kid wasn't sure what to answer. He tried, "Non."

"I think I look Jewish. Maybe a little. I don't know.
Let's just say I look Jewish just for the occasion."

The kid seemed scared enough. He wasn't going to
make a scene so we could now focus on the other guy.

"Come on. Come on, mes tabarnaks," the guy said as
he banged his bat on the wall.

Phil and I were stopped in our tracks; there wasn't
much room to move and certainly not much room to
fight. Were we gonna rush him, wait for him to bail. The
more time we spent waiting was more time for accidents
to happen or people to show up. We looked into the
bathroom to see if there was anyone else there waiting to
jump us in the back: no one.

"Osti d'Anglais d'marde," the nazi was shouting,
pointing the bat at us. "T'aime ça les queues mon criss,
avoue, hein."

"Quoi?" Phil said.

"T'aimes ça les queues mon criss?" I repeated,
startled. Couldn't believe the shit that guy just said.

Karl, I guess, got fed up with this stalemate bullshit.
He sighed the way you sighed when the fucking line at
Starbucks wasn't moving fast enough, folded the paper
walked between us. Just like that. Oh, and he pulled a
gun out of his fucking jacket out of nowhere."

"What the fuck," I said. I didn't even know he had a gun on him.

"Tabarnak," the Nazi shouted as he looked to the kitchen where we assumed the back door was.

Karl didn't wait. He just shot the guy in the leg. The bat went flying, the guy was screaming like a pig being gutted.

"Woah," I shouted. I didn't expect any of this. "Woah," I repeated. He looked at me and all I could see in his face was *what's wrong?* Sure, the guy was a white supremacist, but as far as I knew, Karl was not that liberal either.

"Well, you want the job done or not?" he asked.

"Not that way."

"Why not?"

"Armed assault?"

"It's a .22. He's a fucking Nazi."

He had me there.

"I don't know guys. Maybe the gunshots and the screams will attract the cops," Ryan said from the other room.

"Neighbours are going to expect this kind of shit down here," Phil said.

"Still."

"Fuck," the Nazi was shouting again and again between repeated sessions of panting. It looked painful as shit. But the poor fella had another thing coming. If the gun wasn't enough, Karl pulled a pair of pliers out of his other pocket. Motherfucker had planned this all along. We didn't stop at home on the way here. So he had it in the car or he had everything on him expecting to fulfill this fucked up fantasy here and now. Shoot a

GRAND TRUNK AND SHEARER

guy and pull out the bullet like in the fucking movies. I was going to need to have a talk with Karl.

He walked over to the man he had just shot, grabbed his chin, looked straight at him as he was squirming to fight the pain.

"So you think you're superior?" Karl slapped him. "You think you're some chosen race, right?"

The guy spat at Karl. Karl smiled and punched him twice.

"Hey, what the fuck's going on out there," Ryan asked from the living room.

"You think you're fucking German?" Karl asked. "Hah! Look at me," he said with a slap. "Look at me. I...I am fucking German."

He punched him a third time, then drove his knee into his chest and stayed there. The guy was pinned down, whining and crying, blood gushing out of the wound through his pants and onto the floor. Karl took the long nose to his wound, stuck the end in trying to pull out the bullet.

The guy shouted in pain some more, legs wiggling around. Shit was fucked up.

"Oh hush, little girl," Karl said. "If you move too much I can't get it, can I?"

I didn't know what to do or what to say. I was just damn glad Karl was on my side. He took a hand to the Nazi's mouth to shut him up, trying to perform some sort of surgery at the same time. When that didn't work, he punched him again in the face as hard as he could so the guy would pass out.

The screams died out, echoed only by a barking dog somewhere in the back alley. The legs stopped squirming. Karl finally pulled out the bullet.

"Lucky motherfucker," he said. "The bullet didn't break. It would have been a bitch if it did."

"What about him, man? You're no doctor. What if you nicked an artery or something?"

"I don't care."

Of course. Why would Karl give a shit?

"Then why take the bullet out?" Phil asked.

"Evidence."

Phil and I looked at each other.

"Jesus Christ, Karl. Sometimes you scare me," I said.

"Just sometimes?" he replied with a smile. He took the bullet, bloodied and disgusting, wiped it clean on the Nazi's clothes, did the same with his hands and put the bullet in his pocket. That scared me even more. "I'll be in the car looking out," he added as he headed towards the door.

"He's still bleeding."

"And he's still not German," was the last thing he said before he walked out, paper in hand, like nothing had happened.

I expected the cops to be waiting for him out there. Then again, this was Hochelaga, and if I was to believe the reputation of the apartment, it was expected by the neighbours, plus they probably didn't want to be snitching on the local SS crew. Any anarchist or communist rival gang would be happy we were busting down the place. Karl *had* used a .22 and only fired once. It was not a loud firearm and could arguably be mistaken for firecrackers or any old regular argument between spouses in the area.

Maybe the fat kid was running towards his crewmates

and we should be expecting reinforcements any time soon. I was expecting it, waiting for it. Shit. Something *had* to happen. No one really lived like this. But then again, *I* did and so did these guys and maybe that was a testament to how fucked up our lives really were: the way you can beat up a man, shoot him, let him bleed on the floor and the downstairs neighbours won't even come to check if something was wrong.

The cops weren't showing up, no Nazi stomping came our way. God didn't seem to care; the law didn't seem to exist.

"When you're done killing the superior race, mind coming in here and talking to the live one I've got here?" Ryan asked from the other room.

"Y' pisse le sang," Phil said to me, worried.

"Do something about it. I'll be in the other room."

Phil kneeled next to the one we shot. Phil took off the guy's belt, put it around his thigh and squeezed. That didn't really do anything.

"Fuck," Phil said and then walked to the kitchen.

"So," I said to the younger Nazi. I put my foot on the table, leaned against it just like Ryan did. "I'm assuming you're aware of what my friends have done to your friends and just how bubbly it really makes me feel inside? So let me make this even clearer by stating just how *personal* this all really is. Do you understand?"

Ne nodded yes.

"Hey, D'Arcy, do you think I look Jewish?" Ryan asked me.

"No."

"No?"

"Not even a little."

"Ah, come on, I got to look Jewish a little."

"Having a beard doesn't make you a Jew."

"What if I put on a kippa?"

"Then yes."

"That's all it would take?"

"The kippa usually gives it away, yeah."

"True."

The kid was still silent, scared shitless. I was enjoying this, can't lie about that. Ryan paused and looked at him with heavy eyes.

"Hey, D'Arcy, let me ask you something else."

"Sure."

"You think *he* looks Jewish?"

"I don't know."

"Take a closer look."

We looked to his left, looked to his right, check out the chin. "I'd have to think about it. Maybe the cheeks a little."

Ryan pulled out a switchblade from his pocket, flipped it open. The snap startled the kid who started to sweat heavy drops.

"Maybe if we carve a little Star of David in his cheek. That would help."

"Hey, hey," the kid said, nervous as a pig in a butcher's shop. "Don't do that, man. Don't do that. I mean, come on."

"Let me ask you a few questions then," I said. "What do you think about that?"

"Okay. Ouais. Alright."

"First question," Ryan asked. "You're scared of the blade cutting into your skin or you're scared of having a Jewish star on your face?"

The kid didn't reply at first. His face said, *What?*

"Take your time."

"The knife, man. The fucking knife." He looked towards the hallway. I looked as well. You could see his friends' legs, motionless there on the floor. The line of blood trickling down the hall was getting longer by the second.

"Good, boy," Ryan said as he put the knife away.

"So next question. Faith in Hate?"

"What?"

"Faith in Hate. You know what it is?"

"Yeah. Yeah. It's a band, man. That's it. It's just a fucking band."

"A band that has certain ties to certain ideas that you seem to be sharing here."

"So the fuck what?"

"Where are they?"

"I don't know."

"Ryan."

The blade came out again.

"Well," the kid said. "It's not like I know where they are all the time. Who the fuck would know that?"

"They slept here when they were in Montreal."

"Yes."

"When was that?"

"A few days ago."

"How many days?"

"Three, I think."

"You think?"

"I think. A week, maybe."

"Ryan?"

"I don't know. Close enough," he replied.

"Alright."

The blade went away.

"Was there a show last week?" I asked.

"Not that I know of, no."

"So what were they doing in Montreal?"

"I don't know. The whole band wasn't here."

"Who was?"

"Bass player, singer, that's it."

"That's it."

"Can't play a show without a guitar player," the kid said.

"You know? I'm starting to think you're too smart for this Nazi bullshit," Ryan said.

"Yeah," the kid said with a smile. He tried to move but that only hurt him so he didn't.

"Their website doesn't tell us where they live these days. We went around a few places, asked questions. I heard they're from Toronto," I lied to him, "is that true?"

"They were. They're not anymore."

"How come?"

"All the gooks and ragheads are buying out the city. They were forced out."

"Forced out?"

"It's what's happening, here too man. How many fucking ragheads now in Montreal, man. Ragheads everywhere, even in Hochelaga."

"Ryan."

The blade came out again.

"Stay focused," I added.

"Hamilton, man! They live in Hamilton."

"No ragheads in Hamilton?" I said.

"I don't know."

"Where in Hamilton?"

"I don't know. Swear to God."

"Hamilton's still a big place," Ryan told me.

"Yeah."

"He's gonna fucking die, man." the kid said, talking about his friends.

"Yeah, I guess he is. Hey, Phil," I shouted.

"What?"

"What the fuck are you doing?"

"I'm on this guy's computer. You wouldn't believe the amount of porn he's got on his hard drive."

"What about the leg. I asked you to take care of the leg."

"Dans une minute."

"Jesus Christ."

"Dans une minute. C'est sur le four."

"What's on the oven?"

"In a minute," he shouted.

I turned to the kid. "Your friend's gonna be fine," I said, not too convinced of it myself.

"What do you want with FIH?" he asked.

"Now if I tell you, that wouldn't be really smart of me, would it?"

"I don't know."

"No, I guess you don't."

"Now we're gonna let you go," Ryan said. "You scream or run or fight, Star of David right in the cheek. You jump from the seat..." He pointed to his face with the knife.

The kid nodded yes. We both let go of the table.

"Phil!" I shouted.

"On it," he said. Then we heard the noise that fresh skin makes when it's put against hot metal. The kind of noise your steak does when you put it into a freshly oiled pan set to Max. The leg started jittering on nerves alone. The scent of burnt meat filled the room with its nauseating stink.

"What the fuck are you doing?" I shouted.

"You said do something about it. So I cauterized it."

"You *what?*"

"I cauterized it."

"I said, like...put a fucking bandage on it until they call a fucking ambulance."

"Well, you could have said so."

"A simple fucking Band-Aid."

"Poor motherfucker," Ryan said.

"Nobody's cauterized anyone since the middle fucking ages," I added.

"Alright, alright. I'm sorry," he added as he walked back to the kitchen. He washed the knife in the sink, lemon-scented soap and all. He rubbed it good, dried it with a cloth and put it back in the drawer. Maybe he thought the Nazi would keep it as a souvenir or something, butter his toast with it in the morning.

I was livid. Everything was adding to a lot, this was just one more thing I was going to have to deal with. One day these guys were gonna come after us and I didn't know if I could blame them.

"Did we get what we came here for?" Phil asked as he took both the Nazi's laptop.

"What are you taking that for?" I asked.

"For the porn?" he replied.

"Jesus Chris," I said as I headed out. "Let's go."

The other kid hadn't moved or said a word. He stayed put in the couch like a good little dog who had learned his lesson.

Phil stopped in the hallway, looked at the kid, simply said, "Hey, there."

"Hey," the kid replied awkwardly.

We probably had given him the worst afternoon he had ever had. Point and case.

"Fais que...quoi de neuf?" Phil said.

"Pas grand chose..."

"Alright. B'en bonne journée debord," Phil added as he started walking again. I was already down the stairs when he reached the balcony. *Have a good day, then.* He had told the Nazi kid.

I was sure he would.

CHAPTER 17

"Man, Montreal is better at riots than at Saint Paddy's parades," Cillian said to me once.

I must've been eighteen, nineteen or something. We had gotten up to Wellington to watch the beginning of the parade. Most people went up to Sainte-Catherine or on Maisonneuve around Concordia University. But the truth was that around those streets, what you had were mostly drunk students and I didn't want anything to do with those kids. I was down here with the Irish families, the workers, I liked that better.

We celebrated Saint Paddy's down here with the rest of us, the way it should be. In Verdun, in the Pointe, in Saint-Henri. Even if the French were in Saint-Henri, I somehow felt closer to them than I did the rich Anglos up the hill in Westmount. Everyone who could even be remotely Irish was always welcome to the parade, of course. You had plenty of French people, every year, no matter what the nationalists would've liked everyone to believe. It was always nice to be reminded that in this city, you could find someone name Kathy Murphy who spoke nothing but French, and some guy named Michel Dugay who always spoke English at home.

"What's with all the military shit anyways," Cillian added.

"It ain't that bad," I replied to Cillian. "It's a Saint Patrick's parade. What did you expect?"

"Yeah, I guess you're right. It's just that riots are really, really fun."

"They really are, Cillian." And just like that, I remembered the last Stanley Cup riot in 1993 and the news footage that ran in loop for days. I was too young to participate, but the truth was that everyone born and raised in this city were eagerly awaiting the next one.

The parade had a decent start. The leader looked stubborn and dedicated. He walked too fast for the younger marching bands to keep up. He marched like he meant it, you had to give him that. We stayed there for a moment, just watching as the bands made their way up the hill. After the cops and the RCMP were done with their PR for the year, we finally got some bagpipes. I loved the bagpipes. If I had it my way, Saint Patrick's parades would be one, three hour long bagpipe festival. Now *that* would be something worth remembering.

The weather was bad as it always was. It was freezing as hell and everyone in the crowd was trying to huddle together in the rare sunspots filtering through the buildings. For as long as I could remember it was freezing on Saint Patrick's Day. I guessed it wasn't meant to be a Canadian holiday but I could take pride knowing that the Irish had been taking this shit for a hundred and eighty-seven years now. The weather was always bad, every year...year after year. It was just our luck.

After the bands, there were a bunch of people from parishes I had never heard of or cared about. They had horse carriages and former Irishman of the Year that looked so old it was a wonder they could sit on their ass for so long without popping a haemorrhoid. I didn't know if they did or not, no Irishman of the year would admit to that, but it really just felt like they got Pappy out of the retirement home and slapped him in the back of a carriage for his annual ride around town.

I didn't even know if we were celebrating being Irish anymore or if the parade just gave us something to do in what would have been a boring-not-yet-spring-afternoon. I didn't know. Maybe I was growing mean. All I knew was when I saw these old guys waving at us, their face saying, *what the fuck am I doing here and why are all these people waving at me?*

I looked at Cillian. He looked at me with his signature half-smile on his face. That look he had when he was looking for trouble.

"You want to start a riot?" he asked.

I thought about it for a second. "No," I said. It would have been nice, but I said no. It was true, though, what Cillian had said. Montreal did do better riots than it did parades. *If only the habs could win the cup sometime this decade that would be amazing.*

"Yo, maybe we ought to go to Boston next year for Saint Paddy. Or maybe New York," he said.

"Fuck New York. And you know what? Fuck Boston, too. If you want a real parade, we're going to Chicago."

"You're gonna tell me there are more Irish in Chicago than in Boston?"

"Well, maybe not as a ratio," I said as I popped open a can, "but Chicago's like twice as big as Boston or something."

"You sure?"

"One third of a hundred is bigger than one half of ten, isn't it?"

He was trying to work that in his head. My brother

had a good heart but goddamned he was dumb sometimes.

"Yeah, I guess you're, right," he said. Then he smiled.

I took a sip and I saw this cop cadet walking towards me. *Here comes a ticket.* But no. He looked angry at me but all he said was, "Sir, there are families around. You could use a bag, you know?" And just like that he handed me a paper bag the city had printed for the occasion. No ticket, no arrest, no drinking in public charge.

I put my drink in the bag, took one long swing at it and said to myself, *Goddamn, aren't we civilized.*

"I'll bring you back to Eire someday," I said. A fire lit up in Cillian's eyes.

"You serious."

"Sure. Why not? Delta has cheap flights every summer. So why not?"

"Dublin?"

"Dublin first, but if we're going back to the motherland, we're going to Cork, my friend."

A large float passed in front of us. It was really just a large flatbed, barely decorated with green ribbons, pulled by a semi-truck. They had set up two large shamrocks on each end and plywood floorboards for the dancers to perform on. There was sort of a ramp up there, but I wished none of the nice young ladies dancing on it would fall down. They really had nothing to cling to. The sound system blasted some modern rendition of the Irish rover. Man, we fucking needed new songs,

"Yo! We fucking need new songs," Cillian said. I loved my brother. "How about getting Dropkick Murphys' next year?"

"I'm pretty sure they hate this city."

"What makes you say that?"

"Last time they played Montreal, they waited for the Habs-Bruins game to finish before playing the show and we beat them."

"And?"

"The Habs couldn't beat Columbus on a good day, man."

He laughed and drank up.

That's when a teenage girl, maybe came up to us with pot-luck stickers in her hand. Cillian's laughter seemed to have attracted her. She was all smiles, light dark jacket on, running shoes, brown hair, freckles, soft hands and beautiful eyes. Cute as hell.

She looked at Cillian, bowed playfully like they all did. He got shy. He wouldn't admit it, but got fucking shy. He smiled, looked down, then looked at her and down again. I couldn't believe it. My brother had, in lament terms, become pussy whipped in half a second. I had never seen him that way before.

Then the young girl put her hands to her mouth and giggled. I could tell she liked him too. Hell, if I had been three years younger, I would have been jealous of him. A girl that cute, damn, Cillian, *you better do something, you idiot.*

She put the pot-luck sticker on my brother's cheek. He almost got as red as his fucking hair. I swear to God. She swirled once, gave him one last, I like you look, then skipped away to the other side of the street.

If I knew better, I'd say he was in love. She skipped back and forth, playing with young kids, bringing happiness to the community. Every once in a while she looked back and tried to find Cillian's eyes, there, somewhere in the crowd.

I was looking at him and was convinced that they held the parade in spring to the young sons and daughters of Ireland would meet and get together, make plans for some more Irish babies in the future. Cillian hadn't realized I was staring at him until she was way out of sight. I had a big-ass, satisfied grin on my face.

"What?" he said.

I smiled some more, looked to the side, then at him again.

He shook his shoulders, pulled his chin up, cleared his voice, all macho and shit. "I just want to get laid, man," he took a sip.

"Ha!" I shouted. "Look who's talking shit."

He was pussy whipped and he fucking knew it.

"I know," he admitted.

"Good," I said as I grabbed him by his shoulder. "Now go and find your girl."

His eyes lit up. "You serious?"

"Shit, the parade is *far* from over. Far from over, Cillian. She's still out there dancing and twirling," I said.

"Right."

He took off running on the sidewalk, trying not to kill anyone because he wasn't really looking at where he was going. He stopped maybe five yards ahead.

"Yo," he said, "where *does* it end?" he asked.

"Square Phillips, I guess."

"Right. I can make it there before her, right?"

"Sure."

He was about to take off again but stopped himself one last time.

"Hey, she *was* hot, wasn't she?" he said.

"Yes, she was. Now go and find her."

He told me he ran passed the entire parade, all the way to Square Phillips where the march was ending. He went back to the tents where the participants were handed coffee and hot chocolate. He told his story to the security guards at the gates. They let him in. Hell, it was the kind of story they would have run on the evening news. He looked for a blanket and some hot chocolate. One for him, one for her.

He must've checked his hair and his face fifty million times in store windows and car mirrors. He didn't have any gloves and his hands were turning blue but a half hour later, he saw her group appear in the distance, still dancing, still handing out stickers to kids on the side walk.

Cillian got up on the statue's pedestal. He couldn't shout her name. He didn't know her name. He wouldn't dare to come down either. He was too scared that he'd lose her in the crowd. But he told me, and he swore this to be true, that he spotted her forty yards away in the parade, and that she spotted him back in a crowd of hundreds, just like that. In a snap, her eyes spotted his with his head sticking out against the statue, freckles shining in the sun, emerald eyes like you can't fake them.

All it took was a smile and two hot chocolates. I swear to God. They dated for almost a year after that. Her name was Emily.

CHAPTER 18

A few days later I received a visit I would have rather avoided. I was coming off my shift and there was this black Yukon waiting there. A large man in a black T-shirt, whose tone and accent could not betray more his Celtic origins.

"Good afternoon, Mr. Kennedy," he said to me. "Could you please spare a minute for us?"

No one was that polite unless they were a second away from blowing your head up. I sighed and looked to where I knew the 61 bus stop was. Normally I'd be walking one city block to a fully loaded STM bus that would take me across the bridge and into the Pointe so I could watch the news while cooking up my supper.

Not that night though. I didn't want my last meal to be the shitty Yellow Brand ham and Mayo sandwich with a side of Mars bars I had for lunch earlier.

Of course, I *had* been running around looking for the murderer of my brother. Someone must've opened their mouth. If you took the boxing gym guy I opened my mouth to, the Nazi beating, the gay bar interrogation, the RASH before that, our visit to the Pitt house and let's not forget that sketchy locksmith we spoke too...I guess it was just bound to happen.

He opened the door. Running away would have been both stupid and useless. My guts were telling me to bolt, but my brain was in charge for once. Any moment I was still alive meant that these guys didn't want me dead yet, that could be interpreted as good news.

I walked into the SUV. It was more comfortable than my house. Still, the noise of the locks being slammed down automatically left a pinch down my throat I couldn't shake off. The driver walked around to his seat. He looked at me in the rearview mirror and simply said, "Seatbelts."

He drove down to the 20, headed north and onto the 13. First I imagined they were gonna find my body someday, somewhere north of Mont-Laurier. I kept hoping he'd take a left, first at Sherbrooke, then at Monkland or Côte-Saint-Luc where NDG became Hampstead. When we crossed those, I kept hoping he'd take a right and head into Ville Mont-Royal.

When he crossed into Laval, I could still hope we were headed for a chat. When Laval became Boisbriand, I knew I was in real trouble. Then Boisbriand became Saint-Jérome and Saint-Sauveur where most of the young preppies that plagued the Montreal middle class spend most of their free time as well as their parent's money.

He took a side road just outside of a smaller village I didn't know, headed for one of the millions of lakes around the area. There wasn't a lake or a road around that wasn't filled with cabins or cottages. If he wanted to kill me quietly, he would have kept driving north to where the mosquitos outnumbered humans a billion to one. That could mean better news.

We got up some driveway. A house appeared beyond a thick patch of pine trees. A Canadian house, not as big as you'd expect, but still beautiful. Two stories, three windows upstairs, perfect stone front. There was the wooden deck in the back and a perfect lake beyond it. It was like the heavens had stopped and came to rest on those waters. The mountains around reflected in the water, the skies were mirrored at the centre of it. There was not a soul on the water. Nothing but birds resting quietly. If I would've had to guess, I would have said the guy had bought the whole damn lakeside just for the peace and quiet.

The doors were unlocked. I walked out. The smell of moist wood filled the air. The breeze was cool, coming from the lake and you could hear all the things you forgot existed when you lived in the city for so long: birds, crickets, the sound of branches waving in the wind, the crunch of pure dirt under your soles. It was peaceful enough to remind me why I still loved this country so much.

I took a deep breath, let the wooden air fill my lungs. The driver didn't say a word. He raised a hand politely, directing me to the deck. The inner door was opened, the house sheltered from the mosquitos by a wooden screen door.

"Ah, you're here," I heard from inside. The accent was unmistakable. I had been summoned to a cabin by the Montreal Irish mob. "Come in, come in," the voice added.

He wasn't asking, he was telling so I swung the door open. The smell of garlic and vegetables was strong. The noise of oil tinkling into a frying pan filled the room. The kitchen was flawless: wooden cabinets, dark stone counter, pots and pans dangling over a central isle.

There was a man there and you couldn't mistake him for some chef. He ran things in the city; I didn't need confirmation from anyone to know that. It was in the way he stood, the way he moved, the ruggedness in his skin, his whole disposition screamed power. That guy wasn't nervous about anything, certainly not nervous about me.

"Beautiful, isn't it?" he asked. "The lake, the trees. Reminds me of Lough Ree. The greens, the rain." He paused. "Do you know where your ancestors are from?"

"Cork. I think."

"Ah, aren't they all from Cork?"

I didn't know what he meant by that.

"My family's from Roscommon, just outside of Athlone. Right in the middle, you see?"

"Never heard of it, sorry."

"Yes. It's not Cork. It's not Dublin. It's not Belfast. It flies under the radar, doesn't it? Have you ever been back to Eire, Mr. Kennedy?"

"No."

"We're gonna have to do something about that. You have to go back every once in a while. It's very much, spiritual."

He pulled out a small bucket of cherry tomatoes. Took a handful and started slicing them with care. It was amazing the way his big Irish paws were so gentle with the tiny vegetables. He was hunched over it, focused on every small movement he was making as if he was wrapping up a small child in a blanket.

"Do you know why I love to cook, Mr. Kennedy?" he asked as he wiped his hands on a dish rag.

"No, sir."

"Because people leave you alone when you cook. That's why I love it. If you're working in the office or having coffee, people will still show up and disturb you, you know? Ask you questions even if you're busy. You can tell them you are busy, but they'll still ask you anyways. I've always wondered why that was but could never figure it out. As I've been informed, you are what they call a team leader for a warehousing company, so I know you know what I mean, Mr. Kennedy. You see? When you're cooking, people won't dare to disturb you. I know it sounds stupid, and I can't really explain it, but it's true. Maybe it's because there's a knife in my hands but I doubt it would be a simple as that."

"Maybe you look more focused when you cook than any other moment in your life."

"That would make sense." He paused for a breath before continuing, "You seem like a resourceful man. So let me ask you a question." He tossed a cherry tomato in his mouth, started chewing on it. "Why are you here, Mr. Kennedy?"

"Your driver asked me to come."

"That was the obvious answer. Don't be so obvious. You shouldn't sell yourself short like that. Nothing good can come out of it. What interests me the most at this point is why we *had* to ask you in the first place?"

"That would be a long story."

"I'm cooking. I have time for a long story."

"Are you sure?"

"As I said, no one ever disturbs me while I'm cooking."

"So what are you having?"

"Linguine? Do you like Italian?"

"It'd be rude of me to refuse anything you'd cook for me."

He stood and stared at me. I felt like I wasn't meant to be invited. Maybe he was just fucking with my head. It was working.

"Is minic a bhris béal duine a shrón," he said. "Many times a man's mouth broke his nose. You don't seem like the kind of guy who speaks without a good reason. Don't make mistakes like that." He paused. "I'm trying to learn Gaelic. Do you speak Gaelic?"

"No. I'm afraid not."

"It's a terrible language to learn. Horrible, really. But you have to do what you have to do. Keep the culture alive. I'm trying to pick it up. What was it Obama said when he visited Ireland? 'Is fearr Gaeilge briste, ná Béarla clíste.' Sounded like that anyways. It's an interesting language. You should pick it up." He started chopping fresh basil leaves into tiny little strips.

I stood and waited. Something was bothering me.

"Go ahead," he said. He looked at me. "Well, you have something on your mind. Go ahead."

"You're cooking Italian?"

"Yes."

"After all that you got to love Eire and go back to Eire, it's so spiritual, learn the language...you're cooking Italian."

He handed me a Kilkenny. I took it.

"Our food's fuckin' horrible."

I laughed.

"Am I wrong?"

"I can't argue about that."

"I mean, there's only so much potato pie a man can have before he turns a gun to his head."

"It's what made us leave in the first place."

"True," he said as he put the stove to simmer. "Now, I'm afraid I have to get down to business. Forgive me for being so blunt but what needs to be done needs to be done. I took the liberty of running a background check on you, Mr. Kennedy. You cleared it, if you must know. Your friend, Mr. Anderson did raise some flags in certain circles, but nothing my organization ever had to deal with, so I am not concerned with him."

He took a moment to fold two napkins, perfectly, nice red ones with polka dots.

"I have to say," he continued, "you going through the roof like you did, especially considering the fact that the front door was open, that reads, *meh!* Do you know why the front door is open?"

"Because no one would normally dare to cross you?"

"What's my name, Mr. Kennedy?"

I hesitated. "I don't know," I admitted.

"Good! Nobody knows. Don't sell yourself short like that. You're smarter than that. So again. Why do we leave the front door open?"

"Because nothing in there is worth breaking in for."

"That's right. And the lock on the roof is only there to keep the fiends from jumping off. We used to have a lot of suicides...terrible business. Suicides attract cops. It drives away the customers, terrible."

"Yeah. I saw you had a stiffy in there."

He stopped cooking. Seemed surprised. "I'm sorry, what?"

"Dead guy on some mattress in the corner. Pretty horrible picture I got to say. Looked like that shit on *Vice*, skin all black with scabs and all."

He ran a finger on his iPhone. Pressed a number on

speed dial. "There's Krokodil at the Pitt house?" he sounded pissed. "How come I did not hear about it before? You didn't know? Clean it. Find it. I don't want to have to call again." He hung up. He grinned and sighed.

"Millenials," I joked.

"Yes, I suppose." He raised his hands, admitting, *what can you do?* "Now where were we?" He picked up a whip, started working on the sauce. "I have been made aware that you recently buried a loved one at Mont-Royal Cemetery."

"Brother. Yes."

"You believe he was killed?"

"Yes."

"And what made you believe that the warehouse on Pitt Street could have anything to do with it?"

"The police said..."

"Ahhhh, the police said. Well that explains a lot now, doesn't it?" He started serving pasta in a large round plate. He seemed happier all of a sudden, like my lack of knowledge about anything, really, was making him happier. It was like I was not some blind spot he had not seen coming. I couldn't decipher whether he was being sarcastic or not. He was one weird motherfucker, that much was for sure. I guessed it came with the business but still. I stood there, just looking at him like a deer in the fucking headlights, not sure of what to do to get out of trouble.

"The police are..." he began. He hesitated, nodded a few times, uncertain of how to phrase what he had on his mind. "The police are *something!* They're not like they used to be. It's like they're not interested in us anymore."

"The Irish mob's not interesting anymore?"

"I'm afraid we're not," he said laughing. "It's a new generation, a new culture, you know? It's a mess, if you ask me. Frankly, I don't know what the heck they're doing with their time because I haven't seen anyone up my tail for a very, very long time. Granted, we don't kill people in the street like we used to do. I mean, Irish body, your brother, floating in the canal? What is this, the seventies? But the cops, I mean. It's like all they care about is paperwork and statistics and pensions and terrorists. It's like you get to kill fifty or sixty guys on the islands now and they won't beat up a drum. Any more than that, well who knows? It's been so long since we had to kill that many people. You want coffee?"

"I—"

"Let's get you some coffee," he insisted.

"Okay, sure," I said.

He reached to the espresso machine. He grabbed the handle put in under the coffee grinder, pulled the lever twice. "If there's one thing the Italians learned how to do better than the rest of us, its coffee. And don't get me started on that French crap or that Colombian horse shit."

"You seem to like the Italians."

"Only when it makes sense." I looked at him. "What? We're supposed to stick to rainbows and leprechauns. Come on! Even the rainbow's for the fruits now, goddamnit."

He locked the handle in the machine, turned it on. The coffee was ready in ten seconds. Then he reached in a freezer underneath the counter, pulled out a mug full of steamed milk with foam.

What the fuck was happening, exactly? The head of the Irish mob was making me a fucking latté. He looked at me with a certain amused look on his face. He knew he was being weird and he liked it.

"Not quite the encounter you expected, right?"

"No, sir."

"Good. But again, don't think this means you're not in trouble," he said as he handed me the cup.

"Am I doing alright?" I asked.

"You're doing better than most," he said, smiling at my question. I took a sip. It was damn good coffee. "Sugar's right there," he added as he picked up his kitchen knife, started chopping peppers. "Now, where was I? Yes, the police. I'm afraid we don't bring them in the loop anymore. They're unreliable and full of themselves. We used to be able to keep them in line with blackmail and such, if ever that was deemed necessary. But now everything's different. They have all these unions and health services. They don't lose their jobs anymore. Heck, they don't even lose their families anymore. Maybe they don't even care about their families all that much. If they get caught bashing on their wives or their kids, they don't even go to jail anymore. They send them to counselling. 'The job was too stressful, I'm gonna do better...' and poof! They're off the hook." I laughed while he continued, "Well at least back in the days, a man had his vices and he had the balls to assume responsibilities for them."

"Why are you telling me all of this?" I dared to ask.

"You're a Kennedy," he replied. "You're a son of

Erin. And your brother was a son of Erin too and for all I know, he was killed for no reason on this land that was built and cared for by our fathers and their fathers and mothers before them. I don't give a rat's ass what anyone says. It wasn't the Chinese, the British or anyone. We built this fuckin' continent. It was us, maybe the Scots and no one else."

"Are you fucking serious?" I asked. "You're making me a latté, saying you might not kill me just because I'm Irish. What am I in the loop now or something?"

"Well, you're hardly in the loop about anything. In fact, I wouldn't say you're in the loop at all. Don't get ahead of yourself. Who knows what can happen? I don't. Maybe you're on your way to killing somebody I hate and I just like to sit by and watch. Maybe that's my real reason, maybe not. The Irish thing's a good story whether it's true or not, you can't argue about that. Let me ask you this: how many people claim Irish ancestry in the world?"

"I don't know."

"Give me a number."

"A couple million."

"Eighty million."

"In Ireland?"

"Worldwide. Eighty million worldwide."

"That doesn't sound bad."

"It ain't good either," he said. Then he admitted. "The glory days of the Irish mob are behind us. We were blessed for being among the first to settle on these shores but that's all we'll ever get. The old island is in economic ruin once more and the rest of us here in America are going poor again. What our ancestors built here, whether it was by the sweat of their hands or the tip of a gun makes little difference. And the Jews and the Italians, the Francos, it's all the same principle. It's not about culture or desire, it's purely statistical." He paused to take a sip of his coffee. "Soon, the people in charge will be the Chinese, the Persian. We had a few good decades, that's it."

"You mean, like the Arabs?"

"They were Persians before that, they'll be Persians one day again. They and the Hindu, that's the future of everything in this world. Business, colonization, war, organized crime—everything."

"Hindu mafia."

"There's organized crime everywhere. India probably worse of them all."

"I never thought about it that way."

"All the Irish had was a piece of the north-eastern tip of America. That's all we got and if you ask me, it ain't bad. This is good land, this is our land but most of all, this is *my* land. This house, this lough, this kitchen. The warehouse on Pitt Street is mine and it will be mine as long as I am alive and as long as my son is alive. You have some land of your own, don't you, Mr. Kennedy?"

"Yeah, I guess so."

"And do you have a son to give it to?"

"Not yet."

"So only half your job is done."

"I'm assuming you'll be expecting something from me because I broke into the Pitt house."

"And you would be correct. You're a good man and I can respect that. Your brother got killed and you're looking for answers. If I had done the job, then I can assure you I would've had a good reason for it. No one could blame you for coming after me. But I didn't. The way I see it, you still have a lot of questions to ask, and a few places to visit before you can let your brother rest in peace. I don't feel the need to get in the way of that just yet."

"Does that mean we're good?"

"Yes and no. Níl luibh ná leigheas in aghaidh an bháis," he took a sip. "You take care of that business of yours. That comes first. When I hear that you're done with it. Then you'll get a visit about that lock and door you owe me."

CHAPTER 19

When I got home that night, I realized I had not cried about my brother's death. Not once. I had walked into the gym and punched it out of me. I had fought and dug for the truth, but not a single tear. The jury was still out on whether I was a real man or a true bastard.

The SAQ was about to close but I snuck in before the teller shut the gates on me. I looked for a forty of Jameson then headed for the register. The cashier looked at me, knowing I was in for a long night. I looked like shit and I felt just as bad. I swiped my card. When the word *accepted* appeared, I just picked up my bottle and I was on my way without a word. She didn't seem to approve. She wasn't gonna do anything about it.

The city streets were still busy, especially for this neighbourhood. The endless flow of hipsters and artists coming out of those towers around Ottawa made me long the days when it was a dump no one would dare to visit. At least back then you could be left in peace when you needed too. Now the canal was filled with idiots on their way to happenings and fancy photo shoots.

One day the young urban privileged of this city were gonna line us up against the river and watch to see how far we'd be willing to swim.

I took a left on Des Seigneurs. Walked over the bridge. *That bridge.* Three blocks into the neighbourhood, I was finally quiet and by the time I reached my door, I was left on my own. I turned in the key, walked in and took off my shirt. The damn thing was sticking to my skin because of the wretched heat and humidity. I took off my pants and sat in my couch in boxers.

"So fucking hot," I said to myself. It was past eleven and the little thermometer out my window still marked twenty-nine Celsius. It was hotter inside than it was outside, goddamnit. My walls were sweating as much as I did, Emma was panting in the corner, unable to find a comfortable way to fall asleep. I felt bad for the poor thing. I thought about calling Patricia, ask her if she could take care of the dog for a few days. God I missed her legs. I imagined her legs across from mine, just her bare legs, talking or watching a movie or something, my hand moving up and down her thigh. I wanted to call her but I didn't. I didn't want to call her every time I was down and feeling like shit. I loved her enough not to put her through that every time I was down.

I reached over and opened the windows, the humid air sifted through. The noises of the port followed in with the wind. The sound of containers being loaded or unloaded, the relentless beeps of machinery and trucks or busses driving up and down Wellington Street, trains pulling in two hundred yards away in the Saint-Henri depot echoed in the night.

I emptied an old glass of water out the window, pulled the table with my foot as I opened the bottle. I poured a few fingers, drank them right away. Then I poured again and kept my drink there for a while.

I didn't feel it. It wasn't coming. I was sitting in the humidity, in my sad, empty room I hadn't painted in years. You could see the cracks in the corner from the building's foundations giving in. One day that whole wall would come down on us but that wasn't what I hated about it. What I hated was the way I just started thinking about a million small details at the most useless of times: the slanted walls, the broken edges on my kitchen counter.

I shoulda fucking sold the place. It wasn't like I had happy memories there. Not that many anyways. It was the house my grandfather had left us in. The house where I lived when my brother died.

If some yuppie would give me good money for it, why wouldn't I sell? It wasn't like fifteen bucks an hour would be *that* hard to find elsewhere. If I could pry my mother away from here, then I should do it. Patricia would probably come along. It wasn't like the old neighbourhood had given her more than a dead husband and a front desk job.

I missed her right that moment, Patricia. It was one of the rare few times she hadn't slept at my house since Cillian's death. When she was around I just fell asleep in a snap. It was hard to explain. She'd push me away if I tried to cuddle because it was too damn hot for any human contact. She'd lie naked, there next to me and she'd just hook my ankle with her ankle and *poof!* That did it. I'd be snoring and drooling in ten minutes. No fucking memory of Cillian keeping me awake.

But Pat wasn't there that night. She had to go home at some point, she'd said. I agreed.

At first I thought I'd be fine, that I needed the time alone to cry my brother. That I was big enough to be on my own. It wasn't coming. I waited there ten minutes, twenty minutes. Half-hour. I was getting drunk, getting hazy. No tears.

I kicked the table, saved the bottle. I drank my glass again then threw it in the corner. It broke against the wall and Emma bolted to the kitchen. I felt bad for the dog, she was stuck with an old grump tonight. Small bits and pieces of jagged glass flew everywhere except for that one piece that was spinning, alone, in the middle of the room.

I tried leaning back. I tried leaning forward, rested my elbows on my knees. I tried breathing deeply then holding it in. Fucking Irish blood wouldn't give up. I started punching myself, punching my head with the side of my fist. Twice then thrice. It hurt but I didn't cry. My head started buzzing around from the liquor and the pain. No tears. All I was giving myself was a big headache. It was too hot to sleep, too late to do anything about it.

Outside, the city port was still busy and busses were still going up and down Wellington Boulevard. The rest of the world didn't know and more importantly, the rest of the world didn't care.

Ten hours later, I woke up from the few hours of sleep I had managed to gather here and there. I felt like shit, hung over and overly tired. I picked up the mess I had made. Fed Emma. Let her out in the backyard and hopped in the shower. It was going to be another painful one as far as the heat was concerned and I didn't want to stroll around town in yesterday's sweat.

The water started pouring on my face. The tension in my limbs started to slack off. The noises of the city were drowned in the noises from the showerhead. It felt good.

After running the white supremacist angle, I wanted to look into the fights my brother could have been involved with. So far we could place the fucking Nazis near my brother's death around the time of death, but that didn't absolutely mean they had done it. I wasn't about to go and kill someone until I learned why they had actually done Cillian. I needed to fucking know.

I'd believe some asshole Nazi had killed my brother. I couldn't fucking understand why they'd do it, but I'd believe it if there was a plausible explanation. I wasn't just gonna hop a car south to Hamilton *just because*. I had my ma to take care of and I had Patricia now too. Getting back at the killer was important, but it was hardly the full picture. I also had to make sure I killed the right guy, otherwise Cillian wouldn't rest in peace.

Something else was bothering me. I knew the mob didn't have anything to do with it. It wouldn't make sense if they did. Also, why would they bother me about paying for a door? If they were ready to kill my brother, wouldn't they be ready to kill me just as well? I didn't know how important the whole *sons of Ireland* thing was to the motherfucker. I was pretty sure they had killed plenty of Irish kids to get where they were. That was weird all together. If they were toying with me, they were doing a pretty good job at it.

And then there was the cop who wanted the case to stay closed. Was it because he was covering up for someone or something? Was it purely ego? Did he simply want to set his foot down and be recognized as a good detective whether he did the job or not? Was career advancement in law enforcement so fucking easy to figure out?

I also didn't know what kind of trouble my brother could have gotten in that would require the murder of an otherwise ordinary tattoo artist. We had Nazis, an incompetent detective, an old-world mobster and a young artist who ended up drowning in the canal with Ajax in the fucking veins. That was a lot to process and little of it made sense.

I didn't know, Cillian had tattooed a dick on some douchebag's back and the guy sought him out for it. *That*, I would believe.

The plan was to visit Cillian's MMA gym. I made my way over there right after lunch, met the coach. He was nice enough to greet me, said *sorry about your loss.* When I started getting into details about the case, he just said, "So they think it was an overdose?" It didn't register with him.

"More or less, yeah. Heroin, mixed with Ajax," I replied. "He drowned in the canal in a matter of minutes. A bad fix they say. I don't believe a word of it."

"Me neither," the coach said.

"Really? Do you have a good reason for saying so?"

"Okay, well, I don't know about Cillian and drugs. He didn't seem like the type. Especially not heroin? And Ajax? I'm sorry but that doesn't make any sense. Again, I can't be absolutely sure about your brother using, but guys take performance-enhancing drugs. They're illegal just the same, but a lot of guys try to get away with it. Usually you see a sharp spike in their performance, that's how you figure it out. Why would they use heroin? Seriously, there would be no gain to it."

"What are the guys using these days?"

"A lot of them don't use anything, really. The whole Dolce diet is still popular somehow. If you'd listen to these guys, it would be the only diet allowed, but for those who do dope, I'd say it would be testosterone replacement, SARMS, diet pills...Decabol's pretty popular these days."

"And guys fall for that?"

"Some of them, yeah. I mean, whoever's doping up to perform are convinced they can get away with anything. Since MMA got popular, everybody wants to be the next GSP, but most of them aren't ready to really work for it, you know?"

"Yeah, I get that. But Cillian?"

"Wouldn't believe it."

"Why?"

"I'm sorry to say, but he wasn't that good."

I laughed. You couldn't fake that level of honesty. "Alright, alright. I hear ya."

"I mean, did the report mention heroin specifically or was it something else?"

"The report mentioned opiates."

"Well, that could mean a lot of things then. Morphine, Vicodin, painkillers in general."

"Vicodin was in the list. Yeah. You inject those?"

"Nah, you just swallow them, that's all."

I didn't like that. I kept coming back to Cillian and his bottle of Advil. "But the report mentioned puncture wounds," I said.

He raised his hands, meaning *I don't know.*

"I'm afraid I can't help you there but I know a lot of guys take painkillers after a solid beating. That you do see a lot."

"So it wouldn't surprise you."

"Not at all. I mean, last I hear Cillian won his fight but he also received a few good blows out of it too. I told him he should wait and complete his training but he wouldn't listen. He had been doing karate for years, right?"

"Yeah. And he was pretty good at it as far as I knew."

"I'd say so, yeah. But then he did like everybody else. He looked into jiu-jitsu and Muay Thai. His technique got mixed up pretty badly, he couldn't combine anything properly. Then he started wrestling because Hendriks had done wrestling. His style just became a mess."

"So he couldn't really fight right?"

"He could fight, but I mean. I asked him to focus on one thing at a time, not to go all over the place for no reason. I have no doubt he could defend himself without any hesitation in the street or in a bar brawl, but competing? No way. I told him not to get involved in a team yet but he wouldn't listen."

He reached under the counter for a flyer. It had the name of the team surrounded by twelve logos from small businesses, clothing companies, garages, auto parts and energy drinks I had never heard of. Didn't look good if you'd asked me. I flipped it. There was the picture of Cillian and his opponent, some guy named Louis Chénier.

"They have most of their fights in Kahnawake," the trainer continued. "I told him he wasn't ready but he went anyways. He came back the next day with the face busted up and bruises all over with a big ass smirk, 'I won,' he told me. But what did that prove? Nothing. I mean I could have kicked him out my gym right there. That's no way to treat your coach. It was so disrespectful."

"So he did have an official fight."

"If a fight on a reserve is official to you. You ask the guys to be patient for two years, maybe three but no. They go on some Facebook group and before you know it, they're off fighting in third tier leagues, shopping themselves concussions at three hundred bucks a pop."

"Three hundred?"

"More or less, yeah."

"The cops mentioned six hundred bucks."

"Still not a lot if you ask me."

I stood and thought about everything for a minute. Not much came to mind. Then I said, "Thank you," as I tapped the cardboard flyer twice. I was ready to get out of there.

"I'm really sorry, again," he said as he started shelving protein bars.

"Yeah, so am I," I replied. There was nothing else to add.

I went straight home after that. I had two things I wanted to look up. First, I wanted to run though everything I had on my brother's death at home. I flipped through the pages, through the notes I had written down from what the cops had told me. I flipped back and forth through reports I probably wasn't supposed to understand in the first place.

While the body has several days old bruises on the

body, there was only one indication of new trauma on the deceased. It consists of a small puncture mark behind the knee, hard to see through the deceased's several tattoos...

The report went on, but I had the information I needed: only one indication of new trauma. So all the bruises were from his fight. If some guy had tried to forcibly take him out, I have no doubt that Cillian would have defended himself. He had to, he could, he would, he *had* to. I knew he was capable. His coach knew he was capable. So that meant that either he knew the guy who did it or that Cillian had been drugged before he could react.

What if the drugs weren't a cover up, but a poison? Who would poison my brother? If he had gotten in trouble on the reserve, he could have ended up dead. I'd believe that. But why would the warriors get involved in the murder of an Irish kid? Even if Cillian had given them a reason to, why would they dump the body in the Pointe?

And it just happened that a van from a well-known white supremacist gang was strolling by at the time of death. Why the hell would Faith in Hate dump the body of a Mohawk murder in the Pointe, in front of an Irish mob house, when the natives could have dumped him in the Saint Lawrence seaway for a cargo to snatch and carry it all the way to fucking Casablanca if it wanted to?

Cillian's murder was a damn cluster fuck. None of it made sense and that only meant one thing. I had a bigger bridge to cross.

CHAPTER 20

I remembered my brother and I having breakfast. I had a triple cheese omelette with coffee and I remember specifically because I had a date with Kathryn Crawford that night and Cillian had asked about an internship at a tattoo shop in NDG. The date didn't go anywhere, but Cillian got the job so it served its purpose.

It was a small place, two artists and one guy who did the piercings. They had extra room and a drawing table, so Cillian went in and asked if they could take him in as an apprentice.

"First they said no," Cillian told me. "But then Annie Hayer walked in."

"Never heard of her."

"Short brunette, bit round, rockabilly chick." Didn't ring a bell. "Small tits, big ass." He added. That could have been a lot of rockabilly chicks.

"Still nothing," I said as I grabbed three sugar packets, held them together, shook twice and poured them all at once.

"Well, anyway," he replied, "I knew her from before and she knew I used to doodle a lot."

"Doodle a lot?" I said. That was bullshit. I raised an eyebrow, looked straight at him.

"Well, I drew a little."

"I never saw you."

"You never asked," he replied as he chewed down a piece of bagel.

"Alright, I'll give ya the benefit of the doubt."

"So she walks in and says, 'Hi, are you in to get some work done?' I said I'd rather get a job. 'As an apprentice?' she asks. I said, 'Yeah.' She says, 'I'm gonna need to see your portfolio.'"

"Did you have a portfolio?" I asked.

"Nah. Not really. I had a few things, but then I got motivated, you know?"

"Motivated? What do you mean, motivated?"

"Well. At first, I wanted the money. I always heard that tattoo artists made good money. But then, you know...She's got a good ass."

"She's got a good ass?" I started laughing. Seemed legitimate enough. "So you gave them a portfolio, and they gave you the job?"

"Well, not right away. I said it was at home and she said, 'It's not very professional to show up at a shop and ask for a job without your portfolio. You're lucky I know you, Cillian, otherwise you could have just fucked off all the same.'"

"She's right."

"I didn't know. So I said I'd be back the next day with it."

"You drew all night, didn't you?"

"Yeah."

"Can I see the portfolio?"

"Nah, it's at the shop. It's not as good as what I'm doing now anyways."

He took a sip of coffee, looked around. I did the same, the day was slow, so was the city. Wellington felt like a good place to live for a minute. I felt lucky I had that. I had seen people move out of the neighbourhood but me and my family were good. I had Ma and my grandparents to thank for that. Now that the neighbourhood was getting better, the whole city was doing better, I could sip on coffee knowing I had a place in it regardless what happened in the future. That's how I felt at that time anyways.

"Yo," Cillian said, snapping me out of it, "you should come in and get some work done, I need the practice."

"You're not touching my skin until you have at least three years' experience."

"Ah, D'Arcy, come on."

"I'm serious. I'm not catching hepatitis over your incompetence." He got pissed.

"Well thanks for the sympathy vote."

"Hey, it's professionalism. You wait for other idiots to be used as guinea pigs. And if the artist proves himself and turns out to be worth your attention, then you go in and get some work done."

He took a bite, ignoring my advice.

"So anyways," he continued, "the first day I walk in and I expected to get on the machines or something. Right? Nothing. 'You're cleaning up,' the owner says. He's a fucking hard ass too. Most arrogant guy I've ever seen."

"Serious?"

"Yeah."

"I guess he has to be."

"Why?"

"He owns a tattoo shop. He probably has assholes asking all sorts of weird and useless questions, all week.

If he tried to be nice to every single one of them, he'd never get any work done."

"That's true."

"He's probably hard on you because he likes you, otherwise he wouldn't bother."

"Of course, but still. I like that at the gym, I don't know if I need that at my work too."

"Alright. What about that Annie chick then?"

"What about her?"

"I don't know. Is she nice?"

"Yeah."

"You fucking her?"

"No," he hesitated. "Well, not yet."

"You want to fuck her?"

His eyes lit up and he smiled. It was that Cillian world famous *guilty* smile. I liked that about my brother. He couldn't lie. He couldn't even *try* to lie. He wore his heart on his sleeve and that was it.

"She's not exactly my type," he said, taking another bite, "but I'd fuck her, yeah."

I smiled. Cillian was an idiot, but fuck he had the heart of a lion. He just had to do things. It's not like he made plans or tried to make sense. If he felt it in his heart, he had to let it out somehow and he didn't care about the consequences. *Fuck the world!*

"Word of advice. Don't fuck where you eat."

"You mean, like, in the kitchen."

"What?"

"Like don't fuck in the kitchen?" he repeated with his mouth full.

"Don't fuck where you eat." *Fucking idiot!* "It's a figure of speech. Don't fuck on the job, especially not if

220

she's your boss. You're gonna fucking lose that job in the end."

"I think you're overthinking it."

"I'm not, trust me."

"You ever fucked on the job?"

"Well, I've fucked on the job, but not with my boss."

"So you don't know what you're talking about."

"Ah, don't play that fucking game."

"But you can't say that you know *exactly* what you're talking about." He smiled.

"I've known others who have. That's good enough for me."

"Well, I think that experience is more relevant."

Arrogant prick. He was busting my balls.

"Alright. You know what? Learn for yourself. Go ahead and learn for yourself."

"She's worth it, man."

"Yeah?"

"Ah, man, an ass like you've never seen. It's like two, big round bricks."

"Square rounds?" I laughed.

"You know what I mean."

"Rectangular circle ass shaped-things."

"It's strong, man," he snapped. "Firm. It's like it reaches out to you. I mean, of course it's not rectangular, it's round. It's an ass. But when she wears them tight, black pants, man." I could see he was picturing it in his head.

"Alright, alright. So she's worth it. Go ahead, fuck around. Why not? It's not like it's the only shop in the city, right?" I didn't know if I was serious or sarcastic myself, but he seemed to like that.

He pulled out his smart phone, started texting some-thing.

"You couldn't sit through a fucking meal without taking it out."

"I'm hooking up with Annie."

"What? You mean right now?"

"You just said..."

I started laughing. Big grunt laugh that disturbed all the little families having breakfast around.

"What?" he insisted.

"I love you, man."

"All right."

I had a sip, smiled again. "How about the boss, then? Is *he* fucking Annie?"

"Nah. He's married, man. He's just demanding is all. I mean, I walk in one day and he's waiting for me there and there's a client in the chair already and he's waiting, the client's waiting and he doesn't fucking know why, you know? And I walk in, stop in my tracks 'cause the boss's looking at me like he's gonna kill me. And Annie's there at the drawing table and she's just minding her own business, drawing and shit, so I say, 'Hey,' and then..."

"You think this is a clean floor?" I said, trying to mimic a boss' voice.

"Exactly! So I go 'Well, yeah.' Man, he was pissed. He starts pointing out dirt on the floor, and I mean, each individual specks of fucking dirt. Says, 'The trash can wasn't emptied, there's dirt on the floor, you left your pizza plate with grease on it on the kitchen table. Don't tell me it's a clean floor.'"

"A tattoo shop's gotta be clean, Cillian."

"Well, it's not like it's a fucking hospital, is it?"

"Actually, it's probably worst."

"How so?"

"If a patient gets sick in the hospital, he sues you. If a client catches an infection in a tattoo shop, some of them will come after you with chains and a baseball bat."

"I can hardly see that happening. The business is fucking mellow man. I don't get why there's still people who are scared of this shit. Most of our customers are fucking students."

"Nevertheless. Your boss want's the floor clean, you keep it clean."

"That's what I did. I passed the broom. I mopped, picked up the kitchen, sterilized every single surface. And when that was done he comes to me and tells me, 'You know? Annie's a better friend than I am, I would have you stand in the corner for an hour with a fucking idiot hat on your head.'"

"Was he serious?"

"*Very* serious. Thank God Annie was there."

"Well, it could have been worse than standing in the corner." Then again, maybe not, Cillian was a full-grown man. That would have been insulting. "Alright," I admitted. "I guess your boss' a pain in the ass."

"I know, right?" He started eating again. "So I stick to my shift for a few weeks and everything's going better. I keep my head down, I shut the fuck up. I clean up the messes and the blood and the floors. I draw everything they ask me to draw and I do my best. Most of it is simple flash art or lettering. I mean, I know I can't wait to find my own angle but I know I'm not there yet either, right? Then one day this client walks in.

The boss welcomes him, talks with him for a minute or two. The guy's a fucking weirdo, man and I've seen fucking weirdos before, you know? He's like fat and stiff with that look in his eyes you can only see through his thick fucking glasses. He looks like he's gonna fucking kill somebody."

"Serial killer or geek with a vengeance?"

"Una fucking bomber crazy. It's like you can tell the guy is smart, but he's just completely insane at the same time. There's just something in the eyes, you know?"

"Yeah, I get the picture."

"So the boss calls me over and he says, 'This is Mr. Beaudoin, you're gonna be doing his tattoo.' And I'm thinking *are you fucking shitting me.* But then again, I was gonna tattoo a real human being for the first time. I'm done with pig skin, right? This is it. But, you know, a creep's not exactly what I had in mind for a first..."

"You would have preferred Annie's ass?"

"Well, I would have preferred Annie's antlers. That way you get to look at the ass while she's leaning against the cushion."

You had to admire my brother's sense of purpose.

"But no, he continued, instead of that beautiful memory I could have had with Annie, or some other chick, I got corpse fucking cadaver loving fucking creepo. And at this point, I'm pissed at my boss, 'cause he probably done it on purpose. In fact, I know he fucking done it on purpose. Maybe he had been waiting for weeks for a guy like that to show up. But a client's a client so I shut the fuck up, right?"

"So what was the tattoo?" I asked.

"He pulls over his shirt on his shoulder and he asks

for letters. He wants me to write, 'Do not embalm. No autopsy.' on his collar bone. He doesn't care about what letters we use. 'The most legible writing you can do,' he said and so I go, 'Okay.' Just like that and invite him over to the chair. I'm thinking *don't fuck this up, that guy will come after you, man.* So I put on some gloves, disinfect my arm rest. I pull out my machine, some needles, white plastic caps for the black ink. The whole works. I ask him to sit down while I get everything ready. I look at the boss and he's smiling, almost laughing, the motherfucker. Good thing the client couldn't see him 'cause he would have nail-bombed the place."

"Don't you think you're laying it on thick a bit?"

"I know what I saw and I stand by it. Anyway, so I do the tattoo and he doesn't give a fuck about the lettering, so it's good practice, I'm not too nervous about doing clean lines and shit. Takes twenty minutes, I cash in my first forty bucks."

"Forty bucks for twenty minutes?"

"I know, right? That's the apprentice's share, man. I'm getting fucked over here. Real artists make more."

"I'm in the wrong fucking business."

"How much do you make?"

"Fourteen." He didn't say anything. "An hour," I added. He was surprised. My brother never really worked another job in his life so he didn't know. He worked as a bouncer and that made good money and he had plenty of good looking women hanging around him. When he got fed up with that, he became a tattoo artist. Punching a regular nine to five and *dealing with Claudia* from accounting wasn't exactly on his radar.

"That's it?" he asked, surprised.

"Shut up," I laughed.

"Well. I'm sorry to say. But it doesn't sound like much."

"Hey!" I insisted. "I know, alright? So what about your guy?"

"I don't know. He said he was happy with it. He said thank you. He didn't tip, but he looked crazy enough for me not to ask. I patched him up, he put on his shirt and that was it. He just left without saying anything else, really. The boss looks over to me, starts laughing his ass off. 'It ain't funny,' I said. He says, 'I know. I know. Let me tell you what, that was good enough. Alright? So I'll send the next eighteen-year-old chick your way.'"

"See. He's not *that* bad of a guy."

"I don't know man."

"He made a good gesture."

"Maybe, but a first is a first, and you can't change that, you know? I'll be stuck with creepo for the rest of my life while all I was dreaming about was Annie's ass."

CHAPTER 21

Two men in the octagon was the custom. The referee was just trying to stay out of the way best he could. There was a camera crew. No movie stars, but the rest of it felt like the real deal: groupies, flashing lights, loud music...

There was a handful of women in the audience. Most of them looked like they could handle themselves in a fight. The rest of the crowd was a mixed bag. A few bikers, some construction workers, some of them looked like they belonged to the downtown business crowd and were here to exercise the right to manliness that was denied to them in their daily grind.

The local gambling website was sponsoring the event and the club jacked up the beer prices to cash in a benefit. The two fighters were in their mid-twenties and I figured if they were here at this point in their career, they would never go pro. I had never expected my brother to go pro. If he did, he would have become so arrogant it would have been horrible. But things didn't work out too well for him in the Mohawk MMA circuit. I had that on my mind and not much else.

We paid our dues at the door, walked in and found ourselves a table in the middle of the room, closer to the rear and the wall.

"Sorry, gentlemen," a guy said. "Tables are reserved."

"How much?" Karl sighed.

"Five Hundred."

We got up.

I couldn't help but to feel I wasn't in my element. These were warriors, Mohawks and for better or worse I was part of the invaders. I felt like part of the invaders. Call it white guilt if you want, I had it anyways. I hadn't personally done anything to piss them off and. I could have argued that it was the British who had dumped my ancestors here, but I doubted that in the heat of the moment, if a riot or a fight was to break out, I'd find a kind ear to these kinds of arguments.

So far no one so much as glanced at us. Maybe they really didn't care or held a grudge. We were rowdy men in a rowdy place and there wasn't much more to it. There was a peacekeeper officer in the corner who seemed to enjoy the show. The waitress was easy on the eyes. Her skin was dark but not as dark as he eyes and her hair.

She wore a black tank top and dark blue jeans with running shoes. She wasn't wearing "fuck me boots," but the *lady* was working it. She had a thin neck, a flat, six-packed belly and wide shoulders. I knew she could kick my ass. Her ears were rugged and thick, that meant she did either Judo or wrestling. I could see a few tattoos here and there, a few good scars too. I could make out the name of her kids on her neck, Amelia and Ross, over a pair of black and white roses.

"You guys want a drink?" she asked with her wide smile.

"Got Guinness?" I shouted over the thunder of the crowd and the fight. Guinness was a tourist beer, but I expected that's all they'd have.

"Of course."

"I'll get the round then," I said.

She nodded and turned around. She had a dream catcher tattooed on a shoulder plate. It looked very traditional. She had a brass knuckle tattooed on the other one, not so traditional.

I checked out her ass. It was just standing there, perfect, sporty. Her calf muscles stood out, strong and sharp. The jeans she had on were perfect for her: how the pockets followed the line of her thighs, how the waist was just low enough.

But then I looked around the room. If Amelia and Ross were her kids, then it meant she had a boyfriend or a husband somewhere on the reserve. Shit, maybe her man was in the pit, fighting, who knew? I gave her one last glance then I twiddled with my thumbs, not knowing what to do. I reminded myself of Patricia and told myself there was really no harm in looking around, was it?

She came back with our drinks in good old Irish mugs. I gave her forty bucks, said keep the change. That made it a six-dollar tip. She smiled and said, "Call me if you want anything else."

I raised my glass, looked at the centre of the room. One guy was bloodied up on the floor, holding his head, looking half-conscious. He seemed angry at himself. He had just lost by decision of the referee thanks to some grappling move I knew nothing about. The announcer called something that sounded like kimura. I didn't know what that meant except that it meant the guy in the camo trousers had won.

I wasn't a fan. I hadn't jumped on the MMA bandwagon. When you trained at boxing, you always had two feet on the ground and you danced or you stood toe to toe and that was it. If you fell, they counted up to ten and you lost or you got the hell back up to your feet. I guess there was something spiritual to that, like honour was better than being technically the best.

It's not that these guys didn't know how to fight. I knew they knew how to fight. I just didn't like it. It was like comparing rugby to American football. In rugby, you weren't allowed to go around your opponent to get the ball. You had to push your way *through* him. They'd still run you in like a freight train, but you didn't have to watch your back in rugby. That made sense to me.

I guess I felt the same about MMA. Sometimes, the guy would get a lucky hit on you and shove you down before you had the chance to get your guard back up. In boxing, you had to knock the guy out for ten whole seconds. Not just nine seconds, ten fucking seconds. There were hardly any lucky breaks or some trick that sounded like kimura. It was a war of trenches.

You don't beat a guy when he's down. You just don't do that.

In the octagon, the winner was smiling with his bloody teeth out for the world to see. The referee raised his arm to the air, his crew cheered him loudly and then both of them thanked each other and headed for the locker rooms. One was gonna cash enough for a few free drinks and rent money for the month, fuck the local groupie, maybe. The other one was gonna drag himself to the nearest pusher and buy himself some painkillers on Visa.

The host walked on stage with a microphone in his

hands. "And now, ladies and gentlemen, the lead event you have all been waiting for. Weighing in at a hundred and ninety-five pounds four ounces, the contender from Mont-Laurier, Qc, François Lisée."

Some guy in Quebec-blue boxers walked on stage. He seemed to boast the whole sovereignist thing as his marketing strategy. Didn't seem to sit too well with the crowd. He walked in with a some rope bandana around his head and did a few prayers, warm up and form that I could only assume were Muay Thai forms.

I could hardly believe he was one-ninety-five. He was too tall for his own good, looked like your run-of-the-mill famished white trash. Seemed nervous, too. His stare was focused but in the wrong kind of way. He just kept on banging his head, amping himself up.

"And coming in all the way from Sault Sainte Marie in Northern Ontario, our own Native champion, from the Batchewana community, Russell H. 'Hell' King." Three quarters of the room cheered loudly. The French-Canadian kid felt alone in the universe and it showed on his face. My money was on King too.

He walked in the octagon looking fierce. Lisée didn't look like he had any chance. There was just something in the eyes of the champion. I had seen that look, hell, I had been told I had that look, at least back in the day. If you walk on the ring or the octagon or in any fight, if your opponent can't look you in the eye straight from the start, you usually know he's gonna lose.

King kneeled down and meditated for a moment. He didn't wear boxing shorts but had the traditional Muay Thai trousers, black and red with a feather and flames.

He had the same rope bandana over his head and a red armband around his huge biceps.

The guy looked like he worked in a mine and used poured concrete as a punching bag to soften the tip of his knuckles. Seeing where he came from, that could have actually been the case.

He prayed and stretched in the same way as the other kid, but you could see his movements were a lot stronger, a lot sharper. This shoulda probably been a no contest. Was there such a thing in MMA? I didn't know. If this had been a boxing match, I would have called it.

The referee gave instructions, both fighters touched gloves and that was it. The crowd turned silent for a moment. Dead silent. I knew it was going to explode the moment one of them drew first blood.

The two men circled one another a few times. Then the white kid decided to strike. The sharp noise of leather snapping against leather resonated through the entire room. They traded a few softer blows, still trying to size each other up. They kicked at each other's legs, the opponent bending inwards every time so it wouldn't break.

Lisée was about to throw another one. That's when King decided to go all in. He rushed and lifted Lisée from the ground, banged his head against the fence. The crowd cheered. Lisée replied with a few elbows to King's back, but even I could see he was in a bad spot. King lifted him again, took the blows and threw the guy on the ground. He rolled on top of Lisée, trading a few short punches before he could muster some sort of a guard.

They rubbed their rugged skin against each other,

trying to get the opponent to allow a mistake, a weakness the other could use. Then Lisée managed to lock King's head and kept him there.

They stood like that for maybe two minutes out of a five minute round and I was ready to call *bullshit* but then Lisée managed to get King into what appeared to be an arm lock but King slipped out to the crowd's pleasure and both fighters decided to get back on their feet.

"I don't like this shit. I mean look at this," Ryan said, pointing to the octagon with his hand sideways. The two fighters were in a mutual head lock, trading knees at each other's ribs. I had to hand it to the French-Canadian kid. He lasted longer than I had expected. "They're gonna make what? A few hundred bucks? Shit, I make almost a thousand a night as a bouncer and I don't get a fucking concussion for it."

"You sound like a suburban mom."

"It's not the fighting I mind. But let's face it. If someone wants to watch me get my head banged in, they better fucking pay me for it. I mean, think about it. The shittiest player on the Arizona Diamondbacks roster will still make a hundred and fifty K a year doing sweet fucking nothing. And I mean *sweet* fucking nothing. The guy's just fucking picking dandelions out in centerfield, taking in the sights. Damn! A hundred and fifty K." He took a sip. He sounded like he was drunk, he wasn't. He was just Ryan. He slammed his glass down on a small shelf resting against the wall like he had made his final point.

The crowd jumped into a cheer. The fight was over. Lisée had over reached with a kick, again. King ran him in the fence, lifted him once more, knocked his head on the ground. A few punches later, the kid had passed out and the fight was over.

Three minutes later the announcer called the winner, half the crowd was already gone. The TVs turned from the fight to "Sports Centre." The Als had lost against the Bluebombers and there was a piece about whether or not Carboneau should have gambled with other NHL players at his annual eighteen hole summer fundraiser.

I drank up. The guys were just waiting in silence now. The jukebox played White Zombie's "More Human than Human." We gave the room fifteen minutes to clear out, finished our beer. When the place was quiet enough I told the guys, "I'm getting another round."

Truth was that I wanted to talk to the waitress alone, trying to get something out of her.

"Hi again," she said as I walked over. She was busy putting dead bodies into old cardboard boxes.

"Hey, if you have a second, I'll take another round."

"Sure thing."

I hesitated, she noticed. I spit it out. "I also wanted to talk."

She was ready to give me that *ahh, you're sweet but no thanks* look and smile but then I said.

"The name Cillian Kennedy ring a bell?" It wasn't exactly what she expected.

"Hmm, not really."

"He had a fight here a few weeks ago. I mean. Could I talk to whoever is booking the fights?"

"That would be me."

I stood surprised. She noticed that too.

"I know, women and combat, right?"

"I didn't mean...I mean. Sorry."

She laughed. "It's okay."

"I mean. There are ladies at my boxing gym, it's just..."

"What gym do you box at?"

"Bellagion's Place."

"Never heard of it."

"Villeray."

She grinned.

"How about you?"

"Underdog."

"*Really?*" Underdog was a big deal in Montreal. If the lady worked out there, that meant she meant business. I felt old and out of my league all of a sudden. I probably was.

"So," I said, changing the subject." About my brother."

"Cillian."

"Yeah. He had a fight here a few weeks ago, six weeks maybe."

"Six weeks ago?" she started thinking. "Yeah, the name rings a bell. It's not exactly a common name."

"It is, in Ireland."

"Right."

"Anyways. He had a fight here, Team Impact. I had the flyer and it mentioned the other fighter was Louis Chénier. Do you know anything about the guy?"

"I'd have to check."

She walked over to the end of her counter. There was a touch-screen computer that doubled as a cash register. A few taps and flicks, she was on the bar's MMA webpage, strolling through fights, results and fighter profiles.

"Yeah, right, I remember now," she said. "The fight was a close call. Lots of comments online. People seemed to think Cillian shouldn't have won the fight."

"How's that?"

"There was a punch to the back of the head while the opponent was on the ground," she was reading. "'It was deemed accidental and Cillian apologized, claiming he was trying to rush for the take down and accidentally hit his opponent while reaching for a grab, but doubt seemed to be enough for the online crowd." She looked at me. "Those things happen all the time. I think people are just drama queens, especially online." She kept reading. "The other guy never seemed able to come back into the fight...blah blah blah. There's still new comments on the page. If your brother wanted to do a rematch, we'd certainly be able to book him a good gig. People want to know if he's legitimate or a hoax, that attracts a crowd, you know?"

"Yeah, I caught wind of that," I lied. "So what can you tell me about the other guy, that Chénier guy?"

She looked at her screen again. "Well, Chénier didn't make the fight."

"What do you mean?"

"He had a motorcycle accident two days before the event. We had to scramble to find a replacement fighter."

"Who fought Cillian, then?"

"I don't really know him. Never heard of him before, either. His name was Michael Cook," she read, "fighting out of Hamilton, Ontario."

She flipped the screen for me to see and there you had it. The photo that ended the fight, next to Cillian as the referee was calling the winner, stood the son of a bitch who had killed my brother. Cheap tattoos, bald shave head, Iron Cross trousers.

There was no doubt about it. Right there on the fucking picture stood the lead singer for Faith in Hate.

CHAPTER 22

Karl was waiting with Ryan and Phil. They were leaning against the car, maybe forty feet away from my door. Everyone's faces were yellow from the lampposts, the city lights were in the distance, above the hill, above the rest of us. I was sitting in my stairs with a beer in my hands, Patricia was leaning back against a post sign in front of me. She had a can in her left hand, resting against her thigh, foot up on the post.

Her back was arched a little, her full breast right in front of me and she had the same kind of loose shirt she wore over only one shoulder. You could see plenty of skin and her half-sleeve on the other arm. She could have worn that shirt every day of her life if she wanted to and I would have been happy.

I might've been dead the next day. I might've gone to jail in two days' time. I had to enjoy the scenery while I could.

She took a sip. I followed the can up to her lips. Looked at her neck, her nails, her lips, hair and eyes. "I mean, you got to do what you got to do," she said. It was hard to tell if she was pissed or not, which probably meant she was.

"So you don't mind me doing it?" I replied. "You know what I'm going there to do. I don't have to spell it out to you, not you."

The truth was that I was getting nervous. The truth

was that I was getting cold feet. Running around and busting heads was fun, but now that I had a name and a face and even an address...it made it real and real was always scary.

"I know. My husband was a soldier, you know?"

"And you want that in your life again?"

"I want you in my life. I know that much."

"And the killing...the..." I hesitated. "It doesn't bother you at all?"

She sighed and took a breath. "I'd rather know that I'm with a man that would do anything necessary to protect me and my own."

I would have never believed she could have taken something like this lightly. I loved that. She also had enough guts to roll with it. That made her the perfect women for me, the only woman for me. She was down to earth, beautiful. A working class queen, not bothered with the so-called righteousness of people up on the hill. There was never going to be any bullshit with a woman like that. It was enough to make me smile.

"So does that mean we're going steady?" I joked.

She smirked and looked down at me. Goddamned that look. She was going to get a house and three kids out of me.

"Oh boy." I laughed.

That made her laugh. Good. I took a sip. I looked over to the guys, they were still waiting by the car. The plan was to leave that night, go half the way, sleep somewhere around Toronto and head to Hamilton during the day to avoid the grid lock.

I was asking a lot of my friends these days. I didn't know if they were tired of waiting on me. If they were, well they didn't wave or anything. I needed *this* anyways so they were going to have to wait. I needed my family around. Patricia was my family now.

I wanted to get married right there in the Ukrainian church right across the corner. I wanted to wake the old priest and have him say our vows in the middle of the night with the not so faint trace of beer still on our breath, with the not so faint trace of revenge still engraved in our hearts. I wanted to marry her just like that, with the purest of emotions, no logic, no plans, no bullshit. I would just drag my sleepy mom across the street, force the guys in, let them sit through my *I do* and make love to Pat before we left. If I had it my way, that's what I would have done.

"Are you going to tell your mom?" she asked.

"I think it's the worst kept secret in the Pointe right now."

"I'd say that much. But did you tell your mom?" she insisted.

"Not yet. I think she knows. I think she'd rather not know. But I ought to tell her, right?"

"She's the head of the family."

"Yeah," I replied. "But I mean, if we do something, when we do something, it's gonna be in Hamilton, so."

"Do you have a plan?"

We kinda sorta, maybe did. The truth was that I didn't know or didn't want to know how the rest was going to work out. Nothing that important was supposed to be simple, so I admitted, "Not really but well figure it out."

"Alright, if you say so." She took another sip and stayed there in silence. Then she finished her beer, leaned over to me, kissed me on the forehead. She lifted my chin, looked in my eyes. I was blinded by her curves, blinded by the shape of her neck and that look in her eyes.

"I love you," I said.

"I know." She kissed me. I took her hand in my hand, kissed the back of it. She pushed my head on her chest, the softness of her breast felt like heaven to me. She was nervous, I *felt* that much. But she knew better than to bring it up. What I needed right that moment was a simple *go and get it done*, not some *I'm so scared bullshit.*

So she just let go of me, said *I love you.* Kissed me again and walked in saying, "I'll tell your mom to come down."

The silence of the borough surrounded me. The noises of the trucks and the port felt like a soothing melody I had grown accustomed to and couldn't live without anymore.

I got thinking about every single mistake I did that I thought were mistakes but that really just made me who I am today. Like the job I decided to take instead of going to school. Like the places I decided to hang out like Irish dive bars up on crescent or hardcore shows in NDG. If I hadn't hung around these places, I wouldn't have met Karl and Ryan or Phil and Patricia.

If we still cared about our mother tongue more than where we were from, then I wouldn't have such good people around me. We were sticking together because we all shared the same hits in life, applied on the same kind of jobs and lived in the same kinds of places. We had class rage down to our bones and that accounted for a lot. You couldn't fake something like that.

"Patricia woke me up," my ma said with her tired, sore voice as she walked out the door. She was in her flannel pyjamas, throwing an old wool blanket over her shoulders.

"I'm sorry. I should have asked her not to."

"It's okay," she said, giving me a kiss on the head. "Make sure the police don't see that?" she added, pointing at my beer. "Last thing we need is another fine. If they had it their way, the city would drain every last one of us with those damn tickets."

"I know."

She sat down. "Pat said you were leaving soon."

"Yup." I took a sip.

"Where to?"

"Ontario."

"What the hell's in Ontario?"

"Not much. I just need to check something out, is all."

"Don't make this old woman worry, okay, D'Arcy?"

"Don't worry, Ma."

"That's easy for you to say." She tucked her blanket in, crossed one arm over the other. That meant she was mad at me but wouldn't say it.

"I won't be gone long."

"How long is not long?"

"I don't know. Few days, maybe."

"I don't like the sound of that. Sounds like something I heard before. Sounds like something your father would have said."

I kissed her on the forehead, said, "You worry too much."

"Maybe you don't worry enough."

"'Ma," I objected. She wouldn't have it. She looked the other way. That was her way of telling me she couldn't handle hearing about it. I gave her some air, let her sit there in silence for a minute. I knew when she was ready, she'd get talking again. It was hard to get my ma to shut up. *It shouldn't take long*, I joked in my head.

"You know?" she said. "When your dad would leave, we used to sit right here in those stairs. We would sit around and have a beer before he'd go north for his shift. Just like you and me right now. Just like that. I mean, before you and Cillian got in the way. We'd try to sit here and have a beer but you guys wouldn't have it. You'd drag us back in and started running around the house with dad chasing you to bed. He couldn't leave until you two were asleep. There was no way around it. He had to sleep there with you for hours if he had to. You'd clench your arms around his neck so hard he wouldn't dare to move."

"I don't remember that."

"Ah, you guys used to be all over him. Up to when you were six or seven. I don't know what happened after that. Maybe you started to realize he wasn't around much. Maybe that was all it took, but once, I think it was in October, he was set to leave and we sat here on those steps and for the first time in years he actually had time to drink it one sip at a time. He managed to drink his whole beer waiting for you guys. You never came down. No tickles, no chases, no hugs, not *just one more minute, Dad* before it was time to sleep. Something changed in him that day. I don't think we ever were the same again." She looked at me, tucked in the blanket over her shoulder. I looked at her without a word. I didn't want to get into Dad. I didn't have time for that.

She helped herself to my beer, I let her have it. She took a swing and said, "God, I haven't had one of these in so long."

"It's pretty bad isn't it?" I smiled.

"It's godawful," she said as she handed it back. "Flat, too. Why the heck would you drink something like that."

"I've just been talking for too long. I probably won't finish it."

"Well, don't leave it on the porch. It attracts the flies and it attracts the cops. I don't want to get stuck with those fruit flies in my house again. It's a mess to get rid of..."

"Yes, Ma."

"The cops just the same, so pick up after yourself."

"I said alright," I added calmly.

She got up, looked at Ryan, Karl and Phil, said, "They're good friends aren't they?"

"Yes they are."

"I like them. You should keep them around." She kissed me. "I'm gonna walk back in now. Call me when you get there."

She walked back in and shut the door. I took my last sip and that was that. Two minutes later we were in the car, heading west towards Atwater. It hit me when Karl got into the tunnel.

"Fuck," I said.

"What?" the guys asked.

Ma was going to be pissed.

"I forgot the damn beer on the stairs."

CHAPTER 23

"You can literally do the worst thing in the world and people will let you get away with it if you have a good reason for doing it."

That was my dad. That was the advice he had decided to give me the day he announced he was bailing on us for a fucking job.

Dad had been working as a mechanic in the mines all his life. Most of the year he was gone in the great white north. He'd drive twelve hours up to Radisson and then they'd take a plan up to the mine. The mineral was shipped out on a freight train all the way to Sept-Iles.

He was gone six weeks at a time, then he'd be home for two weeks, more or less, and then he'd be gone for six weeks again. He'd say shit like *I'm doing this for the family. It's all I know.* But that was bullshit. Most of the guys who do that say that it's for a down payment on a house, they're doing it for the money, they're doing it for the family. But the truth was, as least the truth about our dad, was that he was doing it because he liked it. Being around his kids, being home at six, that wasn't his thing.

So he kept working the mines until one day he came home and said plain and simple, "I'm tired of all of this, travelling, the airplanes, the driving...I'm tired about it. I want to live where I work."

There was no way in hell my mother would leave Montreal for some isolated back country village with two thousand inhabitants. She wouldn't sit all winter waiting for the husband to come back home with two rental DVDs and a case of beer, knowing her two kids had no other future than to work the mines themselves.

"I won't follow you up there. I just won't," my mother told him.

Dad offered Fort McMurray. Tar sands were becoming a thing, he said. He could get a job there, the city was a bit bigger, the money was good, Edmonton was eight hours away or something. If she wanted to go out, they could make it a weekend.

"Don't sell me your snake oil," Mom replied.

Eight hours north of Edmonton was too far for my mother. It was too far for me also. I was glad she said no. They split assets right there. And by that I mean that my mother was given the block. It was her father who had bought it anyways. He pretty much gave her everything else but the car and six grand to start over there.

I didn't know if Ma cried. I guess she did, on her own time. But she never spoke about it. Not that day, not ever. I know she didn't cry right that moment. She just started cleaning the house. Took out the vacuum cleaner and got to work. The house hasn't been that clean since.

Dad was never around much to start with, and when he was, he spent as much time in bars than at home. Every time he came back, it was the same. He'd spend a few hundred bucks in two or three days right after his tour. He'd buy rounds to people he didn't know because he didn't have any friends here. Then he'd feel bad about it. I'd bust his balls and he'd buy us something, he'd take us out.

When I heard the vacuum cleaner start that day, I expected something like that at first. He had often left before. Why would that fight be any different? I didn't know. Next thing he did was come to my room. I was fifteen. Cillian was at his karate classes. I was on the PlayStation. It was nice and sunny outside, but I was on the PlayStation. I could have been playing football or rugby or skateboarding. I wasn't.

We had this old, massive TV with a small screen. It was resting on my old wooden cupboard that used to be my granddad's, six feet over my head. Cables dangled down all the way to my PlayStation that balanced very lightly on a narrow bookshelf next to it.

He walked into my room, sat down on my bed without being invited. I was leaning against the wall, so asked me to sit closer to him. He took the remote out of my hands, pressed pause. I didn't say a word.

He looked at me, sighed and looked around in silence. The bookcase was full of comics he had bought me that I never read. There were a few posters on the wall, things like Angelina Jolie in *Tomb Raider* and Slipknot back in the "people = shit" days. I had this Erin Go Bragh flag over the bed that my uncle had given me. My desk was full of unfolded clothes and I was glad Dad didn't look underneath them because there were a few condoms under there and I didn't want to get into *that discussion* not with him, not right now, not anytime.

The next thing he said: "You can literally do the worst thing in the world and people will let you get away with it if you have a good reason for doing it."

That sounded weird. "What do you mean?"

"What I mean is that regardless what you do, you are

always better off being honest about it. Be upfront about it. Nobody likes a snake."

"Okay."

What the fuck's a fifteen-year-old supposed to reply to that anyway?

"I guess what I'm saying it that you should always be honest. You have to be honest to yourself and honest to others. Okay?"

"Okay."

"Even if you're doing something bad. You'd be surprised at how most people will let you do something bad if you explain to them why you're doing it. If you have a good reason, most people will understand. It's like your mother. You know. You heard us fight, right?

"Yeah."

"It wasn't like a big fight, right?"

"No. No, it wasn't."

He leaned towards me with a smile on his face. "We've had worst fights before, haven't we?"

I smiled too.

"You see, we didn't fight because your mother knows I *have* to do this, you understand?"

He sat there, didn't answer at first. At least he tried to make it look hard. He tried saying something. He shook his hand, stopped himself then shook it a few times more and *then* it came out.

"I have to go now. You understand that?"

"I know. You gonna be back in six weeks? So what's the difference?"

"Nah, kid. Not this time. It's gonna be more than six weeks."

"How much more?"

"I found me a better job, alright. One that doesn't require me to drive so much for so long when I come back. I'm not as young as I used to be, see. And I feel like I could fall asleep on the wheel and crash the car, you know? You wouldn't want me to crash the car, would you?"

I didn't answer at first. This wasn't your regular Dad's leaving fight anymore. Three minutes ago I was blowing shit up on Twisted Metal. That was it. That was my life. Go to school, play twisted metal and that was it. Dad showed up every other month and we go to a hockey game and we'd have a good time for a day or two and then things would become about the money again. I'd go back to school like every other day and jerk off alone in my room at night thinking about Jennifer Kreisky.

"So we're gonna move?" I asked.

"You could if your mother would. But I think that ship has sailed, boy."

"So where are you going to live?"

"I don't know yet, but that'll be my problem, alright?"

"Sooo...Where are *we* going to live?"

"You. You're staying right here, kid. The house is yours, the block is yours. When you get older you can just put up a wall back where we opened it and have your own apartment downstairs. Just like we planned for years, right? It'd be cool to have your own place, right?" I didn't answer. "Don't worry about that, alright. Your mom's a good woman. She always took care of you. She'll keep doing that. No reason not to."

I didn't know if I was pissed that he was leaving. I

guessed not. I was worried maybe up to the point when he said that my life wasn't changing at all. We were keeping the house. I was keeping my room. As far as I was concerned, I was just going to see my father a little bit less and a little bit less often. That wasn't even a big deal. I could have shut up right there. I could have. I didn't like him that much and I was old enough to know better but I was also old enough to know I had a right to be pissed. I guess I wanted to take a jab at him. So I did.

"You know? Mom says you could get a job right here at CN. Right here in Pointe-Claire. Every time you get in the car and leave, she stands in the window and says, 'He could get himself a job right here at CN. I don't know why he keeps doing it. He could get a job *right here* at CN.' She does that every time."

"She's probably right," he admitted. "But I love what I do. You get it? I really do, D'Arcy. I love what I do, so I got to do it. One day you're gonna find out what you like to do and you're just gonna have to do it, you know?"

He was looking for approval. I wasn't gonna give it to him.

"Okay." It's all I said. And I said is as neutral as possible. No emotion one side or the other. Just okay. *You try and make fucking sense of that.*

He couldn't so he said, "Alright." He got up, gave me my remote back. I started playing again. The noises of explosions and car crashed filled my small room. I got right back into the game, killing enemies, crashing cars, dodging machine-gun fire. I was making a run for one of the pink homing missiles and then some health after that.

"You're good at this game?"

"I'm alright," I replied without looking at him.

"Is it fun? It looks fun."

"It's alright," I replied. He could have died right there and I don't think I would have reacted differently. I probably would have stepped over his dead body on my way to the kitchen for a Coke and some cookies. He was leaving for good, so *fuck him.*

He took a deep breath, reached for his wallet.

"Here," he said as he handed me a fifty dollar bill. "You get yourself another one okay. Something you can play with your brother."

"Alright," I said as I took the money.

"You tell your brother I love him, alright?"

"Sure."

"Alright." He gave me a kiss on the head, I shrugged my shoulders. He went for the door. "You make sure to tell him, okay?"

"Okay."

"Okay," he said one last time. He closed the door behind, him. Three minutes later I heard the car pulling out the curb. He had packed his shit before he had even spoken to my mother and me. We weren't meant to have any say in it from the start.

Guessed I should have been surprised. I wasn't. I really wasn't. I got right back in the game. I managed to kill Sweettooth and still had three quarters' health for Axel. I was playing with Warthog so everything was just dandy. Cillian would be back from his karate classes in an hour or so.

You tell your brother I love him, alright?"

I never did.

CHAPTER 24

We had found Michael Cook's address in the Montreal bonehead's computer. We had been on the westbound 20 for so many hours I couldn't even tell how long we had been at it anymore.

Truth was I had doubts. Maybe I didn't want to do it anymore. That was what was going through my mind. I didn't know if it would ease my suffering or if Cillian, being dead, would actually benefit from it in any way. It was fucking me up real good but everyone expected it of me and that probably fucked me up even worse. I started secretly hoping that everything would just line up and happen on its own, like the guy would just trip and fall on a fucking nail sticking out of his floor when we were gonna knock on his door. That was wishful thinking.

"Hey, D'Arcy, you know there's gonna be some legal repercussion to what we're about to do, right?" That was Phil making sense.

"I know," I said.

"So what are we gonna do about it."

I didn't know yet and felt lucky we weren't there yet. The forest landscape made way for the endless suburbs of Toronto. We crossed Ajax, Scarborough, North York. Everything looked the same. Rexdale, Mississauga. They all looked the same to me. If it wasn't for the airport, I would have felt we were running in circles. Oakville, Burlinton. It wasn't till we were on Queen Elizabeth's

252

way and we could see the Dofasco plant that I felt like I was in a city I could relate to again.

Hamilton. Also known as Stab City Canada.

We stopped by Home Depot next because it was the only place we knew we could gather the things we needed to kill a man. It felt good to stretch my legs too. A twelve-hour drive and a sleepless night would've fucked anybody up. I wasn't any different.

The A/C kicked me in the face. For a minute I just felt like the good son who was out shopping for something for the house. Nothing more. I even started looking at the specials on furniture for my mom. I imagined myself buying a burgundy swing chair with matching cushions, walk up to my ma's apartment and say, *Look what I've been up too for the last two days.* But that was hardly why we were there, was it?

"Fais qu'on fais quoi rendu icitte?" Phil asked.

"I don't know yet." I replied.

"Why don't we just stab him?" Ryan said.

"He's a trained MMA fighter," Karl replied. "Odds are good that he'd know how to get the knives from your hands and kill you with it."

"You'd be surprised."

"I don't want to find out."

"Well, you trained in self-defence?" Phil replied.

"A few years of Karate as a teenager hardly counts. I wouldn't want one, single guy to take out the entire Kennedy heirloom on his own."

"How about a sledgehammer?" Phil said as he picked up the largest one they had on the racking. He looked like a kid with a flashy new toys. "First we could, like, smash his toes, like *BAM!*"

"What if he's got steel toe caps?" Karl asked.

"Then the cap's gonna bend and cut his toes and there's gonna be fucking blood everywhere."

"That doesn't work?" I said

"How can you know?"

"They tried it on Mythbusters."

"They did?"

"Doesn't work."

"Fuck," he said as he put the hammer back.

"We could still use it," I added. "I mean, for the front door or something." His heart wasn't into it anymore. "A blow to the head, maybe?"

"Yeah." He smiled again. "And there's gonna be fucking blood and brains like it's *The Walking Dead* back in season one."

"We need to keep it down a little," I said.

"Fence pole?" Ryan asked.

"Aren't those like eight feet long?"

"Yeah, keep him at a distance."

"What? I'm gonna joust the fucking Nazi? Plus, where am I gonna fucking put it in the car?"

"Through the open window." Phil started again, "That would be *awesome!* Imagine you're driving and I'm getting out of the window and we're like chasing the guy on the street and I pull out this eight-foot-pole with like a spikey post cap and throw this shit at his head."

"You're on the fanlist for comicon aren't you?" Ryan asked.

"So?" Phil replied. "Don't tell me that didn't sound cool."

"Alright, alright," I said.

"Man, I need to start taking notes," Phil added.

"You're not taking notes," Karl said.

"Why not?"

"Evidence?"

"It's hardly evidence," Phil replied. "I'll leave your names out of it."

"You're an idiot," Karl added.

"Heille on se calme, le cave," Phil replied, telling Karl to get off his back.

"That's gonna be enough," I said. "Keep it in your head," I said to Phil. "Write your zombie movie later at home if you fucking want to. We're here for Cillian, remember?"

We weren't gonna kill the guy with a fence post sticking out of a car, we were probably not going to go after him with a sledgehammer either. We kept walking in the alleys, not knowing exactly what we were looking for.

"You know we are arguably wasting our time here," Karl said. I didn't know if I should reply. "We could have stopped in Cornwall for a gun." He continued, "We could drive to Cornwall and back in fourteen hours."

That was true. We could actually do it. Hell, we could send Karl alone to see his cousin while the rest of us wait in a hotel in luxurious Hamilton. But I wanted nothing to do with guns in the first place.

"I don't know, man, we're here already."

"Alright. Alright!"

So far the only good thing we had was a few pars of rubber gloves from the cleaning supplies.

Karl sat himself in one of the plastic Adirondack chairs under a beige gazebo. It was on sale at $799 and I started considering it for my backyard for a minute. Ma would like the colour; the legs seemed strong enough for the price.

Ryan sat himself on a cushioned bench with floral patterns on it. I rested a shoulder on top of a barbecue and started playing with an oversized spatula. I started feeling clueless, like I was trying to kill time so I wouldn't have to go through with it. I hated the feeling. I hated myself for feeling it.

"How are we gonna get rid of the body?" Phil asked.

"That's a good question," I said.

"Do we have to get rid of the body?" Ryan added.

"I don't know? Do we?" I asked Karl.

"Why are you looking at me every time you have a question like that?"

"Well..."

"I don't kill hookers and dispose of the corpses in the woods, if that's what you're asking me."

"You leave them where you drop them?" Ryan joked.

"Exactly."

"No, but seriously," I said. "We have to think about this."

"We need a pig farm," Phil said.

"Like in *Snatch*?" Karl asked.

"Yeah, it could work, but, we don't have a pig farm," I said.

"How about a chainsaw?" Phil said. "I can see them from here."

"There you go with that whole subtlety thing again."

"Câliss! Heille vous-êtes plates en osti. I'm gonna go and see if I can find something."

"Inspiration?" I joked.

"Yeah, fucking inspiration. I mean, how often do you get to do this? You guys just can't appreciate what life's giving you," he said as he walked away.

Ryan put his hands behind his head, leaning in the beige and pink seat. "He's really enjoying it, isn't he?"

"At least someone here is," Karl replied. He was looking at me. I didn't know what that was supposed to mean.

"I think he's right. We should be enjoying it," Ryan said.

"What do you mean?" I asked. I didn't enjoy this. I didn't think I was going to enjoy it. I didn't think it was something you were supposed to do. Were the guys thinking this was a joke or were they really into it? I didn't know which one was worst.

"I mean think about it," Ryan continued. "We're gonna get to kill somebody. How many people can claim that? How many people in the world can say that they've killed somebody?"

"Probably a lot in fact," Karl said but you could tell he agreed with Ryan. "You know, humanity's shit."

"Well, yeah, obviously, *humanity's shit,* but I mean, even then, there aren't *that* many people who can say that they've killed someone."

"It's not something you can really brag about either," Karl added.

"Of course. But still, how many people can know they did? It can't be that many, not up here anyways."

"That much is true."

"That much is fucked up," I said.

"Hey, D'Arcy. I'm not claiming to be a saint," Ryan replied. "And if you'd ask me if I have any remorse or second thoughts, I don't alright. As far as I know, the guy's a piece of shit and the country'll be better off without him."

"I know."

"But then what's the problem?"

"I just can't think it's that easy, alright?"

"It's the Catholic guilt," Karl said.

"It could be Catholic guilt," I admitted.

"We're all Catholics here," Ryan replied. "I don't feel guilt, you don't feel guilt," he said to Karl. He looked in the distance; Phil was coming back from the front aisles with something behind his back. "He's definitely not feeling guilty." Phil skipped the last few metres up to us like some kid who had found the perfect toy.

"Dude, I got it," Phil said. He pulled out a garden hose from behind his back. "We choke him with a hose." It was a bright pink garden hose.

"You can't be serious." Ryan said.

"Yeah, it's like flexible, so it won't leave a trace and shit."

"It will leave a trace," Karl replied coldly.

"How do you know?" Phil replied. Karl smiled. "Man, I'm really trying here."

"I know," Karl said with as much compassion as he could muster. "We appreciate the effort."

"I mean..."

"Don't blame yourself."

"He's right about one thing, you know?" Ryan said.

"What's that?" I asked.

"Well, think about it. Your brother was drugged, alright but then died of drowning, didn't he?"

"So we should choke him?" Ryan asked.

"I'm gonna drown him," I said. I said it coldly too. "He drowned my brother. I'm gonna have to drown him."

We all looked at each other. It made sense and I was glad that the guys had come to the same conclusion as I did.

"Where are we gonna do that?" Ryan asked.

"Lake Ontario. Simple as that."

"It's a busy fucking port."

"There's like fifty million miles of shoreline, there's got to be one place we can work with."

"True."

"Can you get on Google, see if you find any spots that are worth it?" I asked Karl.

He pulled out his smartphone.

"No wifi. It's gonna be long distance data," he said.

"What?" I snapped. "You don't even break a sweat at killing a man, but you fucking freak out about your data plan?"

"Are you gonna pay for it?"

"You didn't mind paying for the gas or the room."

"I was just about to talk to you about that."

"Are you serious?" Of course he was. "Fine," I added. He started typing.

"So we're gonna need to tie him up?" Phil said, trying to sell us his fluo-pink garden hose again.

"You had to pick the pink one?"

"Each one you buy gives two dollars for breast cancer." He was serious.

"Weights and a rope, Phil," I said. "Weights and a fucking rope."

CHAPTER 25

When darkness fell, Karl turned to me and said, "It's time." We started driving through Hamilton. I started looking around. Everywhere in the city, the same house. They all looked the same, every single street. That single, square brick house, thirty inches apart from none another, so fucking close you wondered why they didn't just slap them together like they did with the blocks in Montreal. I hated Oshawa. I hated Toronto. I hated Hamilton. I hated all of Ontario. It didn't feel like home at all. The sooner we would be done with this shit, I would happily drive back the 401 to city blocks that felt like home to me, condos or no condos, I was going to live with it.

We found the house exactly where Google said it would be. It was just as shitty looking as the rest of the city. Worse maybe. It didn't surprise me, but it was really bad and coming from a guy who grew up in the Pointe, that said a lot. Two stories, narrow house with an A framed roof. Front porch looked like it was ready to give in. Yard was a mess. It was standing, almost alone, in the space between some residential area and the remnant of industrial heritage on the other side. In a sense, Hamilton was Canada's Cleveland. Not quite Canada's Detroit, but who could say it wouldn't stoop that low one day.

There seemed to be someone in the house next to our

target. But that was all. Behind was a barren parking lot. The warehouse across the street didn't have any windows in it.

The only thing that weirded me out was the Buddhist temple at the end of the street. Right there, between a shipping yard and a scrapyard, a fucking Buddhist temple. Red columns, green rooftops, lion statues, arch doors....a Buddhist fucking temple. It felt weird and out of place, but it was there all right.

Since we knew sweet fuckall about the guy's habit, life, job or roommates, we decided to stake the place out for a while in the shade of the temple. After two or three hours watching the house, we figured there were at least eight people in there at the moment. We didn't know if they lived there or if there was a party going on. It didn't really matter. Maybe it was a party and we should come back another day. But I was *there*, this was *now*. I wasn't going back to Montreal, No way. There were probably people over every night so we were fucked no matter what.

"I counted nine," Karl said.

"Yeah? Certain?"

"Absolutely."

"Fuck, nine is a lot," I said.

"Yeah!"

"We set fire to the house?" Ryan asked.

I looked at him through the rearview mirror. "Sometimes you scare the shit out of me."

"Still. They're all Nazis, the more the better. And we know he'll be dead."

"Makes sense," Phil said.

"But there would be no way to make sure he's dead," Karl added.

"I don't know," I said. I needed to kill the guy, but the idea of burning down a house, let alone nine people, didn't feel right. Burning anyone to a crisp wasn't me. "I want to drown the guy. I'm serious about that."

"What then? We come back?"

"Nah, I'm here. I'm doing this."

"So am I," Karl said.

"It's gonna be a hell of a fight."

"You shoulda let me buy that pickaxe and shit back at Home Depot," Phil said.

I looked at the door, looked back towards the boulevard we had come from. Two more boneheads, one guy and one girl, walked in the house, that made it eleven.

"I got an idea," I said as I put the car in reverse. "Google me the nearest liquor store."

"You think it's time to get drunk?" Ryan asked harshly.

"I see where you're going," Karl said as he started typing.

"Can you get me a beer while you're in there?" Phil asked.

I looked at Karl; Karl looked at me. We pinched our lips, nodded sideways, *why not?* Karl found a place maybe ten blocks away. We drove over there and parked up front. There was no need to be subtle about this.

"You do deliveries," I asked the teller when we got in. He was a Hindu guy and I sorta felt bad because I was going to send him or his friend to a house full of white supremacists, but then again, I was going to buy him a hella lot of liquor, so...

"The delivery guy is out," he said in a perfect Canadian accent. "Twenty minutes, maybe?"

"That's perfect."

Karl dropped two cases of six Fin du Monde, strong Quebec-made beer that had ten percent alcohol in it. I asked for two forty ounce Jack Daniels, two bottles of Jäger, two more cases of Miller. Me and Karl looked at each other again, *why not?* Add one of Southern Comfort and, some vodka and a bag of BBQ chips to make it believable.

I gave him the address. He looked at it, looked at me, not too sure he wanted the sale anymore.

"Is there a problem?" I asked.

"That'll be four hundred twenty-three dollars and fifty-six cents," he said.

A week's pay on fucking liquor. Goddamnit. I paid cash, all twenties, felt like crap about it but then we headed out the door and back to the car.

"Hey, where's my beer?" Phil asked.

"I forgot alright,"

"You forgot?"

"We gotta go, alright."

"But I wanted a beer."

"You'll have one later. Now put on your seatbelt," I joked. It seemed to shut him up.

A few moments later, we were back to our lookout point under the shade of Fah Hoy Temple. The delivery guy showed up a half-hour later. He rang the bell nervously, one bonehead walked out.

"What the fuck do you want?" he yelled.

The delivery guy rested half the cases on the porch, went back to his car. They argued and their hands waved around. The Nazi was aggressive; the Hindu guy was just trying to do his job. Then after a few moments, the delivery guy drove off. Nazi finally took the cases with a smile on his face. As far as I could tell, no tip was handed to the poor guy.

"What the fuck was that?" Phil asked.

"That was the plan."

"I don't care about the plan. You bought all of that booze and forgot my beer?"

"Shut up," I said with a smile. He was right though.

Someone put up the music as loud as they could. I resonated through the empty lots around and I could decipher Stars and Stripes' "Drop the Bomb." A not so subtle song about nuking the Middle East. Why did I know about that song? Because Stars and Stripes was the band every skinhead, myself included, secretly loved even if they weren't exactly politically correct.

Soon, they'd be too drunk and too stupid to do anything about us walking in there to finish him off, finish them off. You poisoned my brother, I'll poison you right back.

Around eleven, a group of four went home, that brought it down to seven. Some guy left with his girlfriend not too long after that. They seemed pretty hammered; could barely make it to their car. They got in somehow, made out for a minute and took off in a semi-straight line.

That made it five. If only two more could rush home to fuck, then we'd be in business. Then at two AM that's exactly what happened. Two more walked out and headed north.

The music, which had been had full blast for hours now, finally died out. The silence felt strange in a city of half a million people. You could make out the beeps and clanks of machinery in the port or the steel mill. But that was it. We waited for a while for lights, movement or sound. At three in the morning, we figured we were good.

Karl gave everyone a pair of gloves. We put on our jackets. I had my poor boy hat. We had a canvas grocery bag for a hood and the rope. Phil had the pry bar. The weights were gonna stay in the car. Then we looked at each other. We were ready.

BANG!

"Grab that one," Ryan told Phil. When we walked into that door, things seemed to run at full speed. I was just reacting.

We expected three guys in there. I looked in all the rooms. There was one of them passed out on the couch. Phil was taking care of him. He flipped him around, ready to punch him cold, but the guy was in a liquor induced coma. No complaint, no struggle. I would've asked Ryan to check if he was still breathing if only I could get my lips to listen to my brain. Phil grabbed his head, raised it six inches and let it drop on. The guy didn't even wiggle.

"This one's out for a while." Phil said.

That made it one. I looked into the kitchen: no one. I looked in the back room. It was a rehearsal space for the band. It was empty. The first flood was covered. Me, Karl and Ryan made it up the stairs. We moved silently into the rooms. We were looking for three people. We had counted three people. There were eleven and then four left and that guy in the car with his girlfriend. Then that one guy? Or was it two? *Fuck!* I wasn't sure anymore.

We opened one door, then a second and a third one. The house seemed empty. There was only one room left.

We opened it. Maybe he was sleeping in with his girlfriend. We looked in there, trying to see the shapes in bed with the dim light of the street coming through the Iron Cross flag for curtains. I could only see one person in there. I didn't know. Maybe we had gotten the count wrong. It was possible I had but I couldn't help but clench my teeth, expecting a knife to hit me right between the shoulder blades at any moment.

We walked in slowly, ready to jump him. He wasn't moving. You could see his chest moving up and down peacefully. That was perfect. Hell, it was better than anything that I could ever have expected. I was at his feet, Karl walked up near his head. He took a T-shirt that was lying on a chair, ready to gag the guy.

That's when hell broke loose. He woke up in a snap. He was drunk, but he was awake alright. He kicked Ryan in the knee. It got off like a reflex. Good kick, too. The big guy screamed then tried to muffle his own pain. That's when a boot came my way. I felt the hard rubber, diamond soles dig into my thigh. The motherfucker was sleeping with his boots on. He probably had just crashed there, too drunk to get undress. I stumbled on my back but Karl got on top of things before the Nazi could move. He shoved the T-shirt down the guy's mouth so he couldn't scream. I found my footing, Ryan got up and, *boy*, was he pissed!

I jumped on his legs. Ryan put a knee in his chest. But the guy was a MMA fighter. He managed to kick me again, twice. I grabbed his knees but then somehow I got hit in the ribs out of fucking nowhere. *Motherfucker!* I put all of my weight on his knees, all two hundred and forty pounds of it. I heard him scream through the gag. Ryan punched him in the face. Repeatedly. Even his big paws didn't seem to make a dent and Ryan had flattened dozens of guys in his life. I had seen it a few times personally. There was a reason why bars hired Ryan on tough nights.

It was a mess. The three of us couldn't bring him down but Ryan just kept pounding and pounding. It was a fucking mess. The guy started punching back with his right. He was swinging at Ryan with a brass knuckle. He kept fucking brass knuckles in his bed with him at night.

Ryan took the punch. He stumbled backwards a bit. The guy was aiming for Ryan's temple and if he had hit that, then Ryan would have probably been good as dead. But Ryan just turned away at the last moment and got it to the ear. He probably just saw a flash of some movement and ducked as a reflex. His years as a bouncer probably saved his life.

Still, it must have given him a hell of a *ring*. He screamed in pain as he started bleeding. You could see he was trying hard not to fall down. Poor fucking bastard.

"Don't get any on the bed," Karl shouted. But Ryan was wobbly, probably couldn't hear him. The Nazi was about to strike again so Karl drove a knee in his face, put his weight on him. That didn't stop him from trying to hit Ryan. I could see the shimmering edges of the brass knuckles against the faint light coming through the edges of the curtain. Each swing was half an inch from Ryan's face.

That's when I punched him in the crouch.

It was a cheap shot. I didn't feel good about it but I did it anyways. It was the only one that seemed to work. He probably wasn't expecting it. I wouldn't have expected it. He bent himself in half the best he could with me and Karl still on top of him. That was enough for Ryan to somehow grab his hand and take hold of the brass knuckles that cost him an ear. He was breathing heavily. He was pissed.

The Nazi was trying to shout, trying to wiggle from under our weight. I could see Ryan had a hard time pulling away the guy's arm.

"You want to play with brass knuckles?" he said, grabbing the fist with his gigantic paws.

He started to pry open the guy's hand. We all knew what he was up to. Karl knew it, I knew it and the Nazi knew it, too. It wasn't gonna be pretty.

He tried to keep his fist as tight as he could. He fought Ryan hard but the Scot was stronger. You could see the tide was shifting. You had to take into account the fact that Karl was shoving a knee into the guy's face and I was on his knees. Hell, I was panting like a goddamn dog. *Cillian took this guy one on one and kicked his ass.*

That's when Karl's knee slipped to the guy's throat. He lost the gag but the Nazi couldn't seem to manage to spit it out so Karl, had his hands free to shove a finger in the guy's eye. More muffled screams. The guy was red, turning blue. It was a fucking mess and I needed it to be over with. So I started punching him in the groin again. Then once more and why not a third time?

Only then did Ryan finally get the upper hand. He started to lift the handle of the brass knuckle. The guy's fingers got squeezed in a vice.

Ryan laughed.

He took his sweet fucking time too. He lifted the handle one millimetre at a time. The fingers were turning blue, his hand was shaking from the pain. Karl just shoved his fist in the guy's mouth, pushing the gag into his throat. If things continued that way, we were gonna choke him before he had a chance to drown.

Clack!

The first finger snapped. More spasms, more muffled screams.

"Heeere we go," Ryan said.

The second and third fingers snapped. The body shook violently.

"Come on. Come on, just one more now."

The last one gave. The noise of bones disjointing sent a shiver down my fucking spine but Ryan kept pushing forward.

"Let's see how far we can get these babies," he added.

The edge of the brass knuckle pushed against the guy's own knuckles, acting as a levee point. Ryan just kept raising the handle until all four fingers were ninety degrees in the air.

No doctor would ever fix these motherfuckers.

That's when the body stopped moving. That's when

the noises died out, at last. I could catch my breath, we could take a rest. We could hear the fair city of Hamilton's untroubled sleep once again. The steel mill was busy, you could make out a Jacob break in the distance. It almost felt like serenity.

"I'm keeping that as a souvenir," Ryan said as he pried the brass knuckle out of the Nazi's grotesquely bent fingers. Some of them had swollen already and he had to crack them back in order to free the weapon. The noise would have made most people gag. I had never seen Ryan be that mean in my entire life, probably never would again either.

"Cover your ear. Look around if you bleed anywhere," Karl said. "Grab the sheets with the guy," he said to me.

We carried him downstairs.

"What the fuck happened?" Phil started asking.

"Did he wake up?"

"Still dead drunk."

We dropped our victim on the floor, looked at the other guy. Ryan was limping his way downstairs, still breathing as heavily as a bear.

"Oh this ain't good," Phil said

"*Move,*" Ryan replied.

Phil wouldn't stand in Ryan's way. Not Ryan looking the way he did, not after what he had just heard.

"Ryan," Karl said.

"What?"

"Give me the brass knuckles."

He did. Karl walked to the kitchen sink, found some Windex under the counter, sprayed it over the weapon. He scrubbed it, then washed everything with cold water and regular soap. He looked carefully at every single edge, making sure he hadn't missed a spot. Sure he wasn't some CSI agent with a kit, but Karl was a sharpshooter and I had to believe he wouldn't miss a damn thing.

Karl touched the weapon with the second guy's hand, then walked to the back door, swung it open and threw the brass knuckle as far as he could in the empty grasses behind the house.

Then he walked up stairs. I could hear him rummage through the guy's room, putting shit in a garbage bag. It took a minute or two and I was getting nervous. *What the fuck is he up to?* I looked at Phil, he raised his shoulders.

Then I saw some smoke and he came rushing down with the bag. He handed it to Phil, saying, "Put that in the trunk, will you?"

He had set fire to the fucking house.

"What about him?" I asked, pointing out to the passed out guy?"

"What about him?"

He lowered himself, ready to grab our victim's legs as if nothing out of the ordinary was happened. He was gonna let the guy choke or burn or escape. He didn't give a fuck anymore. Neither did I.

"Well," he said, "grab the fucking head."

So I did.

CHAPTER 26

The port was deserted, at least this entire segment of it was deserted. A few hundred yards away there was still one two ships from the Canadian Steamship Company anchoring to one of the active docks. That was a few hundred yards away. We had picked an isolated spot in the east end of the docks because it had fallen bedlam.

Three were growing in the cracks in the cement, in crevasses that had been filled with dirt overtime. Some of the roots could be seen dangling over the lake outside of the pier.

I stood there, at the edge of the dock. Hamilton's industrial core was still somewhat busy with its flood lights covering every inch of metal in a yellow hue. The waves were coming in from the west, the wind was dry and warm. Miles away across the lake you could see the Toronto sky lit up by millions the millions of light bulbs alive in the city. It's not like you could actually see it, but you knew it was there just from the hue or at least if seemed that way to me.

I took a deep breath. This time it was real and I hoped I was ready for it. Ryan and Phil were dragging the bastard on the cement. He had woken up but he was gagged and hooded. His hands were tied behind him, feet just the same. The way it had taken the three of us to take him out, we weren't taking any chances.

His hand was a bloated mess, swollen worse than anything I had ever seen before. What was left of his fingers were purple stubs sticking out in weird directions. He was struggling and squirming about. I wanted him to hear the waves, to know where we were. Phil punched him in the guts just because he could.

"Shut up," he said. It didn't really work.

Karl was coming in with the rope and the weights. "How much do you think we need to keep him down?" he asked as he dropped the weights on the ground. The Nazi tried to shout something, started squirming some more.

The weights were actually metal plates that were meant to hold fence poles, about five inches wide, three pounds apiece. We asked the guy at Home Depot how many we needed to fence off forty-five thousand square feet.

"That's a pretty big fence," he said.

"It's an important contract," I replied. He sold them to us in bulk.

I stood at the edge of the pier, looking at the dark waters ahead. My brother had been killed by a shot of liquefied Ajax, injected in his veins by the bastard behind me. He was left to drown, incapacitated, in the waters of the Lachine Canal.

Those were the same waters that were facing me, only a few hundred kilometres up the river. I turned around, looked at my friends, looked at our guy, Michael Cook. *The same waters.*

"You want us to get it over with?" Ryan asked.

I turned back, took a long, slow breath. I knew I didn't want my friends to do my work for me. I just needed to let this sink in a bit more.

"I'll take it from here," I said.

"Are you sure?"

"Wait in the car."

They walked down the pier, across the trees that were sheltering us from the world. I didn't rush to the Nazi. *Go on and take your time.* He was there, still trying to get free, trying to scream. I didn't even look at him that much. I didn't believe he could escape, get loose, try to kill me or anything. I was at peace.

The lake was speaking to me. Simple as that. It was peaceful and serene. I could be here throwing rocks at the water and it would have had the same effect on me. There was something about water that brought peace to a man's mind. Living in the city, you tended to forget that. It's funny the things we took for granted when we didn't really need them.

I could end up dead in a few weeks when the rest of his gang comes after me for what I was about to do. I could spend the rest of my life in prison for this. They could find me inside and do me in some random corridor. I could be found dead or dying with a prison-made plastic knife in my liver. Maybe they would come after my mom to get back at me. Maybe they'd kill her and let me live with it, maybe.

The road ahead had nothing good in it for me but I was too far in to change anything about it now. It should have bothered me, or at least it should have bothered me more.

I looked down. The waters splashed against the pillars fifteen feet below me. The waters were most likely cold as hell. It might have been summer in Canada, the waters certainly were still cold. I didn't remember any single time when I jumped into a lake and found the waters to be nice. It was always cold. I wouldn't be cold enough to give him hypothermia. Maybe that was bad, maybe that was good. There would have been something nice about him freezing, to know that each, tiny, minuscule veins in his hands, in his skin, could explode as his blood turns to ice. That might have felt like the poison he shot in my brother's arm before dumping him.

My breath became heavy and I knew it was time. I clenched my fist and finally turned to him. I had to stay there, *stay in the moment, stay in the moment.* The bastard *had* poisoned my brother, with Ajax no less, and left him to drown. He *had* done it. It was not like I had made the story up, police officers fished him out of the canal, I saw his body at the morgue. I saw my mother's tears at the wake and heard the bagpipes at his funeral.

Everything had happened for real. *It did.*

I walked over to him. He had stopped moving, gave up on escaping. Maybe there would be peace in the world thanks to what I was about to do. Killing a man wasn't supposed to feel that serene.

I dragged his feet towards me. He tried to kick me so I kneeled against his knees, put all my weight onto them. He screamed in pain but not loud enough so that anyone would hear it. I went around his ankles a few times, passed the rope in between his legs so it wouldn't slip, locked it with a knot. Then I did it a second time altogether. I wasn't taking any chances with this.

Karl had set up the small plates in three neat rows, had tied them up real tight. They looked like three loafs of meat wrapped up by a professional butcher. It was a good job, a clean job the way you'd expected Karl to do it.

I gave it one more tug to make sure. I could hear the guy breathing heavily through the hood. I looked at his chest go up and down in spasms. I looked at his arms, at his skin and his tattoos. He had swastikas tattooed, SS bolts, white supremacist logos, an upside down cross, probably for the KKK. It was like he was collecting racism.

I got up from his knees, he sighed of relief. He crouched there, hands behind his back. I pulled a knife, cut the tie-wraps to his hood, pulled it off and took out his gag.

He looked at me with such hatred in his eyes that I could have been scared. He had blood running from his nose and the cuts in his cheeks. He had blood in his eyes, blood in his teeth but there was no fear in his stare. There was hatred. Hatred and nothing else. I haven't seen hatred like that since, don't think I ever will again.

I looked down at him.

"Cillian Kennedy," I simply said.

He didn't answer. He kept breathing heavily, looking at me like I was in a gas chamber and he was about to drop the can in it.

"Cillian Kennedy."

He didn't answer. I punched him as hard as I could. He spat out the blood, smiled at me with his bloodied teeth, vein sticking out the side of his head.

I punched him again.

"I could be here all night."

"Looks like I ain't going anywhere myself." He smiled.

"Cillian Kennedy died in the Lachine Canal in Montreal thirty-five days ago."

He twitched. That was enough for me. But I needed to hear him say it.

"So what? Another drunken Irish who can't swim."

Don't bite to that, I kept thinking, *don't bite to that.*

"Understand me," I said. "You *are* going to die here tonight. There's no question about that. At some point I will push those weights in the lake and you will follow them down into the water. But I needed to know why you did it. I needed to know what my brother could have done that warranted that kind of death. I want to know why you killed him. I wanted to know why they had to drain the water out of his bloated body so that I could have a last look at him before they put him in the ground. He fought you in a cage three days before he died."

"So. Doesn't mean I killed him, does it?"

"He fought you and won. He won that fight and you lost it."

"He won jack shit. I won that fight."

"That's not what the card says."

"Well, the card's wrong," he said. He paused for a moment took his sweet time to answer. "The back of the head," he continued.

"What?"

"He hit me to the back of the head. While I was down," he spat something. Most of it was blood. "There are only a handful of rules in the book and that fucking Mick couldn't even follow them."

"So you killed him?"

"Ah, wouldn't you like me to admit it?"

277

GRAND TRUNK AND SHEARER

"The purse was what? Six hundred bucks and you killed him."

"You know what? You're damn right I killed him. I killed him and I loved it. And it wasn't about the money either. I've been waiting for a long time to kill a man and I always expected it'd be a nigger or a kike, but I'm damn glad it was a mick. You should have seen the beads of sweat on his forehead when we stuck that needle in his arms. I told him, 'This is Ajax. You'll be dead in ten minutes.'"

That hit me right in the gut. I started to sob, fought to keep it in.

"Ahhh, the smell of fear on this guy. He just pleaded and pleaded, said shit like 'This ain't cool, man.' Can you believe it. A man about to die and all he can do is say *it ain't cool*. He started crying after that. Crying and sobbing like a fucking baby. Not so tough in the end, was he?"

I couldn't hold it back anymore. I cried like a fucking baby, heavy sobs, hands shaking, body twitching, the whole thing. It was like it had finally hit me and I was glad it did. I just let it take over, fill me up with the sorrow I had been looking for.

"He made noises just like that. He made noises like he was about to curl up in a ball and cry for his mom to pick him up," he tried to look me in the eyes. "I see that it runs in the family, too. Are you going to call your mother to finish a man's job. Takes three guys in the middle of the night just to get me out of bed. I'll make you a deal. If I make it out of here tonight, I'll do the same for you. I'll drive up to that faggot town of yours. I'll stick a needle full of Ajax in your arm and throw your dead body in the river. I'll do the same for your friends too."

"He wasn't dead," I sobbed. I swallowed it. "He wasn't dead when you threw him in the river. He drowned before the fix killed him. He was in shock and he couldn't swim but he choked to death before the heart gave up."

"Well I'm glad to hear that. The longer it took, the better I feel about it. Now. If you're gonna kill me, kill me...but I don't think you're gonna do it. You don't have it. Hell, we didn't chat for ten minutes before we killed him. We just dumped the body and didn't look back."

I took a deep breath. I stood up, looked down at him. I looked at the blood on his skin, the scars in his face, the red of his teeth spoiling his smile. A last wave of sobs caught me, hands started shaking.

I can't say it was easy. My head wasn't working right anymore. My head felt like it was stuffed with cotton. The noises, the lights, everything was hazy. I wished it could have been like in the movies. I wished I could have stood tall, pushing him in the river like he was a piece of rag and stand there, all macho about it.

It wasn't like that. It wasn't like that at all. I felt shivery, shaky and scared. I grabbed his face, still can't figure out why. Then I said, "Alright," I sobbed. "We're good now, Cillian. We're good now."

My shaky hands let go of his face. I crumbled to the ground next to him. My legs couldn't hold my weight anymore. My arms felt like they were full of lead. I tried to push the first weight but it felt like the heavens were holding it back. I was going to hell for this and I knew it.

It was like God finally had decided to show up in my life and tried to stop me from doing it.

It was about time but it was too fucking late too.

The first weight slid out the edge, just barely. I saw it go down so slowly, dragging against the rugged edge of the pier. All it took was for me to move something half an inch. It was so insignificant it felt like I had *barely* killed him. Then it went down and I saw the rope jitter. The second string of weights went down and the third right after that. That was a hundred and twenty pounds dangling from the pier, attached to his legs.

He tried to crouch lower to the ground, tried to lower his weight so he wouldn't go over. He screamed in pain but mostly he screamed in fear. Everybody screams in the end. The shouting in my ears was snapping me back to reality. This *was* happening and it was happening really fast. My sense came back to me in and it wasn't pretty.

He was trying to focus all of his energy on his balance, trying to stay alive. For a moment it worked but then I could hear his knees scrape against the gravel and the concrete. I could hear him scream in pain through his teeth as his skin tore open from hundreds of little shards. That was enough for him to move out of position. A mere second and that did it. His legs were pulled out from under him. His head smashed into the ground in front of me then his body slid over. His head banged once more against the edge and then he disappeared in the dark waters ahead.

I looked over and for a moment all I could see what the splash in the water where he had sunk. For a moment I thought it was done. But he reappeared to the surface. The rope was too long to pull him under, but too short to let him up. He couldn't swim because he was tied up but it was a mess.

This whole story was a fucking mess. My brother, the search for his killer, my revenge, my murder. All of it was a mess. I could see his blood mix with water running over his face. He managed to grasp some air every now and then but the small waves caught up to him and he choked on them every time he tried to breathe or scream.

All that came out from under me was the splatter of water and the muffled complaints of a dying man. I was okay with that and I shouldn't have been.

I had stopped shaking. It didn't hit me, the fact that I had killed a man. It didn't make me cry anymore. It didn't make me weep or feel weak or strong for that matter. It opened up something inside me or maybe it closed it. To this day I still can't explain it.

I was hunched on the edge of the pier, looking down at him. It took him a while to drown. If I had to guess, I'd say he managed to keep himself alive and afloat for a solid eight minutes. I had to hand it to him for that but that didn't stop me from watching every second of it.

When the air was finally drained out of him, his body just floated there. The waves hit it gently like it was a piece of driftwood. The cops would find him easily. We were gonna have to get out of town quick and silent before the sun would be up but I was in no rush. It was like the whole world was a joke to me now. Nothing felt quite as important or as relevant. Everything was just there and then it would be gone one day and it wasn't even that big of a deal.

I walked out of that pier expecting a bunch of squad cars waiting for me at the road. I was ready for it. Maybe I wanted it to happen. Maybe I needed proof that the feeling I had inside of me was wrong. The world would punish me for this and morals we had been instilled generation after generation were not entirely vain. I wanted that to be true. If only it could have been true.

Nothing.

Not a single police officer in sight. Karl, Phil and Ryan were there waiting. I didn't say a word. Nobody did in fact. No one asked about what had happened, how it happened. It was their kill as much as it was mine, in a sense, but something had changed in me and they weren't ready to ask about it. I wasn't ready to tell either. This one was going to take some time to sink in. The drive home was eight hours, maybe nine. It was a long time to stay silent but we all did.

When we got home the next morning, Patricia was there waiting for me. I made love to her that day. Barely said *Hi*. I took her in my arms, took her in my bed, came in her. We made love four times that day and once more the next morning. I came in her every single time. Barely said a word.

She moved in with me soon after that. The kid was on the way. She wanted a son, my mom wanted a grandson. I didn't know what I wanted, but I expected that my days were numbered. Every morning I got up expecting to be jailed or killed. It never happened.

Nine months later, my son was born. We named him Keenan. He cried hard and strong, with the blunt of the Celtic blood running through his veins. Patricia was weeping and happy and I guess that I should have been too. The kid was going to be both hard-headed and cocky, that much was for sure but I was worried. Hell, I was scared.

The nurses and the doctors checked him, cleaned him. He was healthy and strong, the way you hope newborns to be. They handed him to me in a neat little white blanked. I looked at him but I couldn't see his beauty or his deep green eyes. The only thing that I could picture when my son was born was the face man I had murdered in Hamilton.

I could see him squirm in the water, trying to keep his head out of the water. I could head him beg and choke and gag as the water made his way down into his lungs. Eight minutes it a long fucking time when you're drowning. My son was beautiful in front of me, crying in front of me. But all I could think about was the sound the Nazi made down in the water.

I had killed a man and gotten away with it.

Family members wouldn't stop me from doing it. Friends had helped me willingly, eagerly; strangers had given me information just because they could just because it made their meaningless life a bit more interesting. What did that say about the world? People looked away and people preferred not to ask any questions. That's how the world worked.

Lies, assault, blackmail, home invasion, arson... murder. Before all of that, the worst crime I had ever committed was being drunk in public. I'd swear to God that was the worst crime I had ever committed. People expected everyone to behave properly just out of sheer goodness but that was all a lie, wasn't it. The world didn't work like that and that scared me. It really did. I used to believe it was supposed to be hard to kill a man. Turns out it wasn't.

It really wasn't.

Ian Truman is a novelist, a musician and a visual artist. Born and raised in the East End of Montreal, he is a fan of punk, hardcore, hip hop, dirty realism, noir, satire and hopes to mix these genres in all of his works. A graduate of Concordia University's creative writing program, he won the 2013 Expozine Awards for best Independent English Novel. He lives in Montreal with his wife Mary and two daughters Kaori and D'arcy Ann.

OTHER TITLES FROM DOWN AND OUT BOOKS

See www.DownAndOutBooks.com for complete list

By J.L. Abramo
Catching Water in a Net
Clutching at Straws
Counting to Infinity
Gravesend
Chasing Charlie Chan
Circling the Runway
Brooklyn Justice

By Trey R. Barker
2,000 Miles to Open Road
Road Gig: A Novella
Exit Blood
Death is Not Forever
No Harder Prison

By Richard Barre
The Innocents
Bearing Secrets
Christmas Stories
The Ghosts of Morning
Blackheart Highway
Burning Moon
Echo Bay
Lost

By Eric Beetner (editor)
Unloaded

By Eric Beetner and
JB Kohl
Over Their Heads

By Eric Beetner and
Frank Scalise
The Backlist
The Shortlist

By G.J. Brown
Falling

By Rob Brunet
Stinking Rich

By Mark Coggins
No Hard Feelings

By Tom Crowley
Vipers Tail
Murder in the Slaughterhouse

By Frank De Blase
Pine Box for a Pin-Up
Busted Valentines
and Other Dark Delights
A Cougar's Kiss

By Les Edgerton
The Genuine, Imitation,
Plastic Kidnapping

By A.C. Frieden
Tranquility Denied
The Serpent's Game
The Pyongyang Option (*)

By Jack Getze
Big Numbers
Big Money
Big Mojo
Big Shoes

By Richard Godwin
Wrong Crowd
Buffalo and Sour Mash (*)

(*)—Coming Soon

OTHER TITLES FROM DOWN AND OUT BOOKS

See www.DownAndOutBooks.com for complete list

By William Hastings (editor)
*Stray Dogs: Writing
from the Other America*

By Jeffery Hess
Beachhead

By Matt Hilton
*No Going Back
Rules of Honor
The Lawless Kind
The Devil's Anvil*

By David Housewright
*Finders Keepers
Full House*

By Jerry Kennealy
Screen Test

By Ross Klavan, Tim O'Mara and
Charles Salzberg
Triple Shot

By S.W. Lauden
Crosswise

By Terrence McCauley
The Devil Dogs of Belleau Wood

By Bill Moody
*Czechmate
The Man in Red Square
Solo Hand
The Death of a Tenor Man
The Sound of the Trumpet
Bird Lives!*

By Gary Phillips
*The Perpetrators
Scoundrels* (Editor)
*Treacherous
3 the Hard Way*

By Tom Pitts
Hustle

By Robert J. Randisi
*Upon My Soul
Souls of the Dead
Envy the Dead* (*)

By Ryan Sayles
*The Subtle Art of Brutality
Warpath*

By John Shepphird
*The Shill
Kill the Shill
Beware the Shill* (*)

By Ian Thurman
Grand Trunk and Shearer (*)

James R. Tuck (editor)
Mama Cried

By Lono Waiwaiole
*Wiley's Lament
Wiley's Shuffle
Wiley's Refrain
Dark Paradise
Leon's Legacy* (*)

(*)—Coming Soon

Made in the USA
Middletown, DE
28 November 2016